FLARES

FLARES

The Grimwood Trilogy:
Flares
Ordinary World
The Midnight Visitors

Four Corners Thrillers:
Chokecherry Canyon
Firepower

Brick Ransom Thrillers:
Seattle On Ice
Bloody Pulp
Billionaires, Bullets, Exploding Monkeys

Standalone Novels:
On/Off
Rosé in Saint Tropez

Flares

Mike Attebery

Cryptic Bindings
Seattle

For my parents,
Liz Attebery and
Tucker Attebery

“I don’t want to write about sinister things.”

Year One

Timeline

1855 – Town of Grimwood is settled.

1869 – Ashton Grimwood founds Grimwood University.

1921 – Alan Grimwood is born.

1945 – Grimwood graduates and begins teaching at the University.

1955 – *Revenant* is published.

1969 – Founding of The Grimwood Writing Center.

1972 – Shooting on Grimwood campus.

1974 – *Black Robes* is published.

1978 – Alan Grimwood dies.

1981 – Grimwood's books go back into print.

1983 – Excerpts of *Doppelganger* are published.

1984 – *The Collected Stories of Alan Grimwood (1950-1978)* published.

...Present Day

Grimwood

GRIMWOOD UNIVERSITY HAD TWO claims to fame. One was a man. The other, an event. And while the man, author and professor Alan Grimwood, wouldn't live to see the benefits of his own notoriety, he did bear witness to the tragedy that would forever sear his family's name, and the college they founded, into the minds of Americans everywhere.

One year after the Attica Prison riot forever connected the name of that infamous correctional facility with the community in which it was located, the town of Grimwood, which for more than a century had enjoyed a symbiotic relationship with the institution Ashton Grimwood established on the hill, quite suddenly found itself at the center of its own ghoulish media storm. While the town would eventually regain a sense of balance and normalcy, the college and its most famous professor would be forever linked with the events that took place a week before Thanksgiving in 1972.

If there was one element of justice in the incident on Grimwood campus, it was the fact that the armed, deeply-disturbed young man who stormed the University's library and took the object of his "affection" hostage – along with eleven other students – never gained the posthumous notoriety so often bequeathed by today's media. Indeed, after he murdered all twelve of his victims, and jumped to his death from the library's tower, his name was almost immediately forgotten to time. To the townspeople, the students of Grimwood University, and anyone jolted by reports of one of America's earliest college shootings, its perpetrator would forever be known as *The Shooter*.

Then there was Ashton Grimwood's great-grandson, Alan, who, after founding a uniquely intensive writing program at the school, was initially most recognized for his teaching, and less so for his writing. But that would eventually change. In 1955, the publication of Alan Grimwood's *Revenant* had gone all but unnoticed. Two years after the tragedy, and nineteen years after the publication of his first novel, *Black Robes* hit shelves and was met with moderate success, owing largely to the dark subject matter and media interest fueled by the infamous campus killings. In the years that followed, rumors swirled of a third completed manuscript, which Grimwood was said to have thrown over The Falls to the east of the University's campus, but other than the accounts of a handful of long-departed alums, the event was never corroborated. It wasn't until Grimwood's untimely death four years later, at the unjust age of 57, that something interesting happened. It began with people digging up copies of *Revenant* in used bookstores. Something about that book's subject matter – which touched upon life and death, fate, and the after-life – struck a nerve with readers, who passed their copies along to their friends before hunting down *Black Robes* and repeating the process. By 1981, both books were back in print. In 1983, excerpts of a fourth book, *Doppelganger* – an unfinished sequel to *Revenant*, which Grimwood was writing when he dropped dead of a massive heart attack – were released by his publisher. *The Collected Stories of Alan Grimwood (1950 – 1978)* followed a year later, and from thereon out, Alan Grimwood became a legend of genre fiction, one with a small but endlessly fascinated base of readers. Grimwood was unmarried at the time of his death. With no children, and no heirs, the rights to his books were passed to The Writing Center at the University, which knew a good thing when it saw it, and made sure his work remained in print, occasionally releasing revised and expanded commemorative editions in order to maintain the copyrights.

What then of the institution bearing the Grimwood family name? A decade after Alan's death, Grimwood University was comfortably ensconced amongst its old-school, upstate brethren. The Writing Center flourished. Twenty years on, ghoulish curiosity had faded, but from time to time, visitors to the campus reported unusual experiences that made their blood run cold. There were even those who claimed to have seen Alan Grimwood himself, strolling the grounds near the place of his death. To an outsider, such stories might have seemed laughable, but it was interesting to note that few people in town, and almost no one on campus, ever called such reports into question.

1.

"I don't want to write about sinister things."

"How do you mean?" Loren asked. "You don't want to tell dark stories, or you don't want to write about the bad things that can happen in life?"

"I guess both... People are here, and then they're gone. We can vanish in the blink of an eye and never see it coming. If you think about that too long, you start to wonder why people bother getting up in the morning, why anyone pursues their dreams at all. Why create stories that emphasize how weak the threads holding all of this together really are?"

"Maybe to remind people that time is precious. Other than your life, what do you really have to lose? Dark stories can be cathartic."

"So, is that the kind of thing you want to say?" Braden asked as he held her gaze.

"To be honest, I'm not sure what it is that I want to say." She could feel her face growing warm. "I guess that's why I'm here, to figure that out."

* * *

The train rumbled through the outskirts of Grimwood, past industrial warehouses and dilapidated buildings, its engine rattling and hissing as it neared the station. Loren Austin sat at the window, watching the upstate town slide into view. She'd been there only once before, when she and her father traveled back east together to check out her first choice college. That was in January, when Grimwood was tucked under a blanket of fresh snow. Now, at the tail end of summer, with the evening light offering the first spectral glimpses of autumn, things were looking a little more stark. Needless to say, it was a far cry from Durango, Colorado.

Why exactly had a solitary, cross-country trip seemed like such a great idea? Both of Loren's parents had wanted to drive her there – perhaps not *together*, but individually they'd been genuinely interested – yet Loren was determined to do it her own way. In early August, she'd packed up her things, arranged to have them shipped to her dorm at the University, and bought a single ticket for the 2,000 mile train ride.

Now, here she was, pondering her desire to arrive all alone for her freshman year. It might have been because she'd never truly been on her own before. Or maybe she'd spent too much time by herself already and grown accustomed to it. Either way, once her older brother and sister moved out, that had left only Loren living at home for much of high school. In a household where her parents wanted little to do with one another, one might think they'd have spent more time with their youngest daughter, but by the time it was just the three of them, Rick and Mary Beth Austin were more than ready to get on with their individual lives, leaving Loren to become entangled in a pair of young romances, both perhaps too adult for her own good.

First, there was Justin, who was sweet, and innocent, up to a point; he'd been her first… well… everything. Two years her senior, Justin graduated high school after their first year together, and the relationship faded. In hindsight, perhaps Loren had kept him at a distance after he went away to school.

Then there was Alex, who worked at her father's brewery. He was in college when they met, and everything about their relationship was more than Loren was ready for. She liked the grown up aspects. He was a reader, and he labored to project an air of intellectualism. Loren liked to think she was older than her years, but over time, she began to realize that Alex was younger than his own, and while parts of the relationship were good, *really* good, none of it was healthy, and eventually the fights and the drama became too much. When he graduated from Fort Lewis College and showed every sign of staying in town indefinitely, Loren ended it, and even then, it didn't feel like it was truly over until she'd finally gotten on that train by herself and felt the distance growing between them.

The journey to Grimwood was transformational. With each mile and state crossing, Loren grew more committed to two decisions: The first was that she'd learn from her older siblings' mistakes and remain as financially independent as possible, which meant she would need to find a job before her savings ran out. The second was that she wouldn't rush into another relationship at Grimwood. Not yet. If there was one thing she realized now, it was that casual affairs were not in her wheelhouse. No matter how hard she tried, or what she was looking for, she inevitably let things become too serious. If she was going to make the most of her time here and focus on her work in the writing program, she didn't want a relationship limiting her options from the beginning.

The train car lurched to a stop in the station and the crowd grumbled up from their seats to gather their things. Loren ran her fingers through her dusty blond hair and tied it back in a ponytail. She stood and stretched, set one foot on her seat, and lunged up to retrieve her bag from the overhead rack, then she sat back down and waited for the crowd to thin. There was no one meeting her there, so she was in no rush.

~

The crowd was thinning by the time Loren trudged up the platform from Track 7. It was hotter outside than it looked, and the thick air hit her like a wall of vapor. She wasn't accustomed to the humidity, and though the initial plan was to walk from the station, she quickly decided a bus was her best bet.

After disembarking at the first downtown stop, Loren was soon dripping with sweat as she tried to get her bearings. Jefferson Avenue, or "The Ave" as the locals called it, ran from the northern most part of town, straight through the middle of Grimwood's University District, and down to The Falls: the point at which the Allen River wrapped around the University's south end and dropped off the edge into nothingness. The entire stretch was a dozen blocks long, with the primary entrance to the University intersecting it in the middle. Both sides of The Ave were lined with restaurants, shops, and bars. At the bottom, just before The Falls, sat the President's Mansion.

Loren took in the neighborhood sites as she walked. After a few minutes, she stopped at the corner of Eldredge Drive, which led through the main gates and straight up the hill to Grimwood University. Recalling her previous visit, Loren knew a terrific store named R.K. Phillips Books sat just a half a block south of the University's main entrance. Normally, she'd have hooked a right and headed to the bookstore without missing a beat, but she was exhausted, and more than ready to find her dorm and settle in.

~

The gum-snapping, auburn-haired girl working the Student Orientation Services table was friendly, if somewhat distracted by a string of guys wearing Greek letters who kept stopping by the table to flirt with her. She repeatedly shooed them away, scolding them in a slight southern drawl as she checked Loren's name off the list. Her accent, and the way she cracked her gum between her teeth, reminded Loren of a young Holly Hunter.

"Austin. *Austin,*" the girl murmured as her pencil hovered over the list of names. "*Loren* Austin?"

"Yes."

"Looks like you're in Valentine. Room 965." She took out a set of keys and a campus map and drew a circle around Judy Valentine Hall. "It should be pretty easy to find, but if you run into any problems, just look for someone in an orange shirt."

~

Judy Valentine Hall, like all the buildings that circled the residence quad, dated back to the University's founding. The three tallest dorm towers were Eldredge Hall in the southwest corner of the square, Nathaniel Grimwood Hall to the east, and Valentine, which ran along the north. Three smaller buildings – Lavery, Taylor, and Esmond Halls – filled in the gaps that enclosed the common space, where intersecting walkways marked the field with an X.

Loren caught her breath as she recognized the towering bronze figure standing watch from his pedestal at the center of the quad. In life, the man – like his monument – was built like a Russian statue. Yet in pictures, there was a warmth in his smile, and a weariness in his eyes, that lent him a quality of self-effacing wisdom. Alan Grimwood and the literary worlds he created had fascinated Loren from the moment she'd first read his books.

Grimwood's work was the primary reason she'd come to the University, to study at the writing center he'd founded, in the place where he'd crafted some of her favorite pieces of writing.

She got off the elevator on the ninth floor and quietly made her way down the dimly-lit hall, checking the door numbers against her room assignment sheet. Though students had only begun moving in the previous day, it felt as though some of them had been living there for months already. Music blared from open doorways, people milled about in the halls and criss-crossed from room to room. She glanced in an open doorway as she passed by, and felt the people inside – two girls and two guys – sizing her up. Finally, she came to a room where the door wasn't propped open, but was slightly ajar. Loren took a breath and stepped inside.

The room was long and narrow. Even in the dim light, the walls showed their age, damaged plaster and decades of sloppy repair jobs clearly visible beneath layer upon layer of thick paint. Loren's eyes settled on a glowing pink lava lamp on the window sill. A girl in black cargo shorts and a purple hoodie was on her hands and knees under a desk covered with computer cables and equipment. The door hinges creaked as Loren dragged her luggage in from the hall. Her suitcase banged into a rolling chair, which bumped against the desk, startling the person on the floor beneath it.

"Fuck." The girl muttered as she jumped and hit her head.

"Oh, I'm so sorry!" Loren exclaimed. She pulled the chair out of the way to help her up.

Like Loren, she was average height, around 5' 4". Her hair was short and unnaturally black, a punk rock chop and dye to match the heavy eye makeup and general "could give a shit" expression on her face as she got to her feet.

"Brooke Winston," she said.

"Loren Austin."

Brooke looked her up and down. "What are you, a business major?"

"No." Loren laughed. She'd never thought of herself as giving off a business school vibe, but compared to this girl, most people likely seemed like stuffed shirts by comparison. "I'm in the writing program. What about you?"

"Graphic design."

"I've heard they-"

"I assume all that shit is yours," Brooke interrupted as she pointed behind the door.

Loren peered at a stack of five cardboard boxes set in the corner.

"Oh yeah, those are mine. I took the train from Colorado, so I shipped my things back a couple of weeks ago."

"I wasn't sure if you'd been here already and claimed that side," Brooke indicated with a sweep of her arm. "So I went ahead and took this one. That all right?"

Brooke spoke with a slightly defensive tone, like she expected disagreement even as she preemptively promised a fight.

"That's perfect," Loren said. "Unless you have a preference."

"Makes no difference to me."

"I'm happy to-"

"You like No Doubt?" Brooke asked, cutting her off again.

"They're all right-"

"Don't Speak" rumbled from the stereo before Loren could finish her thought. No sooner did the music start, than Brooke went back to assembling her computer.

OK then, Loren thought as she turned to her pile of boxes.

* * *

Braden McNutt stood on Grimwood Library's front steps. He was 5' 10," with an athletic build, a mop of brown hair, and piercing, pale green eyes. Perspiration shimmered on his brow from the uphill climb to campus. He dropped his duffel bag on the sidewalk, dried his face on the sleeve of his shirt, and took a moment to take in his surroundings.

Years of hard work, much of it with his grandfather's support, had brought him to this place, and now that he'd arrived, his head was swimming with possibilities. He was determined to make the most of every opportunity The Writing Center would make possible.

Braden had explored the library on his first campus visit two years ago, when he and Pops wandered the catwalks and corridors for hours, discovering countless study spaces and hideaways hidden among the stacks. In the process, they'd stumbled into areas they suspected were connected to the incident, but the library's macabre history didn't interest them. They didn't want to know where the tragedy had unfolded, or where the shooter leapt to his death, the library's collections, and the sheer *scope* of the place were what boggled their minds.

Though he was tempted to take another quick look around the library, there would be plenty of time for that later. Picking up his room key was task number one, but he couldn't resist making a quick loop around the academic side of campus before he followed the quarter mile walkway to the dorms.

Grimwood Library stood watch at the top of The Falls. The Student Union, was tucked between the library and the President's Mansion, it housed the academic dining hall, the campus bookstore, and the college radio station – WGRM

89.7 FM. Directly to the north of the library, an expansive red brick square called The Lookout, offered unobstructed views of The Falls and the final stretch of the Allen River before it cascaded over the edge behind the library. The Writing Center was adjacent to The Lookout. Walking west, you came upon the Administrative Building and the bulk of the university's other specialized colleges.

Braden picked up his keys and paperwork from the orientation tables and paused to get his bearings. He was assigned room 1050 in Eldredge Hall, which was one of the bigger dorm towers. He stopped in the lobby on his way in, looking over a bulletin board covered with flyers. A notice for a part time position at R.K. Phillips Books jumped out at him. He tore off a tab of contact information, glanced around for observers, and quickly moved a flyer for the Anime Club so it covered the job posting, then he hopped on the elevator and headed up to his floor.

~

"Hey!" a voice called as he opened the door.

Braden pulled the key from the lock and peered into the room. It was as deep as it was wide, a painted cinderblock cube, with two sliding windows on the farthest wall. Music was playing, nothing he recognized, but it sounded good. His roommate was stretched out on one of the beds, flipping through a copy of *Rolling Stone*. He tossed the magazine aside and jumped to his feet as Braden lurched through the doorway.

"Let me help you with that."

"I'm good, thanks," Braden said as he dropped his duffel on the floor, relieved to be rid of the thing.

"Is that all you brought?"

"For now at least. And I'm starting to think *that* was too much!"

"I'm impressed, man. I thought I traveled light, but you've got me beat."

Braden surveyed the room, spotting a laptop, a stereo, and a mini fridge.

"I'm Hank Pierce by the way." He nodded at Braden's room assignment as they shook hands. "The paperwork says Henry, but I go by Hank."

Hank was tall, with at least two inches on Braden. He was muscular but wiry, with short-cropped blond hair, sharp features, and an easy grin. Braden was typically slow to make friends, but he had a good feeling about his new roommate.

"Braden McNutt."

"Good to meet you, Brady. You want a beer?"

Braden wondered how his fellow underage freshman had managed to get set up with beer already, but judging from his personality, such arrangements were likely effortless. And a beer sounded great right about now.

"I'd love one."

"So, are you a business major?" Hank asked as he handed Braden a bottle of Grimwood ESB.

"No, I'm not. Do I look like one?"

"Not especially, but you do seem to have your shit together."

Braden tried to twist the cap off the bottle, then looked around helplessly. Hank motioned to an opener fastened to the side of his desk.

Braden laughed as he pried off the top. "You think I have *my* shit together? You certainly remembered the necessities."

Hank took another bottle out of the fridge and twisted off the cap.

"Wait a minute, how did you do that?" Braden asked.

"You're drinking the good stuff." Hank held up his own bottle. "This is Genesee."

Braden took a sip of his beer and looked at the label. "It's good. Is *everything* around here named Grimwood?"

"It would seem that way," Hank replied as he sat back on his bed and stretched out his legs. "So, do *I* look like a business student?"

Braden took in Hank's wrinkled t-shirt and dirty jeans. "Not at all."

"Good." Hank laughed. "I actually am one. Business major. Music production minor. If I had my druthers I'd reverse the order, but I'm testing an alternate route."

"How did you settle on that?"

"Well… I want to start my own record label, but *everyone* wants to do that, and most of their labels crash and burn, because 99% of the folks who start them love music but have no clue how to run a company. Myself included. I figure a business degree will teach me how to stay afloat, while music production shows me the nuts and bolts of making records."

"That sounds like a good plan to me."

"How about you?"

"I'm here for The Writing Center."

"Yeah, I can see that." Hank studied him for a moment. "You have a *booky* look about you."

"Surprisingly, that isn't the first time I've heard that. Actually, I just saw the bookstore downtown is hiring. I thought I might walk down there later and fill out an application. Hopefully they'll think I look 'booky' too."

"That would be a good gig. I've got an interview with Red Tomato tonight. I'll probably end up slinging pizzas again like

I did in high school. Hopefully I can switch to deliveries before too long though, get some of that tip money."

"Do you have a car?"

"Yeah." Hank pointed at the fridge. "That's how I got the bigger stuff here. You?"

"Back home, but it needs repairs." Braden set his bottle on his desk and heaved his heavy duffel bag onto his bed.

Hank sipped his beer quietly as he watched him unpack.

"Where are you from?" Braden asked.

"Albany. How about you?"

"Huntington, Long Island."

"Couple of New Yorkers," Hank noted.

"I'd be willing to bet we're not the only ones."

~

"What do your parents do?" Loren asked as she looked around Irwin Brown Dining Hall, which everyone simply called Brownie's.

"You know those Wall Street assholes who keep blowing up the economy and getting even richer with the bailouts?"

"Yeah?"

"That's them. I apologize."

"Oh…"

As Loren pondered what to say next, a group of kids Brooke recognized came lumbering into the room. There were three guys and two girls. All of them were dressed in a similar style: something between punk rock and hobo.

"Any siblings-"

Brooke cut her off, "Some people I met at summer orientation just showed up. I'll catch you later."

"All right," Loren said as her roommate picked up her tray and hurried to catch up to her friends.

Rather than returning to the dorms after dinner, Loren walked the wooded path that ran behind Brownie's and down to the sport fields. The sun was dipping behind the trees, sharp orange light singeing the edges of the green leaves. The campus was oddly quiet. Other than a group of students tossing a Frisbee on the football field below, it felt as though she had Grimwood to herself. Loren sat on the grassy hillside and looked out over the town.

Eventually, the Frisbee throwers left. Loren stuck around a short while longer, thinking. When she eventually started back, the woods had grown darker. She stepped up her pace as she followed the path, and was almost to the clearing to the south of Brownie's when she stopped short. For the second time that day, Loren recognized the broad-shouldered figure weaving in and out amongst the trees off to the side of the trail. Only now, rather than an alloyed casting, he appeared to exist in the flickering flesh. Loren caught sight of him again as he re-emerged a short distance away, briefly appearing to look her way, before he turned and disappeared into the shadows.

Grimwood.

* * *

They walked downtown as the light faded. Hank was headed to his interview at Red Tomato, and Braden figured this was as good a time as any to fill out an application at R.K. Phillips Books.

He and his grandfather had made a point of visiting the store when they toured Grimwood two years earlier. They always sought out bookstores on their trips, bringing home stacks of books they'd picked up along the way. Pops had worked in publishing, which he compared to letting an alcoholic work the corker at a winery, half the product never made it to market.

As far as bookstores went, they agreed that R.K. Phillips was one of the best. Owing to its roots in Alan Grimwood's hometown, the store was a bit of a literary touchstone for fans of the author's work. As such, they carried a wide assortment of Grimwood related volumes, including first editions of *Revenant* and *Black Robes,* and every annotated rerelease and biography that hit the market. As far as *non*-Grimwood books were concerned, the store carried one of the most expansive collections of new and back catalogue titles Braden had ever seen, all of it housed in a two-story, red brick building, beautifully decked out with dark wood shelves and well-worn oak floors.

The wide planks creaked underfoot as Braden stepped into the store and took it all in. A rounded bank of shelves arched across the righthand side of the sales floor. Antique schoolhouse lights hung from the pressed tin ceiling overhead, casting pools of light over the tables of hardbacks below. An imposing wood counter anchored the left wall, along with a staircase leading up to the second floor.

Braden headed to the front counter, where a short, middle-aged woman with close-cropped brown hair was pulling books off a rolling cart, checking them against the computer inventory, and stacking them on the counter to be shelved. She looked up as Braden approached.

"Can I help you?"

"Yes, I was hoping to fill out an application for the part time position."

She handed him a form and a pen. "Fill this out and drop it off at the information desk upstairs."

"Thanks," Braden said as he took the paper and looked for a place to sit.

He found a wide chair in the back corner of the store and carefully filled in his contact information and work history, particularly his seasonal work at The Book Revue in Huntington. He looked it over carefully when he was done, and started up the stairs.

A packed author event was going on in the back room, with a line of people flowing out into the hallway. A handful of customers was queued up at the counter at the top of the stairs, waiting to buy their books from the young, blond-haired girl working the register.

A honeyed gravel voice began talking behind Braden as he waited for a good moment to hand in his application. The voice grew louder as the speaker wrangled a customer from the back room to the information desk, and Braden turned to see a woman in her early fifties, with dark, curly hair, swoop past the line of customers and duck behind the counter.

"Beth," the woman said to the girl at the register. "After you're done with that sale, can you look up a book for me?"

Beth seemed to be under a great deal of pressure to keep up with the line of customers, which was growing by the minute, but she hopped to attention at this request, "Absolutely, Roxanne," she said in a way that told Braden the woman must be someone important.

Roxanne waited a nanosecond before she continued her discussion with the customer she'd brought with her. "Don't write her off yet. I know her latest isn't for everyone, but her *first* book was something special." She turned back to the girl, who was sweating a little as she punched in a credit card number. "Beth, what was the title of D.J. Norman's first book? The one where the victim gets shot in the back in the first scene?"

The register began making a high-pitched beeping noise that suggested something had gone haywire. Beth opened her mouth helplessly, but no sound came out...

Braden cleared his throat, "*Sub Rosa.*"

Roxanne looked at him intensely. "What was that?"

'The first D.J. Norman book was *Sub Rosa.*"

Roxanne snapped her fingers and pointed at him. "That's it," she said as she darted down the stairs. She returned a few moments later and handed a paperback copy to the woman she'd been helping.

"You'll love this book. Let me get it for you… Beth!" Roxanne called over the wail of the still-beeping register. "Mark out a copy of *Sub Rosa.*"

Braden stifled a laugh as Beth's eyes nearly bugged out of her head. He was just looking the application over one last time when Roxanne stepped toward him.

"Thank you, that would have driven me crazy," she said. "Can I help you with anything?"

"I was just dropping off an application for the-"

Roxanne snatched the paper from him. "I can take that." Her eyes scanned the form, then she looked up. "Expect a call tomorrow," she said as she walked behind the counter and disappeared into the back office.

Braden looked at Beth, who appeared to be in a state somewhere between bemusement and all out panic.

"I think you got the job," she said.

So that was Roxanne Phillips.

~

Braden decided to take the long way back, wandering past a diner called *Brick's,* and down to the University District's farthest end, where he could look up the hill and see the President's Mansion peering down over him. A steep, concrete staircase made its way up the embankment from the street. Braden started climbing. Aside from a shallow landing midway up, the stairs rose four precipitous stories at an alarming angle. By the time he reached the halfway point, Braden wondered how in the hell such a dangerous set of stairs was still accessible in the age of the personal injury lawsuit. He was out of breath and sweating when he finally reached the top, where he could hear The Falls thundering in the distance, and feel their cool mist settling on his face.

He trudged across the President's back lawn, past The Student Union, toward the library. Tomorrow was the first day of classes. If someone had asked him a year ago how he saw his freshman year beginning, he would never have imagined he'd be arriving on campus by himself. Pops would surely have been there. And if he couldn't make it, Jeremy would no doubt have taken his place. Ultimately, neither was a possibility. Instead, Braden was strolling the Grimwood grounds alone, remembering the people who couldn't be there.

Retracing his path from the afternoon, Braden glanced up at the tower in the dim light. He passed the entrance to the library, and climbed the steps to The Lookout. The late summer air was thick with humidity, but the heat was gone. Braden crossed the square, and was nearly to the lookout point, when the shadows around him wavered. Three figures emerged from the darkness, and began walking along ahead of him. Braden stopped short, watching as the spectral figures circled one another, as if in discussion, then they turned in opposite directions and vanished.

Flares.

2.

THE FIRST CLASS OF Hank Pierce's college career was about what he'd expected. *Boring.* He knew his two-track strategy was bound to cause some degree of frustration, and the dry business lecture he'd just sat through had more than confirmed his suspicions. His eyelids were heavy as he left the business building and staggered to a nearby coffee cart.

"Large black coffee," he said as he dug through his jeans for cash.

The vendor slid a cup across the counter and took his money.

Hank took a gulp from the steaming cup, burning his mouth, but welcoming the surge of caffeine.

Next was the main event, his first music class. Then he'd report for work study in the Administrative Building. After that, he'd try to finish as much homework as possible before his first night at Red Tomato.

He'd scheduled his classes back to back, leaving just five minutes to get from the business building to the School of Music. Hank hurried across the crowded courtyard, feeling much more at ease amongst the art crowd than he had in the business building. Where the business students were dressed in pressed shirts and slacks, the art students wore what his father would have dubbed "rags." With his faded jeans and threadbare Sub Pop T-shirt, Hank felt right at home.

The lecture hall was set up stadium style, the seats looking down on the presentation floor below. Hank took a seat near the back. He dug a notebook from his bag and stretched out, sipping his coffee as he surveyed the room.

A lanky guy with unkempt dark hair and a bag strapped tightly to his back stepped slowly down the aisle. He slipped into the row just ahead of Hank's, and slid the straps from his shoulders, taking a seat and looking around the room with a relaxed, pleasant expression on his face. Hank peered his head around to get a look at the band name printed above faded tour dates on the back of the newcomer's shirt, and wasn't at all surprised when he made out the word TOOL. For some reason the most mild-mannered people seemed to get the most enjoyment out of Maynard Keenan's art metal band.

~

Braden settled in a seat by the aisle as Professor Mark Price took roll. The course was The Novel, which he'd realized, with some disappointment, was focused on the reading and analysis of around a half-dozen books, and *not* on their actual creation. His enthusiasm for the curriculum in check, Braden looked around the room.

There were a couple cute girls in the auditorium, particularly one near the front, who, he learned from the roll call, was named Kate Murphy. She was tall and thin, with strawberry blonde hair and a hesitant, self-conscious smile. She had an inviting way about her, and Braden found himself staring, right until the moment she turned around and looked directly at him. The intensity of her gaze caught him off guard and he looked away, embarrassed at getting caught. Despite a couple of high school romances, Braden was never all that confident around girls, they usually had to make the first move, and he could never tell if his flustered responses were a help or a hindrance. When he looked back in Kate's direction, he could see the faintest hint of a laugh line at the corner of her mouth as she looked toward the front of the room.

Professor Price was nearing the bottom of the roster. He flipped to the last page of the class list. "And I have one late addition. Loren Austin-"

"Here," a voice called from the back of the auditorium.

Braden turned to see her heading down the aisle toward him. She was average height, with a trim, athletic build, shoulder-length blond hair, and piercing blue eyes that sparkled beneath dark eyebrows. Their eyes met for a split second… then she blinked and strolled past, taking a seat in front of him in the next row.

"Glad you could join us, Miss Austin," Price said as he pulled a stack of papers from his briefcase and handed them to a student in front. "Please take a syllabus and pass it on."

Something about Professor Price struck Braden as old fashioned. He dressed and behaved like a man from a different era. Braden recognized the look, because his grandfather and his friends had all dressed the same way, even in their later years. A tailored grey suit, emerald-green tie, and hair combed straight back. Braden pegged the professor as being close to 60, but once Price began to speak, his exact age was harder to pin down. While his movements were youthful and easy, they seemed out of step with the thick veins of gray that ran through his slicked back hair. And his eyes were those of a significantly older man; lines etched the corners and crinkled around the lids. When he smiled, parenthetical lines appeared fleetingly on each cheek. Braden instinctively liked him.

"Since you're all enrolled in The Writing Center, I think it's safe to say that the bulk of you want to be writers, or perhaps some of you have progressed a bit further in your thoughts on publishing, and want to be editors. Whatever your intentions, The Novel is one of the first courses taken by every student in the program."

Price gathered the extra copies of the syllabus as they found their way to the front of the room. He set all but one on top of his briefcase, then leaned against his desk and looked over the sheet of paper.

"So, why the novel? Why not short stories? Simple, because you've all had claptrap like *The Lottery* beaten into your heads throughout high school English, and while Shirley Jackson's story has kept her heirs in the money for decades thanks to the apathetic textbook industry, after four years of reading that kind of short-form, doomsday drivel, I'm amazed *any* of you got through the public school system with any interest whatsoever in the printed word. I like to think Grimwood is a bit more developed in our approach to storytelling, so while I'll cover the deserving classics, like *Jane Eyre,* and *Great Expectations,* I won't be making nods to the favorites of level-one high school English teachers everywhere. You all have the list, so you can see what we'll be reading. Bronte, Dickens, Vonnegut, the *greats* like Dashiell Hammett and Raymond Chandler, Nick Hornby's *High Fidelity,* some Stephen King, and of course, early John Irving. Books that live, and breathe, and serve a purpose. Other than Jane Eyre and Dickens, have any of you ever read these in a class environment before?"

No hands went up.

"Excellent. Then I'm doing something right. So, what's the purpose of a novel? I think there are a few of them, actually. For the writer, they let you process what has happened in your life, right wrongs, live through tragedy, *change* history, maybe try in your own way to help others avoid making the same mistakes you've made. Novels follow the plots writers think life should adhere to… Or maybe they're just a way of living out fantasies and getting revenge. Those are great reasons too. For readers, it's some of the same objectives, an escape from life, a way to come to terms with the things you've lived through. There's something soothing in knowing that someone somewhere – a character and therefore a *writer* – has experienced, felt, thought, seen, tasted, and lusted after all of the same things that you have. Books are communion between one person and another. They instill ideas and bring people together. What in life is better than a couple curling up and reading a book aloud to one another on a snowy winter night? What is more intimate than sitting in a leather chair, blanketed in the glow of a reading lamp, processing the dreams and ideas of someone miles, continents, or even decades and worlds removed from the time in which those words were set to paper? Novels are life pressed into ink and passed through time. The power to capture and deliver a message from one heart and mind to another, no matter the time or distance, is *invaluable.*"

Though he was listening to Price's impassioned speech, the more the professor expounded on intimate exchanges and the meeting of minds, the more Braden felt his attention shifting to Loren as she played with a lock of her hair, repeatedly twirling it in her fingers and running her hands down the length of the strands. She pulled a hairband from her wrist, twisted her hair together at the back of her head, and fastened it in place. Before Braden knew it, the lecture was over.

~

In addition to the pizza-tossing gig he was starting that night, Hank had been assigned a work study position in the university's development office for the first quarter. By the time he arrived for orientation, a handful of other students were there already, waiting for the tour to begin.

A stern older woman greeted him at the front desk as he signed in.

"You're *late*."

"Sorry," Hank said. "My last class-"

"Does not interest me in the least. Don't make a habit of it."

The rebuke threw him for a moment, then Hank caught sight of one of the other students, a striking red-haired girl, who was wagging her finger disapprovingly as the woman continued to reprimand him. The frown on the girl's face intensified as she stabbed at the air with her index finger for comic emphasis.

"You might think it's OK to be late from time to time-"

Finger stab, finger stab.

"But it all adds up-"

Finger stab.

Hank fought to suppress a smile.

"And I assure you, your peers will *not* look kindly on having to pick up the slack if you fail to keep up with your work."

Out of the blue, the woman turned and looked at the red-head, who was standing at attention now, an angelic expression on her face. The girl shook her head in agreement with the stern words of warning, but she turned in Hank's direction one last time, a devilish twinkle flashing in her light hazel eyes.

"Now," the woman said as she stood up from her desk with a groan. 'We can begin the tour." She picked up a clipboard and led the group down a long, narrow hallway.

The other students followed close behind, listening attentively as their guide spoke, but the red haired girl held back, waiting for Hank to catch up. When he did, she leaned toward him, whispering in his ear with a smile.

"You'd better shape up, deadbeat."

Hank smiled. "I guess so."

She shoved his shoulder lightly, then hurried up ahead.

Hank watched her as she caught up with the rest of the tour. She was tall, with long red hair that bounced as she walked. She didn't appear to be wearing any makeup, and she didn't need it. Hank found her intriguing, and hoped they would be working together at some point.

~

Loren sat at her desk looking over the syllabus for The Novel. From *Jane Eyre* to *The World According to Garp* in ten weeks. If the professor lived up to his opening lecture, this could be an interesting course. It was certainly refreshing to hear an instructor echo her opinion of the typical high school reading list. She could never understand why English Department heads believed grim morality tales would make the average high school student *want* to read once they were out of school. Her suspicion was that they didn't really care.

She picked up *Garp* and flipped to the author photo on the back. John Irving could go over the top with his macho "know your weight class" schtick, but she treasured several of his books. He was also easy on the eyes, like Alan Grimwood's New England cousin. She set the book down and thought back to class that morning, when she'd briefly made eye contact with that boy near the aisle. She didn't know that he was her type, or if she even *had* a type, but he was cute, with shaggy brown hair, a soccer player build, and just enough of that adolescent flush in his lined cheeks to suggest he was a freshman as well. She usually went for older guys, but there was something about him. She pictured those pale green eyes and wondered what he was doing…

~

There had been a distinct… hiccup in time when their eyes met. Braden had never felt anything like it. As though he'd briefly dropped out of reality and watched from a distance. He'd struggled to focus on anything else since. All he could think about was a girl he hadn't even spoken to, who he knew nothing about.

Loren Austin.

He'd caught her name at least, that was something.

Braden looked over the class syllabus in the light from his desk lamp. He fished another slice from the pizza box Hank had brought back from work. His roommate was fast asleep on the other side of the room. Braden knew he should be sleeping now too, but he wasn't tired. He scanned the list of books they would be studying. He'd read one or two of the titles in the past, and had long meant to read a few of the others. But all he really cared about at the moment was the fact that for the rest of the quarter, he'd get to see Loren Austin on a regular basis. Hell, he might even work up the nerve to talk to her.

He wondered what Jeremy would have thought. In a perfect world, Braden would have told him all about her by now. That's what they'd always done. Talked about girls. And he knew what Jeremy would have said.

"Ask her out, man! What have you got to lose?"

That was Jeremy's answer to everything. And of course he was right. Live your life without fear of the consequences. *Life* is consequences. In the end, what did any of us really have to lose? Worst case, you embarrassed yourself. Best case, you made a connection.

***

"Have fun-" Loren said as the door swept past her face.

She just caught sight of Mark, who appeared to be the one semi-decent member of the group, raising his hand in a weak wave before the dorm door slammed shut.

Loren's relationship with her roommate hadn't just failed to take off, it had exploded on the launch pad as Brooke hooked in with her moody friends and deflected any and all of Loren's friendly overtures. In the past week they'd exchanged perhaps a dozen words, most of which involved Loren inviting Brooke to dinner, and Brooke grunting what could only be interpreted as a "no." The few times they crossed paths, Brooke was always with her morose cohorts, who made even less social effort than she did.

Including Brooke, the group was made up of three girls and three guys. Loren suspected Mark had a slight interest in her roommate, since he was the only halfway friendly member of the bunch. She'd picked up the other names, but was unsure who was who. The other two guys were Evan and Devon. The girls were Miranda and Carol. Carol was the one with bleached blonde hair and a caustic personality to match. While Miranda sported long black hair, with blood red streaks, and the type of charisma that had likely inspired Joseph Guillotin to start tinkering. As for Evan and Devon, their personalities were as interchangeable as their names.

Be that as it may, *they* also had something to do that night.

Loren heard a beer bottle shatter somewhere in the distance. The signature sound of a Friday night. She eyed the pile of books on her desk, briefly considered working on one of her class assignments, but instead grabbed her keys and walked out the door. She might as well explore the campus.

~

Thornfield Hall was such a great, gothic setting.

Braden closed the book and surveyed the warmly-lit, wood-paneled room around him.

Speaking of gothic settings…

He'd walked to Grimwood Library after dinner and spent an hour wandering the stacks and corridors. The place was just as mindboggling as he remembered – like something from a Jules Verne novel – full of crisscrossing catwalks, spiral staircases, and soaring iron bookcases. Walkways and ladders were welded into the very structures of the towering shelves, creating intricate balconies that circled books on every imaginable subject.

The main hall was four stories high, with wide study tables that stretched back into the shadows, their surfaces lit by scattered banker's lights. Above everything loomed an enormous, domed ceiling, where an eerily-painted night sky was sporadically shot through with stars.

Braden had climbed a set of stone steps to the library's top floor and wandered back to a shadowy room called Ashton Study Hall, where he'd settled into a secluded workspace, lit by the warm glow of a single desk lamp, and begun to read *Jane Eyre*.

Hours later, his eyes growing bleary, Braden stopped to consider what he was doing there on a Friday night. His grandfather would have told him to go out this first weekend, make some friends and learn the lay of the land. He was always pushing Braden to be as well rounded as possible, urging him to expand his interests beyond literature and writing, and Braden had done his best to do just that, but over the course of the last year, pushing himself had gotten harder. There were times he just wanted to do his own thing, and often he did, perhaps too frequently…

He sighed and gathered up his things, heaving his backpack over his shoulder and backtracking through the dimly-lit corridors, listening to the sounds of his own footsteps padding softly on the worn stairs. He emerged on the first floor, and was almost to the exit when he caught sight of the girl from class. Loren.

She was standing just inside the library's front doors, taking in the scene. Recognition flashed across her face when she turned and saw him.

"Hey," Braden said.

"Hi."

"I think we have a class together."

Loren smiled and nodded. "The novel."

"Isn't this place awesome?"

"*Totally*," she said as she looked up at the painted ceiling. "It's almost overwhelming."

"But in the best possible way, right? I'm Braden by the way."

"Loren."

"Nice to meet you, Loren," Braden said as he looked her in the eyes. "I guess I'll see you in class." He started for the doors.

"Braden-?" Loren asked. Braden stopped and turned around. "Would you have any interest in, I don't know, going someplace and getting a cup of coffee?"

~

Hank set down his beer and grabbed a pen.

"All right," he said into the receiver as he jotted down a message for Braden. 'First shift at the store is Monday at six.' I'll let him know."

He hung up the phone and stuck the note on Braden's desk lamp with the heading: *You got the job!*

Hank finished the last sip of beer, tossed the empty bottle in the trash with a *clink*, and debated his next move. He could open a Genesee, or he could head out and see what was happening around campus. Since he didn't feel like another drink, he figured now was as good a time as any to wander the dorm tower and get to know some of his classmates.

The halls were filled with the sounds of music and chatter. Hank recognized most of the songs as he drifted past the open doors. Some of the occupants nodded at him from their rooms, but for the most part, the people inside were either seated at their desks, absorbed in their work, or gathered in groups, oblivious to passersby.

He reached the end of his hall and took the stairs down to the next level. This floor was significantly more quiet. He passed several closed doorways before he came upon a small lounge space tucked into an alcove away from the main hall. A girl with damp red hair was seated on a couch inside, reading a book. She was dressed in pajama pants and a tank top, which was slightly wet from the twist of freshly-washed hair draped over her shoulder. Hank took a deep breath as she turned in his direction. It was the girl from the work study tour.

"Well, well…" she said with a grin. "I was wondering when you'd decide to show up. Late as usual."

~

"I latched onto *Revenant* in middle school. My grandfather was a big Alan Grimwood fan, so as soon as he thought I was old enough, he gave me that first book. I must have been around twelve."

"I was probably the same age," Loren said. "I used to plow through book after book at my town library, so one of the librarians would set aside stacks of stuff she thought would interest me. At some point she slipped a Grimwood title in there, and that was it. I read *Revenant,* then *Black Robes,* then anything else I could dig up."

They were seated in Brownie's, working their way through their second refill. Braden picked up his coffee, studying the soft lines under Loren's eyes as he took a sip.

"And what about this place?" he asked.

"Brownie's or the university?"

"Grimwood. When did you know you wanted to come here?"

"When I figured out I wanted to be a writer," Loren said. "I knew my favorite author had been a professor before he died, so it was heartbreaking to think I'd missed my chance to learn from him. When I heard about The Writing Center, I figured it was the next best thing."

"Same here."

Loren locked him in her gaze.

"So what do you want to write about?" she asked.

"What do *I* want to write about?" Braden murmured. "Well, despite my deep fascination with Alan Grimwood… I don't want to write about sinister things."

"How do you mean?" Loren asked. "You don't want to tell dark stories, or you don't want to write about the bad things that can happen in life?"

"I guess both." He took another sip of coffee as he gathered his thoughts. "People are here, and then they're gone. We can vanish in the blink of an eye and never see it coming. If you think about that too long, you start to wonder why people bother getting up in the morning, why anyone pursues their dreams at all. Why create stories that emphasize how weak the threads holding all of this together really are?"

"Maybe to remind people that time is precious. Other than your life, what do you really have to lose? Dark stories can be cathartic."

"So, is that the kind of thing *you* want to say?" Braden asked.

"To be honest, I'm not sure what it is that I want to say." She could feel her face growing warm. "I guess that's why I'm here, to figure that out." Loren was quiet for a moment, then asked, "You really think Grimwood wrote about sinister things?"

"Yeah, I suppose I do."

"I've always felt the opposite. His books are creepy, and the stuff about reincarnation and the afterlife can be disturbing, but I've always found his ideas about life and the passage of time inspiring."

"Maybe sinister is the wrong word…" Braden said. "I suppose his stories *are* life affirming in their way. I could just be looking at things from a funny perspective these days…or letting the mystique around this place cloud my thoughts on his writing."

"That's understandable," Loren replied. Then a thought occurred to her. "What about mysteries?"

"What about them?"

"Do you consider mysteries sinister books?"

"They can be. But they're sort of their own thing, right? It all depends on the writing. Some mystery writers revel in the gory elements, which aren't my thing. And thrillers are all about the action. But there are others who use the stories as an excuse to play with language-"

"The whole blonds and stained-glass-windows thing."

"Exactly," Braden said. *"That* I love. I guess I'm with Professor Price: I think Dashiell Hammett and Raymond Chandler are hard to beat."

"I want to take a stab at a mystery like that some time."

"Me too. It would be fun. Maybe we could write it together."

"Maybe," Loren replied as she studied her companion across the table.

There was something about this guy.

It was a fun talking to someone who spent time thinking about the same things she did. And though he had opinions, a *lot* of them, he didn't put them out there and hold his positions like some arrogant blowhard. There was give and take in their conversation. He had an open mind.

Loren dropped her eyes for the first time since they'd sat down together. She watched Braden's hands as they held his coffee, his thumb rubbing the smooth porcelain where the handle met the body of the mug.

This wasn't part of her plan.

She liked him, but she wasn't sure what, if anything, to do about it.

~

Hannah Merritt wished she was wearing a bra.

For some stupid reason, the thought that she might end up talking with anyone tonight had never crossed her mind. After her shower, rather than staying holed up in her room, she'd pulled on lounge pants and a tank top and decided to bring her architecture textbook out to the lounge. Her father had managed to get her a single room in the dorms, which was helpful for studying and sleep, but it was more isolating than she'd expected. Perhaps she was less anti-social than she realized.

Still, the thought that someone, let alone a guy, might sit down with her for an extended amount of time hadn't occurred to her. And even then, it wasn't until they'd been talking for a while, and she absentmindedly pulled a hairband from her wrist and gathered her damp hair into a ponytail that she realized how obvious her lack of a support really was.

His name was Hank, and he was a gentleman about it, but it would have been understandably difficult for anyone, let alone a college guy, not to let his gaze betray him. To his great credit, aside from an involuntary darting of the eyes and a slight flush in his cheeks – which took a few minutes to dissipate – he'd done an admirable job pretending not to notice, but eventually his thoughts tripped him up.

"So, I was, uh…"

He stopped, and Hannah almost had to laugh.

"I'm supposed to start the radio station job next week," he said finally.

"How often are you doing that?"

"I think one night a week to start. Between classes, work study, and Red Tomato, I don't know how much more time I'll have. What about you?"

"Me?"

"Are you working anywhere other than the development office?"

She shook her head. "I feel like a brat, but I'm not. Aside from the work for my scholarship, my dad is helping me with everything else."

"That's cool," Hank said. "That's the way it should be, right? You'll probably get a lot more out of your classes without the distractions. You're certainly not a brat."

"I'm afraid I can be though. You don't know me."

"I don't know you… yet," he said with a grin.

Hannah narrowed her eyes. "…Yet," she repeated with a lopsided smile, then she shivered. "Would you mind if I grabbed a sweatshirt?"

"Not at all," Hank said as she got up and ducked around the corner.

~

"That is one *full* backpack," Loren observed as they stepped out into the cold night air.

Braden adjusted the straps on his bulging bookbag. "I know. I need to lighten the load somehow."

"How much of that is textbooks?"

"Most of it actually," Braden replied. "I have a paperback and a notebook in here, but almost everything else is for classes. It's ridiculous though."

Loren studied her new friend's expression as they walked.

"Can I ask you something, Braden?"

"Sure."

"You said your grandfather passed away, but how did you end up living with him in the first place?"

"It's sort of hard to explain. My father inherited a ton of money from his aunt when he was in his twenties, so he mainly likes to travel and have a good time. After my mother left, he became more unreliable than ever. Which, if you knew my father, is *really* saying something. So my grandparents stepped in and raised me. First the two of them, then just Pops."

"Did you ever see your mother?"

"Not that I can remember. She and my Dad dropped out of the picture when I was really young."

"So where did you live your senior year?"

"After Pops passed away, I stayed at the house."

"By yourself?"

"Mostly. Our old cook was still there part time."

"*Cook?* Did you grow up in an episode of *Dynasty?*"

Braden laughed. "I don't think so, but maybe. Pops was a little old fashioned that way."

"So, you were on your own all last year?"

"Well, no, I had my friend Jeremy. He was kind of like a brother to me."

"And where is he this year?"

"Originally, he was talking about going to Grimwood too." His eyes darted Loren's way. "But he passed away unexpectedly last spring."

"Oh, I'm so sorry. What happened?"

"He died in his sleep, but they never really figured out what happened. Which…"

"-kind of makes it worse."

"Yeah."

"I can see why you might be looking at Alan Grimwood's books a little differently these days."

"But in a way, that's the beauty of it," Braden replied as they approached The Lookout behind the library. "I reread *Revenant* this summer, and after everything that's happened the last two years, it was like a whole new experience."

"What do you make about Grimwood Library and the whole…"

"-Incident?"

Loren nodded.

"You're the first person to mention that since I've been here."

"I guess it's sort of an unspoken thing," she said. "There are so many stories about what happened, and what people have seen. For some reason, I tend to believe them."

"I do too. My grandfather called them flares."

"Why flares?"

"He had a theory about life, and whatever is on the other side – that both existed on simultaneous planes. Like two parallel sheets of glass. Flares are individuals caught between the planes, like stray fragments of light."

"Flares…" Loren repeated. "I like that."

"Whether they mean to or not, every so often their images reflect off of one of the planes, and it makes their presence known. He called that flaring."

Loren was curious to know the backstory on Pops' theories, but she was suddenly reminded of the curious event her first night on campus..

"I feel funny asking this," she said. "But since you've been here, have you *seen* any flares?"

"Three of them." Braden motioned toward The Lookout. "Right here actually. My first night on campus."

"Who do you think they were?"

He raised a finger towards the library's tower. "I assumed they were… victims. What about you?"

"I'm pretty sure I saw Alan Grimwood the same night."

~

There were times Brooke wondered if she ought to take Loren up on her invitations to hang out. But what would they possibly have to talk about? The girl was from the middle of nowhere. Utah? Colorado? What did they have out there? Mountains and cows? Besides, she didn't want to spend all her time with her roommate. She needed to be around people like her friends in the city.

They were at some townies' house tonight. Evan knew them through friends. Brooke leaned against the wall and took a sip from her plastic cup. Whatever was in this drink, it was strong. She'd downed three of them in the first hour, and they'd started to kick in about midway through drink two. She ran her fingers over the texture of the wall, only dully registering the painted, bumpy surface.

Her teeth were tingling. Always a good way to tell if she was trashed. She liked to think she could hold her liquor, but she may have overdone it. She probably shouldn't have nabbed those pills from the medicine cabinet either. Old habits died hard.

Her friends had ditched her. Except for Mark, and *that* just wasn't happening.

Evan and Carol had wandered off to find a spare bedroom. Miranda was sitting on a couch across the room, attempting to stare through her hand. Apparently pot gave her x-ray vision. If Devon were around, she might have been interested in talking to him away from the group, but he'd scampered after some girl in a torn plaid skirt the minute they arrived, leaving Brooke to drink punch and keep one eye on Mark.

The music was getting louder, and her cup was once again empty, so Brooke lurched toward the kitchen, smashing her shin on a coffee table as the room skittered past her eyes in tracer-vision. She rubbed her leg and staggered ahead, holding her cup out to the shapeless face at the punch bowl.

~

Monday morning came fast.

She and Braden had exchanged numbers, and though she'd considered calling him Saturday night, Loren ended up staying in to work on class assignments. Same thing on Sunday.

What was keeping her from making that move? Fear of once again getting into something before she was ready?

She kept thinking of him though.

A groan emanated from the covers of Brooke's bed. She hadn't come back to the room Friday or Saturday night, and had been largely absent on Sunday as well, until she staggered in the door around 11 p.m., smelling like sweat run through a charcoal filter – the unique stench of someone expelling alcohol from every pore of their body. Her roommate had clearly overdone it, as the body's usual methods of excreting booze weren't enough to keep up with the sheer volume of alcohol Brooke must have consumed. At 11:16 she'd rushed down the hall to vomit in the bathroom sink. By 11:30 she'd moved from the sink to one of the toilets, where she'd stayed for at least the next hour, until Loren came in to brush her teeth, recognized a familiar pair of purple jeans under the stall door, and helped Brooke back to bed, where she'd remained ever since, one hand dangling over the trash can placed beside her for emergencies.

Loren didn't judge – she'd been known to help herself to a bit too much Puzzlebox Pale at her Dad's brewery. Though she briefly considered waking her roommate to see if she had any morning classes, Loren ultimately decided it wasn't her problem, opting instead to crack the window and draw the curtains before she grabbed her backpack and left.

~

Jason Pepper grew up in Grimwood, so the University had always been a presence in his life. In high school, visits to the University District were a kind of rite of passage among town kids, whether it was trips to the bookstore or meals at one of the restaurants along The Ave. Later, they'd start to go to shows at the district's all ages clubs. The more rebellious ones would pursue fake IDs, and if successful, would return to school Monday morning, boasting of alcohol-fueled weekend adventures. Jason was a part of the fake ID crowd, but for him it had nothing to do with alcohol; all he cared about was music, and the bands that played all ages clubs had a well-earned reputation for sucking.

He never imagined he'd become one of those townies who grabbed his pillow and teddy and trudged up the hill for college, but as his interest in music production grew, Grimwood started to seem like one of the best options. And of course, there was Susie… but despite what his mother thought, she hadn't been the deciding factor. Not ultimately.

As with most things, Jason didn't care what anyone thought of his decision anyway. The only voice he'd listened to was the one in the back of his head that told him he could go to Grimwood, but he couldn't be a day student and keep living at home like he was still in high school. Up until the last minute, he and Susie had planned to get a place together off The Ave. When that fell apart, his last minute dorm request nabbed him a single in Esmond Hall, which suited him just fine. Unlike home, he could play his music until all hours without complaint. And it was a three minute walk to Brownie's.

He ducked into the warmth of the dining hall as a breeze whistled through the early morning air. The cold was creeping in more each day. That, and the early hour, meant he had the place largely to himself. One of the first things he'd learned in the last week was that college kids and breakfast did not mix. The only child of a nurse who often worked the morning shift, he'd been raised to wake up early, a habit he was finding hard to shake. It was doubly troublesome today, as aside from the night shift at the campus radio station, his Monday was a blank slate. Fortunately, breakfast came with unlimited coffee refills, which he was aiming to stretch out for as long as possible.

Brownie's reminded him of the lobby to an old school hotel, with lots of dark paneling and wide-planked wood floors. The majority of the tables were lined up in the large, sunken center of the room, with booths tucked into moody niches that lined the sides. Jason collected his meal, filled his mug with coffee, and headed for a booth in the farthest corner, where he spread out his books, pulled on his headphones, and listened to music while he ate and worked on class assignments.

He was on his fourth cup of coffee when a girl walked into the largely empty dining hall who was looking very much the worse for wear. Still, she was a cute. Not too tall, not too short, jet-black dyed hair – chopped like a rocker, with a pretty face. But something about her struck him as sad.

Jason watched as she crossed the main dining area and took a seat alone at one of the tables. Seeing the way she nursed an orange juice and gingerly poked at her plate of scrambled eggs, he suspected a hangover. She took tiny bites of her food while barely taking her eyes off her plate. Jason watched her steadily from his booth, and wondered if they'd ever cross paths.

~

"Monday nights can be quiet if there's not an event," Mary Ellen said. "So it's usually a good time to catch up on shelving. God help you if Roxanne comes in and doesn't see you either waiting on a customer or restocking books."

Braden was following the store's floor manager, a short, fiery woman in her mid-thirties, who clearly knew her way around a bookstore, but lacked the ability to filter any of the words coming from her mouth. She was introducing him to everyone on shift that night and training him on the register. No sooner would they walk away from one staff member, then she'd give him the dirt on that individual's strengths, weaknesses, and personal delectations. So far he'd met Dan – the receiving guy, Claire – who worked in the café, and Jan – one of the other booksellers.

Mary Ellen eyeballed him for at least the third time that night.

"Speaking of Roxanne... are you a family friend or something?"

"No, why?"

She led Braden to the other side of the store, where she observed a tall, long-haired young man in his early-20s, who stood at the register, flipping through a magazine and scratching at a patchy goatee. The sour expression on Mary Ellen's face told Braden all he needed to know about her opinion of this particular staff member.

"We get a lot of applicants around here, so it can take a few interviews before we fill an opening. But Roxanne insisted we hire you immediately. Only one employee has *ever* had an easier time getting a job here." She nodded her head towards the guy at the register. "Cole Phillips, Roxanne's son."

A slamming noise reverberated from the front of the store.

"I'll introduce you to him some other time," Mary Ellen said.

Something rumbled again.

"What is that?" Braden asked.

His tour guide arched her neck to peer around a display. Braden followed her gaze until he saw a blond-haired girl, perhaps a year older than himself, yanking books from a cart and hurling them in a pile in front of the cookbook section. She grabbed two more books and repeated the process, then looked over at Cole to see if she had his attention.

She didn't.

Mary Ellen headed back to the main side.

"That's Faith," she said. "Cole seems to see the store as his personal dating pool. Half the female undergrads we bring on staff end up quitting because of Warren Beatty over there. Looks like we'll have another opening soon."

She walked over to a cart next to the front counter, where a short-haired woman in her late 40s was standing at the register, checking books against the computer inventory.

Mary Ellen looked at her watch and headed for the stairs.

"I've got to get an order in before eight o'clock." She turned to the woman at the register. "Jan, could you show Braden the basics of shelving?"

"I think we can manage that," Jan said with a smile. She waited until Mary Ellen was gone, then she pointed to a floor diagram taped above the register. "All the book sections are organized by numbers, which are shown on this layout." She pulled a book from the shelving cart and pointed to a number on the back, just above the barcode. "When the new books come out from receiving, you type the ISBN into the computer, check that the number of copies you're shelving matches the number the inventory says we have on hand, then find it a good spot on the proper shelf," she concluded as she walked over and shelved the book she'd been using as an example. "Easy as that."

"That sounds pretty straight forward," Braden said.

"Give it a shot and tell me if you have any questions."

He went to work, quickly shelving a handful of titles with no problem.

"I'd say you've mastered it," Jan said. She glanced down at her watch, then out the front window, where the light was fading fast. "It's eight o'clock. Why don't we see how much we can clear off this cart before closing?"

"I'm game," Braden replied.

The two of them set to work.

He was shelving a copy of *Chokecherry Canyon* in the mystery section when the front bell chimed, and a gust of chilled autumn air swept through the store. A girl with strawberry blond hair was standing at the register when Braden returned to the counter.

"Can I help you?" he asked as the girl started to turn around.

"Hey, aren't you in my class?" she asked.

Braden blinked.

It was Kate Murphy, the classmate with the self-conscious smile from The Novel.

"Oh yeah, I am. How are you?"

"I'm good," Kate replied, watching him intently with her light green eyes. There was a little crinkle of laughter between her brows and nothing self-conscious about the grin she gave him now. If anything, her demeanor was so self-assured that it threw Braden off balance. "This must be a great place to work."

"So far so good," Braden replied. "This is my first night."

"Congratulations."

"Thanks. We'll see how it goes. I could be a goner next week."

"Somehow… I doubt that," Kate said as she set a copy of *Jane Eyre* on the counter. "Speaking of class, I'm already behind on my reading. Can I pay for this?"

"You know, I haven't quite gotten up to speed on the register yet-"

Jan crossed the floor. "I can get that for you," she said, taking the book from Kate's hands as she ducked behind the counter.

Kate continued to look at Braden as Jan rang her out. He nodded awkwardly.

"Happy reading," Jan said as she slipped the receipt inside the book and handed it back to her.

"Thank you," Kate said. "I'll see you in class, Braden."

She remembered his name.

For some reason, that *really* threw Braden off his game. He could feel his face going red.

Jan looked at Braden as she and Kate waited for him to respond. When the silence grew especially uncomfortable she chimed in.

"He'll see you in class," Jan said, suppressing a smile as she tapped Braden on the shoulder playfully.

Finally, he snapped out of it. "See you class."

Kate's bemused smile only grew wider as she headed out the door. "Have a good night."

Jan waited until Kate had left before she shook her head at Braden in mock disappointment.

~

No TOOL shirt today.

After an afternoon shift at Red Tomato, Hank raced to the radio station on campus, where he arrived just in time for his first shift. To his surprise, the first person he ran into in the lobby was the lanky kid from his music class, who was once again wearing his bookbag tight against his back – almost like a parachute – but he wasn't wearing anything Maynard Keenan-related today, just an unzipped black hoodie over a white T-shirt and jeans.

Hank smiled as he put out his hand. "I'm Hank Pierce."

"Jason Pepper," his classmate replied. "Are you here for orientation?"

"I am-"

They were interrupted as a big guy in a Hawaiian shirt and a bushy beard came lumbering into the room. Hank was immediately reminded of Wolfman Jack in *American Graffiti.*

"You guys here for the training?"

"We are," Jason said enthusiastically.

"All right then. I guess that makes you Hank and Jason," he said, nodding his head as they raised their hands to identify who was who. "I'm Howard Lester. Let's get this carnival started."

Howard led the way down a darkened hallway. They passed a sign emblazoned with "89.7 FM," followed by the station's call letters.

"Welcome to WGRM, where the equipment might *look* old and dated, but… it doesn't work all that well either."

He motioned to a small kitchen on the right. "Help yourselves to coffee and soda. You might find some food in the fridge, but I can't guarantee it's from this quarter, so you'll probably want to steer clear. If you're working a late shift and worse comes to worst, order a pizza."

"Actually, I just started a gig at Red Tomato," Hank chimed in.

"Do you get a discount?"

"I think it's free."

"All the better! We'll order some tonight!"

They came to a glass door, which Howard opened, ushering them into the broadcast booth.

"Have a seat. You're about to see the magic happen."

Howard dropped into a desk chair that creaked under his weight as it rolled a few feet to the side, coming to a perfect stop in four indents worn into the old linoleum floor. He reached for the microphone arm, which creaked slightly as he brought it closer.

Jason and Hank took a seat on a dilapidated sofa against the far wall, where they could easily take in their surroundings. A window at the far end offered an opaque look into a dark room.

"Now, the *bad* thing about running such an outdated rig is that we have to wing a few things that *should* be easier in this day and age," Howard said as he tinkered with the console in front of him.

"We can't queue up much in the way of advanced programming, so if you're ever manning the booth on your own, bathroom breaks can be an adventure. The *good* thing about this setup is that we aren't just slapping our own soundbites on either end of a generic feed. We actually pick the songs we're going to play and put our stamps on the program. The DJ still *deejays*, which is a rare thing these days."

Jason pointed to the darkened window.

"What's in there?"

"That's our old recording studio. You guys stick around long enough, I can tell you some stories about that room. It looks like shit, but there are folks who swear it's got one of the best mixing consoles in the world. You ever find a band you want to put on tape, assuming they don't mind a little asbestos exposure, you could probably cut an album in there."

"Really?" Jason's eyes were wide.

"That's awesome," Hank said. "And… you're joking about the asbestos, right?"

"Who's to say? Don't take me too literally kid. I'm on the radio, so I talk a *lot* of shit. Speaking of which," he looked at his watch, "I need to get on the air."

Howard slammed his coffee cup down on the desk, punched a button on the console, and started howling into the microphone like a dog.

"It's five o'clock on a Monday night. Do you know who's manning the border?! Look to the north, look to the south, man the battle stations, cause *this* is *The White Russian's Rockabilly Bedlam Ball!*"

Jason and Hank again exchanged looks of delight. This guy was going to be interesting.

~

Howard broadcast for two hours before he signed off, putting on a *Best of WGRM* tape as he headed out the door.

"That's all the magic for today, fellas. I'm needed at the Pig 'n Whistle." He grabbed his coat and headed for the door. "Help yourselves to whatever you can find in the kitchen. I usually keep something special in the veggie crisper. You're welcome to partake. The next deejay should be here by eight. If no one shows up… good luck!"

Then he was gone.

"Veggie crisper?" Jason asked.

They headed down the hall to the kitchen, where Hank opened the fridge and pulled out the bottom drawer. A 1.5 Liter bottle of Kahlua rolled forward, stopping with a *thunk*.

"I think I see where the White Russian gets his name. Should we?"

Jason shrugged his shoulders. "The man offered."

~

Howard's Kahlua paired rather nicely with the slow-cooked coffee that had been simmering in the pot all evening. Forty minutes and three mugs later, Jason and Hank were just about up to speed on the lives that had led them to Grimwood campus.

"Well, your Mom is right," Hank muttered as he slumped back in the couch. "Susie sucks."

Jason was sitting in Howard's creaky chair. "She had her good points."

"Like what?" Hank asked "You dated the girl all through high school. She gets you to enroll at Grimwood with her. You guys put a deposit down on an apartment together! Then three weeks before classes start, her first choice college sends her a last minute acceptance letter and she leaves you in the dust? How does she not suck?"

Jason shrugged. "I'm just glad I'm here. This might sound bad, but I'm sort of glad that's over anyway."

"What could *possibly* sound bad about that? If you're happy, then godspeed."

"What about you?" Jason asked. "Are you dating anyone?"

"From Albany? No. My last relationship ended around the start of the year. I was kind of focused on school and the whole 'plan' after that."

"What's the plan?"

Hank sat up straight, self-mockingly reading off a mental checklist as he punched his fist into the palm of his hand. "In-state school for cheaper tuition. Business school to learns the ins and outs of running a business. Music production classes and the radio to learn the ins and out of the music biz. All work. No play."

"That sounds… intensive."

"Yeah, my old man loves it. He's pragmatic to a fault. My mother wants me to find a balance."

"You strike me as someone who *would* have a balance."

"I usually am. I may have swung a little too far in one direc-tion." Jason mused. "Actually, I am sort of interested in this one girl at the moment. Hannah. She's from Chicago. We're supposed to hang out again tonight after I'm done here."

"Then you're human after all. That's a relief."

"What about you? What's your plan?"

"Me? I'm trying to enjoy school as best I can. And eventually I want to start my own label."

Hank's ears perked up. "Oh yeah, do you have a name?"

"I do. Cradle to the Groove Records."

Hank crinkled his nose.

"What? You don't like it?"

"Are you saying groove like "Groovy?"

"No, like cradle to the grave, but groove. Like, *record* groove," Jason said, growing impatient as Hank still looked unconvinced. "Anyway, the name is still up in the air, but I've been going to as many shows as possible on the weekend. I'm keeping an eye out for bands that I might be able to work with at some point down the road."

"I'm not so sure about that name, but maybe we should join forces…"

"Maybe we should," Jason mused, though he still seemed rather irritated.

~

There was no mention of the vomiting adventures of Sunday night, but when Loren invited Brooke to dinner at the end of the day, her roommate surprised her, accepting the invitation with a simple "Sure."

Of course, once they got their food and sat down, conversation was sparse as usual. By the time Brooke's usual cohorts rolled into Brownie's, she and Loren had fallen silent. On seeing her friends, Brooke inhaled the rest of her food and excused herself.

Loren watched as Brooke headed over and joined the group, once again taking note of the indifference with which they greeted her. After they'd left, she pushed her tray away, pulled *Jane Eyre* from her bag, and started to read.

~

Hank was meeting Hannah inside the Student Union after his shift at the station. She sat on a bench just inside the main entrance, flipping through a textbook. The over-achieving voice in the back of her head was telling her she should be getting a head start on class work, but a tingling sensation in her stomach told her this was just as important.

The doors opened with a *whoosh,* the sound of crisp leaves blowing in on the cool evening air. Hannah looked up from her book as Hank approached with a grin.

"Hi."

"Hi," she replied.

He tilted his head to get a look at the cover of her book. *"Foundations of Architecture…* Nice play on words. So, is that what you're studying?"

"Yeah. An architecture major from Chicago. Who'd of thought, right? But in my defense, if you grow up in that city and *don't* learn to appreciate the buildings, you're *probably* a narcissistic asshole."

"Why didn't you go to school back home? They must have a ton of good programs."

"Too many people interested in the same thing. I didn't need the added pressure. *Why?* Are you saying you wish I wasn't here?"

Hank looked her in the eyes and placed a reassuring hand on her. "Yes. That's exactly what I saying."

"Oh shut up." She shoved his hand away and gathered up her things. "You want to get something to eat?"

"Absolutely. I'm starving."

"I think Spike's is still open."

Spike's was a greasy spoon in the basement of the Union. The specialties of the house were burgers, fries, grilled ham and cheese, and anything else that could be griddled into submission. The place was designed like a bunker, with dining wings that split off in every direction from a central hub. A massive TV in the middle of the room was tuned to *The Simpsons*.

"Have you eaten here before?" Hannah asked as they entered.

"Not yet."

"The food is pretty good. The place reminds me of a SPEC-TRE boardroom from one of the Sean Connery Bond movies."

Hank peered in the entrance. "It does sort of have that look. How do you know Bond movies?"

"Are you kidding? I grew up with a middle-aged father in a single parent household. What else would we bond over? Excuse the pun."

"Interesting…" Hank said as they grabbed their trays and slipped into line.

~

After dinner, they wandered down the hall to the game room, where they shot a game of pool, then played *Dance Dance Revolution* until they were both sweating. They were doing pretty well by the time they realized that, aside from the two of them, the place was empty, and the student manning the front desk was clearly anxious to go home for the night.

"Think we should head out?" Hank asked.

"Probably. It's late."

They trudged up the basement steps and out through the main foyer.

"That was fun," Hannah said as they exited the building and started down the moonlit walkway in front of the library.

"Yeah it was."

"Hey."

Hank stop and looked at her as she lingered in the shadows. "What?"

"Come here."

Hank stepped forward, and Hannah put one arm behind his back, pulling him closer before she kissed him.

"I had a good time." she said.

"I did too."

"We should do this again."

"Absolutely."

~

"So, this girl is just one floor below us?" Braden asked.

"Yep."

"Do you think that might get awkward?"

"Not if everything goes well."

"And how is it going so far?"

Hank grinned. *"Good."*

"I'm happy for you, man. What's this girl's name, anyway?"

"Hannah."

As they were talking, a group of guys began assembling in the lounge just outside Hank and Braden's open dorm door. The noise of the crowd was getting increasingly louder.

"What's going on out there?" Hank asked.

Braden arched his neck to see. "I have no idea."

"Hey!" Hank called to a gangly kid with a buzz cut.

"Yeah?" the guy shouted back as he walked over to their door.

"What are you guys doing?"

"We're getting a group together to head over to Brick's for some plates."

"Plates?" Braden asked.

"Yeah, Brick Plates."

Hank looked dubious. "What the heck is a Brick Plate?"

"You don't know?!"

"Nope," Braden replied.

"Brick's is a diner on The Ave. They serve a little bit of everything, but Brick Plates are the specialty of the house. Huge scoop of macaroni salad, pile of home fries, two massive burgers, all topped with hot meat sauce and swirled together."

Braden's mouth hung open. "That… sounds horrendous. Why is it called Brick's?"

"Supposedly the owner is named Brick, but most people think it's because bricks are what you're shitting after you have a plate. You guys wanna go?"

"What do you think, Brady?" Hank asked expectantly.

"I think… I'd better pass," Braden said.

Hank hesitated, but eventually shook his head. "We'll take a raincheck."

"Suit yourself. You'll have plenty of opportunities. Everyone gets there at some point."

Braden waited for the kid to leave, then he whispered to Hank. "Think we should have gone?"

"I've gotta admit, I'm a little curious now."

"Me too."

"Thing is, I ate dinner at Spike's. That *and* Brick's in one night… I'm not sure the human GI system can handle that much grease."

* * *

In each of the lectures so far, Professor Price had worn suits so dark that they reminded Braden of something one might wear to a funeral. In both cases, he'd also worn a distinct shade of green, an emerald tie in the introductory session, and today, an open-collared shirt in the exact same color.

At the end of the second class, almost as an afterthought after wrapping up his lecture, Professor Price stood and cleared his throat.

"Just one more thing. I wanted to let you know about an upcoming event I believe would be well worth your time. Daniel Buckley, who usually writes rather darkly humorous detective novels, will be giving a talk here on campus Friday night. His new book is supposed to be something different than his usual work. As freshmen, I encourage you to come to as many of these events as possible during your time at Grimwood. As writers, it's important to hear from as many different people working in the field as possible. He'll be speaking right here at The Writing Center at eight o'clock. I hope you can all make it."

"Wanna go?" Braden asked Loren, who was seated next to him.

"Sure."

"Why don't I stop by your place at six and we can head over?"

"Sounds good to me."

"By the way, where exactly *is* your place?"

"I'll write it down for you," Loren said as she dug out a piece of paper and pen.

~

What was she even *doing* here?

Brooke squinted at her reflection in the mirror. Her vision was fractured and out of focus, as if two lenses had been knocked out of alignment. It didn't feel like she was really even there. *There* being the common bathroom in the three bedroom dorm suite Evan and Devon shared with one other student.

They'd met up as a group earlier in the evening. Carol had slipped into Evan's bedroom the moment they walked in the door, her typically bored expression at odds with the sounds that bleated out into the lounge area as soon as they shut the door.

Brooke had waited in the living room with Miranda, Devon, and Mark, drinking Honey Browns and watching some goofy show on the TV, but eventually, she'd grown restless and headed into the bathroom, where, just as she used to do at her friends' apartments in the city, she opened the medicine cabinet to peruse its contents.

She didn't know who "Peng Hsiao" was, probably the third roommate, but his name was on a pill container on the top shelf, along with the words *"for pain."*

Bingo.

She'd taken two pills before popping the container in her pocket. That was five minutes ago. Or maybe twenty. Whatever the case, the pills had only done half their job. She was feeling no pain, but her thoughts were *swimming*. The whole point was to quiet her mind so she could have a good time, but if anything, she was more wound up than ever. The way things were going, she'd need to pop a handful to get some peace.

Brooke splashed water on her face and tried to reason her way through the rising doubts.

She was here, at Grimwood, to study design, away from parents who didn't see her, and friends in the city who – consciously or unconsciously – did everything they could to throw her off course. Yet, she was already falling into old habits – barely making it to half of her classes each week. The bulk of her time was spent with this new group of malcontents, drinking and hanging out, with nothing to show for it.

She needed to make a change.

There was a knock on the door. Brooke fumbled with the handle and pushed it open.

"I've been waiting for half an hour," Carol said. "Are you done in there?!"

"Yeah," Brooke said, feeling in her pocket for the pill case before she slowly stepped out of the bathroom.

Mark was staring at her.

"Are you OK?" he asked.

"Yeah. I'm fine."

Miranda looked at her, a cigarette hanging from the corner of her mouth.

"Wanna have a smoke before the club?"

It felt like she nodded, but she wasn't sure.

Then they were on the balcony.

"What's the name of this place we're going to?"

"The Shack," Miranda replied.

The words seemed to echo.

They were followed by a jumble of images.

Walking on The Ave.

Standing in a line.

A passed bottle and cigarette after cigarette.

The next thing Brooke knew, they were listening to a band made up of three twenty-something guys in flannel shirts, each of them scratching at foot-long beards. They'd never get booked for a gig in the city with that look, but she had to admit, they were pretty good. The only weak point was the lead singer, who was also the keyboard player; his playing was fine, but his voice was just an octave too high, like a flamingo that had been punched in the throat. Still, the beat, and whatever she'd ingested, had Brooke bouncing and lolling from side to side.

Curiously, her head kept swiveling slowly in the direction of this lanky guy wearing a backpack up ahead. He was tall, with a mess of brown hair, and skinny as all get out. And he was dancing to the music like Kermit the Frog.

A skinny guy with a backpack.

What was wrong with her?

Brooke watched him for a minute as her fingers rubbed the plastic pill canister in her pocket.

~

The trek to The Writing Center echoed their walk from a week earlier. Yet, as the crowd streamed into the building – past posters of a smiling Dan Buckley holding a copy of his latest release – the crisp night air, and the rustling of leaves overhead and underfoot, left no doubt that Fall had arrived.

Braden recalled reading one of Buckley's books years ago. It was a page-turner, but nothing particularly memorable. He recalled the main character, a sardonic cop, was more interested in tackling recipes than fugitives. He'd felt no compulsion to read another installment in the series, but the law-enforcing gourmand was clearly more popular than Braden realized, as the auditorium was packed with attendees. It seemed half the town was there.

As he and Loren made their way through to their seats, Braden spotted a table covered with books near the front of the auditorium. Mary Ellen, from the bookstore, was manning the cash box and looking *especially* irritated at being there.

"That's one of the people I work with."

"She looks delightful," Loren replied, noting the scowl.

"Yeah, I don't know what to make of her yet."

A gentleman squeezed past them, carrying a copy of *Cheap Thrills* under his arm.

Braden motioned to the cover.

"Have you read any of his books?" he asked Loren.

"A couple. They were all right. You?"

"One. I thought the same thing. It was *Cheap Thrills* actually."

"I looked up the new one after Professor Price said it was something different."

"And?"

"It sounds interesting," Loren whispered as the lights dimmed and the crowd began to applaud. "It's set in the South of France."

~

The black-haired girl from Brownie's was there tonight.

Jason caught sight of her as he was doing his Snoopy dance. If he weren't so into the music, he *might* have been worried about making a fool of himself. Instead, he registered her presence, and continued to boogie. The Fisher Brothers was one of his favorite local bands. He likened them to a talented trio of in-bred musical hillbillies.

The Brothers paused between songs to rub their itchy beards, and Jason wondered, not for the first time, whether they were suffering from eczema, contact dermatitis, or both. Any band manager worth his salt would have advised them to bring in a stronger lead singer on day one, and shave off their beards on day two. Since there was nothing he could do to keep the band's onstage antics from causing those around him to scratch at their necks unconsciously, Jason took a moment to see if he could figure out who that cute girl had come to the show with. As best he could tell, she was part of the group of dim-eyed emo kids standing in a loose huddle at the back of the room. Incredibly, she looked even more strung out than the last time he'd noticed her. Her eyes sagged at half-mast as she took weak sips from a plastic cup. She wasn't looking so good. He made a mental note to keep an eye on her.

Midway through the next song, Jason caught sight of her again as she was stumbling away from her group, working her way through the crowd to the bathroom. When he looked again, the door was closed and she was nowhere to be seen.

~

Dan Buckley seemed like a character Greg Kinnear might play in an independent film. He was handsome, and clearly accomplished, but while his books were neo-pulp detective stories, he dressed and spoke in a way that betrayed a far more serious way of thinking about his writing career, even as he presented his opinions with a charming sense of wit and self-deprecation. For a man in a tweed coat with leather elbow patches, he sure made fun of himself a lot.

With the bulk of his talk completed, Buckley was answering a question posed to him by one of the upperclassmen in the writing program, a short guy with prematurely gray hair and black glasses.

"Tobin Cinder is like a chloroform donut," Buckley said with a sigh. "He might be a food snob, but his adventures are the literary equivalent of bedtime junk food. The right amount will help you forget your worries and slip away to dreamland, but as a writer, if you handle that stuff for too long, you start to get listless. Don't get me wrong, Tobin has made me a good amount of money over the years. And he's covering the costs of my hotel room and the high tannin cabernet I'll be drinking tonight, but I've gotten pretty tired of the guy's company. I was ready to try something new this time. As writers, that's a luxury we can and should take advantage of. We're not stuck punching a clock and marching in step with drones X, Y, and Z. We're not angling for promotions or hoping for a solid third quarter. When *is* the third quarter anyway? I've never known."

The crowd laughed, and Braden immediately recognized the sound from R.K. Phillips; that discordant combination of polite chuckles and over-the-top guffaws unique to public readings and literary events. Braden and Loren exchanged looks as Buckley waited for the murmurs to die down.

"As writers, we just have to hope and pray that someone out there will buy into the stories we make up, and tell their friends, who will tell *their* friends. And hopefully they won't all pass around the same copy of your book, but go to the store and purchase a copy of their own. If enough people do that, and you can repeat the process a few times, then maybe you'll be lucky enough to take your audience for granted and have the opportunity to try something totally new. Which, like I've said, is what I've done with *Purple Haze*. Currently available for $25.95 hardback – makes a great gift."

He paused for more knowing laughter.

"But to answer your question, to ensure you continue developing as a writer, you have to *keep writing*. As long as you're staying objective, and you actually give a damn about what you're doing, you'll improve over time. Even the most hacky among us continually develop our style. As long as you're reading other writers' work, and staying curious, you should be OK. Now that said, if your books don't seem to be doing as well as they have in the past, that could be a sign that you need to mix things up. Of course, let's see how this book tour goes, right? If *Purple Haze* is a disaster, you better believe I'll me returning to Tobin Cinder's sweet, chloroforming embrace in a hurry. I don't want to become an M&M, but a writers got to eat."

The student who had asked the question arched an eyebrow and brought the microphone to his mouth for a follow-up question, "M&M?"

"Mental midget," Buckley explained.

The crowd erupted into laughter.

"That's pretty good," Loren whispered to Braden.

"I think that's about all the time they're allowing for the blabbing portion of the evening, but if you want to get a jump on your holiday shopping I'll be up front for the foreseeable future, signing books."

~

Unless he'd missed her, she hadn't come out of the bathroom during the last two songs. When the band launched into its next number, Jason started making his way through the crowd.

The bathroom door was locked. He jiggled the knob loudly. When there was still no response, he pounded on the door with his fist.

"Hello?!" Jason shouted. *"Are you all right?"*

His eyes settled on a towering security guard at the back of the room. He hurried through the crowd to him, shouting over the noise, and somehow managed to get the guy's attention. The two of them hurried back to the bathroom.

"How long did you say she's been in there?" the guard bellowed.

"At least 20 minutes, probably closer to 30."

The bouncer tested the knob and pounded on the door. Still nothing.

He looked around, debating what to do – "Ah fuck it."

He motioned for Jason to get out of the way as he stepped back, angled his shoulder, and rammed his full body weight against the door. The door buckled inward on his second attempt, the doorframe splintering to pieces.

Brooke was lying on her back by the toilet, her mouth caked with vomit and blood.

"Call 911!" The bouncer shouted as he lurched inside.

~

When faced with the option of buying or not buying a book, Braden usually purchased two. If he wanted to make a living writing, it just seemed like good karma. But with Dan Buckley, he was oddly apathetic, and while it was clear that Loren would have stuck around and waited with him for a signature, she was obviously ready to go, and the more Braden thought about it, the less inclined he was to wait in line and pay Mary Ellen for a copy anyway, so they headed back to the dorms, where Loren suggested a much more appealing option.

"Do you want to come up and hang out?"

"That would be great," Braden replied.

Loren felt through her pockets for her keys as they rode up in the elevator together. She was all too aware of the connotations of "coming up" and "hanging out," and while she was in no hurry to jump into anything, there was a tingle in the back of her brain telling her that something here was different.

Her floor was unusually quiet. By the second week of school, even the wallflowers had Friday night activities. Though she knew her roommate wouldn't be back tonight, or likely for the rest of the weekend, Loren took off her coat and tossed it on the couch in the lounge outside her room, nodding at the TV as she unlocked her door.

"Wanna see what's on?"

"Sure," Braden said as he snuck a peek through the door.

"Would you like the grand tour?"

He smiled. "Just curious."

She held the door open. "It's not much to look at. Sorry."

Braden looked around the warmly lit room, his eyes settling on the shifting, amorphous pink glow of a lava lamp on the window sill.

"I like the retro touch. Is that yours?"

"It's my roommate's. Not at all what I would have expected from her, but to be honest with you, I like it too."

Braden studied the shifting shadows creeping and stretched across the walls.

"Now *I* want one," he said as he walked out to the lounge couch and took a seat.

Loren's gaze moved from the lava lamp to Brooke's mini fridge.

"You want a Coke or something?" she called out to him.

"Sure, that sounds good."

~

The Fisher Brothers had stopped playing by the time the paramedics arrived. The crowd in the club murmured anxiously as people tried to figure out what was happening.

In the whirl of confusion, not one of the girl's cohorts had stepped forward to help, so Jason Pepper claimed he and the girl were together, and rode in the ambulance to the hospital. The EMTs were too busy to ask him any questions about the patient, which was good, since he didn't know so much as her name. It also helped that he knew his way around once they got to the hospital. Jason's mother was one of the first nurses to meet them at the entrance to the Emergency Room.

"What are *you* doing here?" Cathie Pepper asked in surprise as her son climbed out of the ambulance.

"I found her," he said.

"Oh?" she replied, not understanding.

Jason followed behind as they wheeled the gurney into the hospital.

~

"Your friend was very lucky."

Jason turned at the sound of his mother's voice. She was standing at the waiting room door, still dressed in her scrubs.

"I don't even know her. I just recognized her from campus."

"I was *wondering*," Cathie Pepper replied. "But with all the garbage they pumped out of her stomach, it would be understandable if she couldn't remember anything. Still, I told her who you were, and she wanted me to give you this number. Can you give her roommate a call and ask her to bring some things down?"

She handed Jason a piece of paper with a campus phone number.

"Also, she'd like to meet you."

~

"What did you think of Dan Buckley?"

"I liked him," Braden said. "He might get a little annoying after a while, but he was interesting."

Loren nodded her head in agreement. "*And* he's a little fox."

"Yeah," Braden laughed. "That was my second thought as well. Candidly, he reminded me a little of my father."

"Oh *really?* I'll have to meet your father sometime."

Braden's eyes narrowed. "I'm just… gonna forget you said that."

"Where did you say he lived again?"

"Moving on."

Loren laughed and took a sip of Braden's Coke.

"So if, like me, Alan Grimwood is your favorite dead author, who would you say is your favorite *living* author? Someone you'd really love to meet some day."

"That's easy. Janet Rylander. She kicks ass."

"The mystery writer?"

"Yeah. Have you ever read her?"

"I haven't."

"You should. She's like the female Raymond Chandler, only better."

"Better?"

"Yep. Beautiful writing, *and* her plots make sense."

Braden thought back to his writer's jealousy while reading *The Big Sleep,* remembering how he'd envied every perfect turn of phrase, even as he'd struggled to understand what in the hell was happening.

"My mother loves Rylander's books too." Loren continued. "She used to pick them up on business trips, then I'd snag them from her when she got home."

"Would you guys ever discuss them?"

"Not really, but it got to be one of our little things. If she was out of town for a while and came home while I was sleeping, I'd wake up in the morning and find a couple of Janet Rylander books sitting at the foot of my bed. The paperbacks would all have that little curve in the spine, so I could tell she'd been picking them up and putting them down while she was running around. I love that."

"That reminds me of Pops with Clive Cussler novels." Braden smiled. "What's your family like?"

"It's… kind of a mess. My parents are married, but they might as well not be. My dad owns a brewery in Durango.

Puzzlebox Brewing. He sort of half runs that and a taphouse in town, but he spends most of his time skiing at Purgatory and chasing women."

"And your mother?"

"She handles the business side of things. And I'm pretty sure she has her own thing going on the side."

"That does sound messy. Any brothers or sisters?"

"One of each."

"So, neither of us has June and Ward Cleaver for parents."

"I guess not," Loren said.

There was no clock in the lounge, but it was clearly late, even by college standards. If she was going to do something, *this* was the time. Her chest tightened with nervous energy as she tried to decide whether or not to go for it.

Loren eased closer to Braden as their eyes met.

Then the phone in her room rang. A loud, vibrating clang.

Loren closed her eyes, exhaled softly, and walked over to answer it.

"Hello? Yes it is."

Braden watched her expression tighten as she disappeared behind the doorframe to write something down. After a few questions, Loren hung up the phone and returned to the lounge.

"Is everything OK," he asked.

"Do you happen to know someone with a car? I need to get to the hospital."

~

"Are those yours?"

Loren pointed to a garish pair of *RUSH: Caress of Steel* boxer briefs hanging off the side of Hank's bed.

Braden gave her a look. "Do they *look* like they'd be mine? Those are my roommate's."

The door was unlocked, but Hank was nowhere to be found.

"Did he leave his keys?" Loren asked.

"I don't know the guy well enough to steal his car just yet."

"That's not what I had in mind. I just thought he might be down the hall or something."

"He's been seeing a girl on the floor below us. Maybe he's down there."

Loren looked at the boxers again. "I really hope he's wearing pants."

They took the stairs down to the next floor, and began wandering from one lounge area to the next. When he didn't see Hank anywhere, Braden started peeking in open doors. A scrawny guy in a black bathrobe and slippers was sitting at a computer in one of the open rooms. He rotated his head like an owl when Braden called in to him.

"Have you seen a guy and girl down here?" Braden asked. "I think her name is Hannah?"

The guy just stared back at him blankly.

"Hannah?" Braden asked again. "No? Thank you, you've been a big help."

He arched his eyebrows at Loren.

"He must be a software engineer," she offered.

They passed a girl who was walking down the hall with a shower caddy.

"Do you happen to know someone on this floor named Hannah?" Loren asked.

"I don't think so, sorry." Then she stopped. "You know, you might try the room just around the corner from the small lounge. That may be hers."

"Thank you."

They made their way down the hall, stopping at a door with a sketch of the Leaning Tower of Pisa drawn in thick marker on a sheet of engineering paper. Dave Matthews' bedroom voice was burbling out from under the door.

"Crash?" Braden asked, recognizing the song.

"Bowchickawowow," Loren said with a sly smile.

"I sure hope we have the right room," Braden said as he knocked on the door.

The music grew softer, but there was no answer.

"Knock again," Loren told him.

He did.

"Yes?" a girl's voice called.

"I'm sorry to bother you, but I'm looking for Hank Pierce."

The music stopped entirely as they heard the sounds of two people fumbling around, banging into furniture and muttering curses under their breath. Finally, the door opened a crack, and Hank's face emerged from the shadows.

"What is it, Brady?"

"Sorry to disturb you. I remembered you saying Hannah lived down here-"

"She does. And you're here because…"

Loren stepped forward as Hank opened the door a bit wider. She caught sight of his bare chest and quickly looked up.

"I'm the reason we're… interrupting you guys," Loren explained. "Apparently my roommate, who I barely know, just had her stomach pumped. The hospital called to see if I could bring some of her things down."

"Oh," Hank said. "Is she OK?"

"It sounds like it."

"That's good."

"You, uh, didn't happen to leave your underwear upstairs did you?" Braden asked.

Hank swung the door open. He was standing there in boxers and a pair of white tube socks. "That's not my *only* pair, man."

"What's with the socks?" Braden asked.

"My question exactly," a girl's voice called from inside the room.

"I get cold!" Hank said as he swung the door all the way open.

Hannah, who was lying in bed in the shadows, scrambled to pull the sheets up over herself.

"Hank!"

"Oh, sorry. This is Hannah, by the way. Hannah this is Braden and…"

"Loren," Loren said with a tight, apologetic smile.

"Nice to meet you," Hannah said. Her face was growing red.

"We obviously caught you two at a bad time, but could you give us a lift to the hospital?" Braden asked.

"I suppose your timing *could* have been worse." Hank admitted. "Sure, I can drive you guys there. Hannah, you wanna come?"

"Yeah, why not?"

~

Jason peered into the hospital room. A wisp of black hair was just visible above the crest of the bed pillow. The room was so quiet that he wondered if she was asleep. He was nervous to go in, but as he got closer to the bed, he saw that she was indeed awake. Her hair had been washed and brushed back. Her face was scrubbed clean. Aside from some bruising where she'd fallen and hit her face, her complexion was clear, in stark contrast to the dark eye makeup she usually wore. She looked up at him, surprisingly alert. For the first time, Jason was close enough to get a clear look at her eyes. One of them was a very light green, while the other was an equally pale brown.

"Hi." She said softly.

"Hi."

"Are you Jason?"

He nodded. "Yes."

"You found me?"

"Well, I had some help. I was worried you might have gotten into some trouble or…"

"Overdosed?"

"Yeah."

"The doctor says you got to me just in time."

She reached her hand out and he took it. Her skin was smooth, and soft, and impossibly cold.

"I'm Brooke."

"Jason."

~

The four of them stopped by Loren and Brooke's dorm room. Hannah was helping Loren get Brooke's things together, while Braden and Hank waited in the lounge.

"So, I guess I don't need to ask how things are going with Hannah."

Hank tried to suppress a smile. "No, you probably don't. What's the deal with you and Loren?"

"We've just been sort of hanging out."

Hank motioned toward the open door. "But you were in her room when she got the call from the hospital, right?"

Braden shook his head. "Nope. We were here on the couch."

"Hmm…"

"I was getting a vibe though."

"That's good. Have you met her roommate?"

"I haven't, but she sounds like a real piece of work. She's barely spoken to Loren since they moved in, and spends most of her time hanging out with a pack of assholes-"

"Yet *Loren* is the one who gets the call when she ODs."

"Exactly…"

The girls were just about finished packing. Hannah removed the contents of Brooke's backpack and stacked it on her desk. There wasn't much there; aside from one textbook and a sketchpad, it was practically empty.

"Not much of a student, I take it?"

"I'm not even sure she's made it to class," Loren said.

Loren set the clothes on the desk and Hannah started packing them into the bag.

"So, we've got the essentials. Toiletries. Extra clothes."

"I think we're all set," Loren said.

"Is there anything else you've seen her with? A blanket? A teddy bear?"

"Trust me, this is not a teddy bear kind of girl," Loren replied as they slipped out of the door. "I think we're good."

"Do we have any idea how to get to the hospital," Hannah asked the guys as she and Loren joined them in the lounge.

"Not a clue," Braden said.

~

The first glimmers of sunlight were seeping into the sky by the time they reached the hospital and were directed down the hall to Brooke's room. They were greeted outside the door by a blond-haired woman in hospital scrubs. She looked to be in her mid-forties.

"I'm Cathie Pepper. I've been taking care of Brooke since the doctors treated her early this morning," She looked around the group. "Can I ask which of you is Loren?"

"That would be me."

"Brooke has authorized me to update you on what happened. The doctors want to keep her here one more day for observation, then she'll be released, but once you've spoken with her, we can get together and discuss next steps."

"OK," Loren said uncertainly.

"Did you want to go in now?"

"I really don't know her all that well," Loren admitted. "I'm honestly shocked that I'm the person she wanted you to call."

Cathie set her hand on Loren's shoulder. "She no doubt picked you for a reason."

Loren glanced at Braden, who gave her a reassuring nod. Then she started down the corridor. The group watched as Loren walked down the hall to Brooke's room, knocked gently on the door, and stepped inside.

A split second later, the waiting room doors swung open as Jason Pepper hurried through, stopping short when he saw everyone.

"What the heck are you doing here?!" Hank blurted out.

"What are *you* doing here?" Jason replied.

"Do you all know each other?" Cathie asked.

"Hank and I just started working at the campus radio station together, Mom."

Hank looked from Jason to Cathie. "Mom?"

"Jason is my son," Cathie said with a shrug. "He's the one who found Brooke at the club."

"Oh. Well, nice to meet you Mrs. Pepper."

"You can call me Cathie," she said as she turned to leave. "I'll leave you all alone to talk for a bit."

~

Loren closed the door behind her.

"Hi," Brooke said softly.

It took Loren's eyes a moment to adjust to the dim light, when they did, she saw her roommate lying in the bed looking much smaller than she remembered. Brooke's short hair was sitting flat on her head. Deflated. Her face was pale and slack.

"Hi," Loren said softly.

"How excited were *you* to come down here in the middle of the night to help your asshole roommate?"

"It's no problem."

Brooke gave her a skeptical look.

"You're being polite. I don't know if I'd have been so nice about it."

"How are you doing?"

"I'll live," Brooke sighed.

"What happened?"

"I was being stupid." Brooke's eyes glistened in the darkness. "More stupid than usual, unfortunately."

"Did you want to talk about anything?"

"Not unless we need to." Brooke was quiet for a moment. "I'm sorry we got off to such a bad start."

Loren slid a chair next to the side of the bed and sat down. "If you don't think it's too late, I'm up for a do over."

"I'd like that. If you can help me downplay this to my parents, we might have time."

~

"So…" Jason said with a smile. "You must be Hannah."

The twinkle in his eyes caused Hannah to whip her head around and stare Hank down suspiciously. "What did you tell him about me?"

"*Relax,* I haven't told him anything!" Hank replied.

Hannah narrowed her eyes, studying all three boys' expressions. Her gaze settled on Jason. "Nice to meet you," she said suspiciously.

"Nice to meet you too," Jason said. "It looks like things are working out with you and Hank. That's awesome!"

"Thank you. Now can we *please* change the subject?"

Braden leaned forward. "Jason, as long as we're making introductions, I'm Braden."

"Brady's my roommate," Hank added. "So, what exactly happened? How do you know Loren's roommate?"

"I don't really. I just happened to be at the right place at the right time"

"And she's lucky you were," Hannah said.

~

By the afternoon, Brooke's doctors had given her the all clear to head home. As Hank, Hannah, and Braden sampled the vending machine coffee, Jason returned to Brooke's hospital room to help her get ready to check out. Cathie Pepper gave Loren the rundown on how things would work for the next 24-48 hours, and was just handing her a piece of paper with her contact information when the rest of the group returned.

"Anything comes up, just call me."

"I will," Loren replied.

"They're releasing her if you want to go get your car," Cathie told Hank.

"Sure thing."

"I'll go with you," Hannah said as Hank started for the elevator.

Braden, Loren, and Cathie watched as Brooke made her way into the waiting area. She was walking slowly, and leaning on Jason for support. A sheepish half smile crossed her face when she saw everyone.

"Sorry for dragging all of you into this," she said.

"You've got a good group of friends here," Cathie said.

"Do I?" Brooke asked as she took in the new faces. Then she turned to Cathie. "Thank you for everything."

"Take care of yourself, Brooke. Loren has my number if you need anything."

"OK."

"And come back and see me when you're feeling better."

"I will."

"Thanks, Mom," Jason said as they prepared to go.

Cathie kissed him on the cheek and whispered in his ear. "You look after that girl."

~

"This may not be up to your usual Saturday night standards," Loren said as she walked into their dorm room carrying two pizza boxes from Red Tomato. "But Hank hooked us up, so the price was right."

"I love pizza." Brooke said as she push herself upright in bad.

"Then you're in luck."

Loren glanced over at her roommate, who was dressed in sweatpants, with her short hair brushed back. It seemed as though the black dye in her hair was fading, but that was likely just another part of the overall shift that had begun at the hospital; without her makeup or her defenses up, Brooke was much more approachable.

Loren set out some paper plates and served each of them a couple of slices. She handed a plate to Brooke, then slipped off her shoes and climbed up onto her own bed with the other.

"This is good," Brooke said. "Do you have pizza in New Mexico?"

"Are you joking? Of course we have pizza. It's not the frontier."

"Eesh, OK."

"By the way, I'm from Colorado, not New Mexico. Those are actually two different places."

"Am I giving off some sort of snotty New Yorker vibe?"

"Maybe just a bit."

"Good to know. I guess I probably do that."

"How in the world did you end up coming to Grimwood?" Loren wondered aloud.

"My parents thought getting out of the city might be good for me."

"So, did you visit before you applied?" Loren asked.

"Of course. I actually really like the art school here."

"Then, why aren't you an art major?"

"If my father would let me, I would be. He's a 'most value for your money' sort, which is why I'm in graphic design. But this year is mostly foundational stuff, which is a lot of what I enjoy anyway."

"Could you ever shift to a different emphasis?"

"You haven't met my father. It would be easier on all of us if I just stick to the plan, but we'll see right? At the moment, I just need to downplay last night so he doesn't pull me out of here and stick me someplace where they can keep a closer eye on me."

"He sounds strict."

"He vacillates between strict and indifferent." Brooke sighed. "Have I told you anything else about him?"

"Something about crashing the economy I think."

"That about covers it. Definitely not the warm and cuddly type. He's the kind of guy who saw *Wall Street* in college and thought Michael Douglas was the hero."

"What about your mom?"

"Can we talk about something else?"

"Sure."

"What's *your* family like," Brooke asked.

"Can we talk about something else?" Loren laughed.

Brooke smiled. "Sounds like we could be an after school special."

"My family is… in flux. Let's leave it at that."

They sat in silence, eating their pizza.

"What do you think of Jason?"

"From the hospital?" Loren asked.

"Yeah."

"He seems cute. He has sort of a Kermit the Frog thing going on-"

'That exactly what I thought!" Brooke laughed. "But there's something about him that I… *like*. My friends in the city would eat him alive, but I keep thinking about him."

"What would your city friends think of the group you've been hanging out with here?"

Brooke rolled her eyes. "They'd probably get along great."

"Go with Kermit!" Loren exclaimed.

"*OK*. Tell me what you *really* think why don't you?"

"I'm sorry, but those guys are awful!"

"Yeah, they do kind of suck. Mark seemed sort of OK, but…I dunno."

"Mark also never bothered to check on you."

"That's true."

"Jason goes to Grimwood, right?"

Brooke nodded.

"You should call him!"

"I don't need to. He called here while you were picking up dinner. He wants to stop by tomorrow to see how I'm doing"

Loren arched her eyebrows. "Sounds promising."

"Yeah. All it took was a near fatal overdose."

"Isn't that how all the great romances begin?"

~

Loren had gone down the hall to take a shower when Jason stopped by. Brooke was alone in the room, lying on her side with her back to the door, lost in her thoughts. How long it would take for evidence of her hospital stay to filter through the insurance system and arrive as a bill at her parents' place?

That wasn't going to be a fun call.

The sound of Jason's knock only half registered.

"Come in," Brooke said absentmindedly without moving.

The door behind her opened with a slow creak.

"Is this a bad time?" Jason asked.

Brooke rolled over and sat up. "No, this is a perfect time."

He wasn't wearing his backpack today, but was clad in a white t-shirt with an open plaid button-up over the top. Even dressed in layers, he looked unusually skinny. Brooke felt the sudden urge to hug him tight and keep him warm.

"How are you doing?" he asked.

"I feel a lot better. I owe you one."

"No you don't. I'm just glad I could help."

"Do you want to sit down?"

"Sure," Jason said.

He looked around the room, trying to determine the least awkward place to take a seat. Brooke turned and hung her feet over the side of her bed, so he walked over to the opposite bed, pulled up the comforter, and sat down.

"I hope your roommate doesn't mind."

"I'm sure she won't. She's cool."

They scanned the room, looking for something to talk about, then they made eye contact, and Jason was again struck by the color of Brooke's irises.

"You have husky eyes!" he exclaimed.

"Excuse me?"

"You have two different color eyes. One brown, one green. Like a husky."

"Oh, yeah. Most people say 'like David Bowie,' but I guess a dog works too. It's called heterochromia iridis," Brooke said.

"I thought Bowie just had a permanently dilated pupil?"

"I think there's some debate. Dan Aykroyd also has the same thing."

Jason made a face. "Stick with Bowie. That's much cooler."

"Cooler than what, Dan Aykroyd or a friggin' *dog*?"

"Sorry. I guess that wasn't so flattering. That was the first thing that came to mind."

Brooke shrugged. "I'm sure you're not the first person to think it."

"Think you'll be up for classes tomorrow?"

"I might need one more day to get my head straight. But I probably can't afford to miss any more than that or I'll fall too far behind."

"Can I ask what you're studying?"

"Graphic design."

"Oh, that's cool," Jason said.

"How about you?"

"Music production."

"Like… making albums?"

Jason nodded. "Hopefully."

"That's awesome."

"Where are you from?"

"The city," Brooke replied, then quickly pivoted. "What about you?"

"I'm from here," he said.

"Grimwood?"

"Born and raised."

"Do you like it?"

"I suppose it's as good a place as any."

"Think you could show me around sometime?"

Jason's eyes brightened. "*Absolutely.* Anytime you like."

"This week?"

"Just give me a call," Jason said.

She looked him in the eyes. "You'll have to give me your number."

~

Loren bumped into Jason in the hall as he was leaving.

He smiled, visibly relieved. "She seems better."

"So far so good."

"If you guys need anything, let me know. Brooke has my info."

"I will for sure."

Jason started down the hall, then stopped.

"Have any of the friends she was with called or come to check on her?"

"Nope. And I doubt they will either."

Loren could see his jaw clench.

"Let me know if they do. I'd love to talk to them about what happened."

Somehow, Loren wasn't sure that was such a great idea. Apparently Jason Pepper was scrappier than his physique might suggest.

~

"Well, that was an interesting weekend. How are you feeling?"

"I'm tired," Loren confessed. "I got a little sleep yesterday, but I'm all off schedule."

She and Braden were standing outside The Writing Center, waiting for The Novel to start. Professor Price hadn't shown up yet, so they were taking the opportunity to stay outside in the crisp air for just a little longer.

"And how is Brooke?" Braden asked.

"I think she's OK. She's hard to read, but I think we actually bonded a bit."

"So, are you two becoming friends now?"

"I don't know... Maybe," said Loren. "I was thinking about getting a group together next weekend to take her out. Would you be interested?"

"Sure, just give me the details."

A few of their classmates were standing on the steps smoking, but threw their cigarettes away as Professor Price approached and began climbing the front steps.

"Did you know he went to Grimwood?" Braden asked as they watched Price head into the building ahead of them.

"I didn't. How did you find that out?"

"I was just reading his profile in the staff directory," Braden said. "Class of '73."

~

With Halloween fast approaching, The Little Theater was show-ing a marathon of Universal monster movies. It was an ambitious schedule, starting at noon with the 1931 *Dracula*, followed by *Frankenstein, The Bride of Frankenstein, The Mummy*, and *The Invisible Man*. After a brief break, the program would resume later that night with *The Wolf Man* and *Creature from the Black Lagoon*.

After arriving halfway through *Bride of Frankenstein*, the group was ready to eat by the time *The Invisible Man* met his end. It was the first time they'd all been together under normal circum-stances. Hank and Hannah already seemed like an established couple as they lead the way down The Ave to Brick's. They were followed by Braden and Loren, with Jason and Brooke bringing up the rear.

"I liked them," Hannah announced, "but those movies had some *goofy* moments."

"I think those were intentional," Hank said. "They were all directed by the same guy. I saw a movie about him once. There were definitely some inside jokes going on."

"So, what is this place you guys are taking us too?" Hannah asked Braden.

"It's called Brick's," Braden said.

"Have you been there?" Hannah asked Jason.

"I have."

"What's their specialty?"

"That would be the Brick Plate."

"What is the Brick Plate?" Loren asked.

"The Brick Plate is the whole reason we're going there," Hank replied.

"Yes," Hannah said, noting their evasiveness. "But what *is* that

Brooke, who had been reserved for most of the night, looked Jason in the eye and smiled. "Yeah, what's in it?"

Sensing his answer could cause revolt with the girls, but incapable of holding out on Brooke, Jason recited a description remarkably similar to the one Hank and Braden had heard in the dorms their first week.

"It's a big plate of macaroni salad, home fries, two huge burgers, onions, beans if you want them, smothered with mustard and a secret meat sauce, all mixed together."

"That sounds *disgusting!*" Hannah exclaimed.

"Why is it called a *Brick Plate?*" Loren asked.

"Well, the owner is named Brick, but most people say it's because once you eat one you'll be…shitting a…you know…"

"Yuck!" Hannah said as she smacked Hank on the arm. "What the hell, Hank?!"

"OK, settle down," Hank said defensively. "There are other things to eat there, too! No one said we all *have* to order Brick Plates."

"I am not eating *anything* with the word *"brick"* in its description."

"Some people call them Garbage Plates," Jason offered.

Loren laughed. "That's really not an improvement."

"Have you eaten them before?" Brooke asked Jason.

"I have," he admitted. "I like them."

"Then I'm game," Brooke said.

~

Brick's was your basic diner inside. Lots of brushed metal and chrome, padded, cracked-vinyl booths, and college kids everywhere. A long counter ran along the back of the restaurant, where an open window allowed a glimpse of the kitchen. Waitresses were cycling through the dining area, ferrying food to tables and bringing soda glasses back for refills.

Jason led the way to a booth and took a seat.

Brooke slid in beside him. His leg was warm against hers. She was feeling remarkably at ease with him, as well as with the rest of the group. She watched Hank and Hannah slide in across from them, and made a promise to herself not to blow this. Loren and Braden sat across from one another at the end of the table.

Hannah reached for the menu, "Well, I might as well see what else this place has to offer." She looked up when no one else reached for menus. "You're all getting Brick Plates, aren't you?"

"We might as well try them," Loren conceded.

Hannah tapped the side of her menu in deliberation. "How are the bathrooms?" she asked Jason.

"They're…diner bathrooms."

She sighed. "Fine, I'll try a plate, but the second I sense it's not sitting well, I'm booking it back to the dorms. I don't want to spend the rest of my night incapacitated in some disgusting bathroom."

Hank, patted Hannah's leg. "I'm sure you'll be just fine."

She didn't look so sure.

An older woman approached with a tray of water glasses and began passing them around the table. Her nametag read: BETTY

'What'll it be?" Betty demanded.

"Hello there, Betty," Hank said.

"Hi," Betty replied flatly.

Hank was clearly the type who liked to get overly familiar with restaurant staff, but this lady was having none of it. "We were just debating the Brick Plates," he said. "But if there's anything else that-"

Betty cut him off. "Six Brick Plates?"

Hank glanced around the table for confirmation.

"…Sure," Hannah sighed.

"Why not?" Brooked added.

"Any drinks?" Betty demanded.

Once everyone ordered, Betty left without another word, and the conversation started down the typical college freshmen questionnaire: Majors, the first few weeks of school, and where on campus everyone lived. Then it turned to the season that had inspired the evening's movie marathon in the first place.

"Any plans for Halloween?" Loren asked.

Brooke perked up. "I was wondering the same thing. I thought Grimwood might really get into it, considering the school's history."

"Are you referring to that thing that happened at the library years ago?" Hannah asked. She was clearly skeptical.

"Yeah, that and the stories of what people have seen around campus," Brooke said. "I take it you're not a believer."

"I find it a little hard to swallow," Hannah replied. "What about you?'"

"I don't rule anything out. I mean, I don't want to be haunted or anything, but it doesn't seem impossible to me."

Loren and Braden exchanged looks. They'd already covered this ground and knew how the other one felt. Braden's gaze dropped to the table, where their fingertips were almost touching. He pulled his hand back and reached for his water.

"What exactly *did* happen?" Brooke asked Jason. "Do you know the whole story?"

Jason was familiar with some of the details. It would be impossible *not* to know about an event so horrific that your hometown had been made infamous by it.

"I don't know names or specifics – I'm not sure if anyone does anymore – but yeah, I have a rough idea of what happened,"

Jason said. The group was waiting expectantly, so he continued. "Just before Thanksgiving in 1972, a student with a rifle stormed one of the top floor study halls in the campus library and took a dozen students hostage."

"Why did he do it?" Hank asked.

"He was delusional. Thought he was in love with one of the girls in the group, but the feelings were not mutual. I don't even know if she knew him. He held them in the building for almost a day while police tried to negotiate with him. Then, he stopped communicating, and a short time later he jumped from the top of the tower. The police thought he'd come to his senses and taken his own life before he did something terrible, but once they got inside, they found he'd killed everyone before he went out the window."

"That's… awful," Loren whispered.

"As far as the haunting thing goes, I've heard some strange stuff over the years. I've never seen anything personally, but one of my uncles used to work maintenance in the library. He had some stories. Said he could feel something change in the air sometimes."

"Like, the temperature?" Brooke asked.

"Like a… mood." Jason said. "That was how he could describe it. That and this distinct feeling that there were still people in the building hours after everyone had cleared out for the night."

"That's creepy," Brooke said as she scooted closer to Jason.

"Did he ever see anything?" Braden asked.

"Nope, but plenty of people have. My uncle just felt them. He called them the midnight visitors."

"I don't know that I believe in them," Hannah said. "But so much for studying at the library."

"I like that name," Loren said. "The Midnight Visitors. It sounds like the title of a Stephen King book."

"Yeah," Brooke said. "But if any of us start to see them, it might be nice to have a shorter name for them. By the time I've shouted, 'It's the midnight visitors!' they'll have gotten me."

"I've always liked 'flares.'" Braden suggested as his eyes met Loren's.

"Why call them *anything?*" Hannah asked. "Just get the hell out of there!"

~

A sense of quiet had come over the neighborhood while they were eating. The air felt lighter as they gathered on the sidewalk after dinner. Hannah leaned her head against Hank's shoulder.

"What did you think of your first Brick Plates?" Jason asked.

"I wouldn't eat it every day," Hannah said sleepily. "But it wasn't the *worst* thing ever."

"I loved it," Braden said.

"Same here," Hank agreed. "I'll be back."

Brooke brushed her fingers through her hair as she looked around the street. The breath caught in her throat as she caught sight of them walking up the sidewalk across the street. Evan and Devon were in the front. Miranda and Carol were in the back. And Mark was being carried along in the eddy between them. He turned slowly in her direction and started to wave. But before he had a chance, Brooke took Jason's hand and looked away.

"Can we go?" she asked.

"Absolutely."

Jason knew something was up.

The group, sensing the same, closed ranks and headed up The Ave.

"The temperature's dropping again," Braden observed, making small talk as the six of them started up the hill to campus.

Loren murmured acknowledgment.

She didn't know why, but she felt the sudden urge to be alone. To stretch out her arms and arch her neck. Between Hank and Hannah, and Jason and Brooke, they were all pairing off so quickly. She'd felt Braden's hand next to hers at the table. She could practically feel his legs in proximity to her own under the table. But as they stepped outside, she'd become aware of both the desire to step closer to him, and the inexplicable need to run. Tension was building in her arms and legs, pulsing under her skin, a tingling sense of pooling adrenaline.

She studied Braden's face from the corner of her eye as they made their way back to Grimwood. There was a sadness about him, she had noticed that the first day. His eyes seemed always to be looking just a bit too far ahead at something in the distance. And while she felt an undeniable attraction to him, a warmth that grew stronger as they spent more time together, just what that *meant* worried her. The ease with which she'd shaken off Justin and Alex had surprised her, but something told her things with Braden, should that happen, would be much different. Deeper. And she didn't know if she was ready for it.

As they rounded the corner to the residential quad, Hannah and Hank peeled away from the group, no doubt headed for Hannah's room.

"We're gonna take off," Hank said as Hannah kissed his neck.

At Esmond Hall, Jason and Brooke also bid them farewell and slipped into the dorms together.

That left Braden and Loren.

They walked silently to the middle of the quad, stopping at the statue of Alan Grimwood, where they stood below their spectral mentor, waiting for something to break the tension that hung heavy between them. Eldredge Hall, and Braden's empty room, towered behind them.

"That was a fun night," Braden said.

"It was."

His lips parted, as if to speak again. But he stopped.

Loren heard the sounds of crackling leaves underfoot as he leaned toward her, and for a moment she *thought* she would meet him halfway, was certain that, conscious or not, she'd decided to see what might happen. But at the last second, she twisted ever so slightly at the waist, and gave Braden a whisper-soft kiss on the patch of cold skin just beneath his ear.

"Have a good night, Braden," she whispered as she hurried away.

Braden raised a hand to his neck as he watched her go.

~

The hot water coursed over Loren's body. She inhaled the steam and turned her back to direct the pulse of the spray onto her shoulders. The heat felt wonderful on her skin as she pictured the tension seeping from her body. When she finally stepped out of the shower and wrapped herself in a robe, her body felt limp and exhausted. She returned to her empty dorm room and collapsed on the bed, asleep almost the instant her head hit the pillow.

Across the quad, in his own empty room, Braden sat on his bed, still dressed, and stared out the window. Condensation was gathered on the cold glass. He reached out a hand, running his fingertips over the icy dampness, and studied the lines they left in their wake.

***

"So, what's happening with you and Loren?" Hank asked as Braden was getting ready for work.

"What do you mean?" Braden shot back.

He was irritated, as he'd been asking himself the same question for weeks. He and Loren were still hanging out. They were still going to classes at The Writing Center together, and grabbing lunch afterwards. It *felt* like a friendship that might be leading to something else, but ever since that night under Grimwood's statue, a chill had moved in between them. They still talked about things, but where once they'd confided in one another, it seemed Loren had taken a step back. Outside of the school week, they hadn't spent any time together for the last two weekends. Meanwhile, the two couples in the group were hanging out consistently. Maybe she'd met someone more interesting, but Braden figured he would have heard something about them by now.

After a particularly awkward night as the fifth wheel, he'd taken to spending his Friday and Saturday nights at the library, working on class assignments and hashing out writing ideas.

"Hey, I wasn't trying to piss you off," Hank said defensively. "I was just wondering if anything was going on there. You haven't mentioned her in a while."

"Sorry," Braden said as he pulled on his jacket and started for the door. "I wish I had an answer for you, but I'm in the dark myself."

~

Two hours later, Braden was standing at the bookstore's upstairs counter, waiting for the night's reading to finish. He kept replaying the exchange with Hank in his head, wishing he hadn't been so short with him. Hank obviously wanted something to work out, he'd just nicked a raw nerve.

Once the event let out, Braden knew from experience that the audience would rush the counter to pay for their purchases and queue up for the signing. Despite every attempt to sell as many books as possible ahead of a reading, customers always wanted to be dazzled by the author before they committed to a purchase. It made for a chaotic process, and this, like so many things, bugged the hell out of Mary Ellen.

The diminutive store manager slammed a pile of hardcovers down behind the register as laughter chortled from the event room, followed by a round of applause.

"Brace yourself for the onslaught," Mary Ellen grumbled.

"I don't care *what* happened, Cole." Roxanne's distinctive growl echoed up the stairs as matching footsteps clomped up to the second floor. "Thanks to you, we're a person short tonight, so you need to help with the drinks *and* man the downstairs register when the crowd thins out up here."

"Faith quit today," Mary Ellen whispered to Braden just before Roxanne and Cole Phillips emerged at the top of the stairs and hurried to the event room.

Faith must have been the disgruntled blonde Braden had seen shooting daggers at Cole that first day.

Roxanne and her son were each carrying a half-case of wine. She set hers beneath the refreshment table and slipped into the back room as the audience members rose from their seats.

Braden watched from behind the register as Cole opened several bottles of red wine and poured them into clear plastic glasses, which he arranged for customers to pick up as they waited to have their books signed. Cole crouched down to carefully level off the glasses, then he peaked over his shoulder like a guilty child, grabbed two unopened wine bottles, and ducked into the staff room just off the hall.

Mary Ellen didn't miss a trick.

"Junior always snags a few bottles to take home with him after events," she explained as the crowd began lining up at Braden's register. "Heads up, it's showtime."

Braden grabbed a copy of *The Cobbler of Kabul,* and watched over the first customer's shoulder as Cole emerged from the staff room empty-handed.

Braden lowered his head and set to work ringing up sales.

Customer after customer filed through the line, and before he knew it, the event was drawing to a close. The back room was almost empty by the time Braden looked up. The table of wine glasses had been decimated, and Cole Phillips was nowhere to be seen. Roxanne emerged from the back room, one arm around the author's shoulder, a coffee table book beneath the other. She stopped at the register and dropped the book on the counter with a *thunk.*

"Braden, can you mark this copy out of inventory and charge it to my AR?"

"Absolutely." Braden replied.

Roxanne turned back to the author. "Braden here will set you up. What a great evening. I can't wait to read your book." She leaned over, delivering a pair of air kisses before she ducked into the back office.

Braden nodded at the author as he handed over the coffee table book.

Roxanne poked her head back around the corner. "Oh, and Braden, we have an opening for a part time bookseller if you know someone who might be interested."

~

He had the softest lips. They were thinner than she was used to (of course, so was he), but when the two of them kissed, their mouths seemed to fit together perfectly.

Brooke leaned her head against the hallway wall and slowly opened her eyes.

"What are we here for again?" she asked sleepily.

"You wanted to pick up some clothes for the weekend," Jason said.

"That's right," she replied as she opened the door to her room.

Loren was sitting inside, studying in the glow from her desk light. The rest of the room was pitch black. "Hey," she said as she looked up from her reading.

Brooke flipped on the light. "How can you see anything in here?"

Loren blinked and looked around. "Oh yeah, it was still light out when I started. What time is it anyway?"

"Just about 9 p.m." Jason said as he stepped inside.

"*Seriously?* I guess I've been at this longer than I thought."

Brooke pointed at the paperback of *Jane Eyre* on Loren's desk. "That must be one hell of a good book for you to be holed up in here on a Saturday night."

"It has its moments," Loren said. "What are you guys up to?"

Brooke sniffed a tank top and shoved it into her backpack. "Just getting some things to take back to Jason's. Have you eaten?"

"Nope."

"Wanna join us at Brownie's?" Jason asked.

Loren hesitated. She didn't want to cramp their style, but she could sure use the company. Brooke and Jason were together most of the time now, she couldn't remember the last night her roommate had actually slept in their dorm; and she was giving Braden some space outside of classes while she figured that out. Another meal by herself sounded bleak, though.

"Would you mind?" she asked Brooke.

"Of course not!"

Loren got up, pulling on her coat as she followed Jason and Brooke towards the door.

"Hank and Hannah may join us there, too," Jason said.

Brooke stopped. "Oh, you didn't tell me that."

"Is that OK?"

"Yeah, of course, I like him. *She* can be a bit much sometimes, but… now we have Loren as a buffer." Brooke grabbed Loren's arm. "Is that all right?"

"Oh sure," Loren said. "Just think of me as your roommate and human shield."

~

Loren couldn't believe how busy Brownie's was on a Friday night. The majority of the booths on the room's perimeter were filled with groups of guys eating soggy pizza and rolling multi-sided dice, while the tables in the middle were occupied by solitary students who sat hunched over their textbooks, styrofoam coffee cups clenched in their fists.

Brooke nodded toward a pale-faced girl with drooping eyes, who was seated with her nose roughly two inches from a text-book, looking as though she was ready to expire. "See the fate we saved you from?"

"How can I ever thank you-" Loren stopped as she saw Hank and Hannah heading down the steps with Braden walking a few paces behind them. He stopped short at the top of the landing, raising his hand with a shy smile when he saw her.

"How's it going, guys?" Hank said as the three of them reached the table. "Look who we dragged along with us."

"Long time no see," Jason said. "How have you been?"

"Not too bad," Braden said as he pulled off his heavy backpack. "I've been wrapped up in work and assignments. I hope you don't mind me tagging along."

"The more the merrier," Brooke said.

Loren noticed Brooke giving Jason's hand a little squeeze, and wondered just how much her roommate really wanted *any* of them there. If Brooke had her druthers, it would probably just be she and Jason tonight. Funny how quickly things changed. Jason was good for her. And of course, coming to Brownie's was his idea, so there was no sense worrying about horning in. Braden's unexpected appearance had knocked her off balance however.

"Hi," Braden said to Loren as the two couples began talking in the background.

"Hi."

He motioned toward the cafeteria line. "Want to get something to eat?"

"That would be good. I'm starving."

"Me too."

The two of them grabbed trays and began picking out their meals.

"So, you're working at the bookstore now," Loren said. "How is that going?"

"So far so good. There are lots of events, which is cool. Aside from a couple of high strung coworkers, everyone working there is nice. Anything new with you?"

"Nothing noteworthy," Loren replied. "Just classes and studying."

"That's why we're here, right?"

Loren watched Hank and Hannah as they started toward the food line, observing the easy intimacy between them.

"Yeah," she said. "I guess it is."

~

"So, are any of your parents coming for parent's weekend?" Hannah asked.

Brooke's head shot up. "Is that happening *already?*"

"It is. From the panic in your voice, I take it your parents will be here?"

"I wouldn't put it past them," Brooke sighed as she went back to her meal.

They were halfway through the first quarter now, and with no mention of unexpected hospital bills, she was hopeful her medical misadventure had slipped under the radar.

Jason put his arm around her. He knew what was on her mind. "If it makes you feel any better, I'm pretty sure my mother will be in town for that as well."

"You *think?*" Hank joked. "It is kind of a slog."

"*Plus* your mother is really nice," Brooke added.

None of them *ever* discussed Brooke's hospital stay, but their minds collectively flashed to Cathie Pepper's reassuring demeanor that terrible weekend.

"I'd be shocked if my folks made the trip up from Albany," Hank said. "But you never know. Is your father coming?"

"I'm pretty sure he is," Hannah replied.

"What about you, Braden?" Jason asked.

Loren watched Braden's expression, knowing full well he didn't have anyone coming to visit him. Aside from perhaps Hank, she wondered if any of the others knew anything about Braden's family life.

"I think it will just be me," Braden said.

"Same here," Loren added quickly.

'Well, no matter who shows up, what do you say we all go to some of the events together?" Jason suggested. "I know my mom would like to see you guys again, and for those of us who *will* have visitors, it might reassure them to see we're making friends here."

"That sounds like a great idea," Hannah said. "What exactly happens over parents weekend anyway?"

"My guess is the school does a little song and dance to make the folks feel better about how much this place is costing them," Hank said. "Maybe dip into the reserve for some food and entertainment; hand out some free T-shirts."

Hannah rolled her eyes. "My boyfriend the cynic."

"He's probably on target with that one though," Jason admitted. "What do they call that?"

"Bread and circuses." Braden said. "Appeasing the masses through superficial means."

"Thank you." Hank pointed at Braden. "See! I'm not the only one."

Loren laughed. "How long have you been waiting to roll *that* one out, Braden?"

"Since high school Latin with Miss Chabot," Braden replied. "Panem et circenses. I had to get *something* out of that misery!"

"Maybe it *is* just for show," Hannah said defensively. "But I'm looking forward to it. What's to be gained from looking at everything sideways?"

"I don't know," Hank said, twisting around to give her an exaggerated once over. "A lot of the times, that's the best angle-"

"Oh shut up."

The group laughed, but Loren's thoughts stayed on Braden and her instinctive protectiveness toward him when the topic of visitors came up. Her eyes kept returning to him as the night went on. She liked him, obviously, but she knew he wanted more from their friendship, and her own feelings were still unclear. She'd arrived in Grimwood determined to keep life simple, but their almost immediate sense of familiarity had caught her off guard.

Hank and Jason were still giving Braden crap for the ease with which he'd broken out the Latin. He laughed good-naturedly and turned to look at Loren. Their eyes met, and the flash of warmth made her want to lean forward and kiss him, even as she pressed her shoulders tight against the back of her seat. Braden's eyes narrowed, like he was asking if she was OK, and Loren stepped out of her mind and back into the conversation.

~

"I'm really sorry about the other night," Braden said as they headed out to the lobby.

The others had gone up ahead, leaving he and Loren behind.

"I am too," Loren replied. "I don't know what happened."

Braden smiled, but his expression showed he knew.

"Can we forget about it and pick up where we left off?" he asked. "I could really use a friend in the writing program."

"So could I," she said.

"Then we're cool?"

"We're cool."

"Good," Braden said. "Then that brings me to another topic. There's a job opening at the bookstore. Would you be at all interested?"

"*Absolutely.* I could use the money. Do you think I'd have a shot?"

"To quote Dan Buckley, you're not some M&M, of course you'd have a shot. If you can swing by the store this week and fill out an application, I'll talk to the owner and tell her I know someone."

~

Hannah heard the clink of beer bottles as Hank slipped back inside her room. The caps hissed as he popped them off by the door, then walked through the shadows and set them on the ledge behind her bed.

"You stopped by your dorm?" she asked.

"Yeah."

"I thought you were just going to the bathroom?"

He took off his robe and stood naked in the dim light, taking a sip from one of the bottles.

"I thought a beer sounded good. You want one?"

"No thanks."

Hank took another swig and slipped under the covers beside her. The cool air made her shiver, but the heat of his body against hers felt wonderful.

"Tell me about your father," Hank said.

"Is that what you ask all the girls once you've had your way with them?"

"Umm, no, and frankly that's disturbing," Hank said.

"I agree. *You're* the one who brought it up."

Hannah ran her hand down Hank's stomach, sending a shiver up his spine.

"You've got goose bumps."

"It's cold in here," he said.

"You weren't complaining five minutes ago," she replied.

"Neither were you."

They lay on their backs and stared up at the shadows on the ceiling.

"So seriously, tell me about your father. If he's coming to parent's weekend, I should probably know something about him."

"You'll like him."

"Why?"

"He's friendly. He's supportive. He always treats people to dinner. And he's never killed any of my lovers."

Hank sat up. "Have there been many?" he asked in mock-alarm.

"No." She kissed him. "You can relax."

Hank slumped back on the pillow, shifting against her in the narrow bed.

"He likes old music. Crooners and big band. He's like a throwback. He's always traveling for work. He has this great den. Big leather couch. Dark wood walls. Heavy cocktail glasses… Scotch."

"What's he look like?"

Hannah laughed. "You mean, is he big enough to hurt you?"

"Is he?"

"Kind of. He played football in college, but he wrecked his knee, so he has a little bit of a limp. You'll see."

"Your Dad sounds like he'd be Frank Sinatra's bodyguard. A den-dwelling, scotch-drinking, football-playing, protective father, and you say I should relax? Guys like that *kill* guys like me for doing what I just did."

"You flatter yourself. It's cute."

"And what about your mother?"

"That is the question for the ages."

"So it's just the two of you?" he asked.

"*Yep.*"

Hannah said it in a way that told Hank that particular topic was closed for discussion.

"Have you always lived in Chicago?"

"Of course."

"Got a little hometown pride have you?"

"Where else would a person ever want to live?"

Hank laughed. "I guess I'll have to check it out."

Now it was Hannah's turn to sit up. "You've never been to Chicago?!"

"I haven't."

"Oh, we have to go."

Hank put his arms around her and pulled her close. "You've got me convinced."

"You better hope my father can't read minds," she whispered.

~

"Do I look OK?"

"You look great," Jason said. "You always do."

Brooke was standing in front of the mirror in her dorm room, brushing her hair, which was growing longer and lighter by the day as the black dye faded and her natural brunette color came through. She made eye-contact with his reflection.

"Thank you, but you're biased."

"That doesn't make me wrong."

"I hope to hell nothing comes up about my hospital visit."

"Didn't you figure his accountant must have paid the bills by now?"

"That's what I'm hoping. For once I'm rooting for my parents to be unengaged."

"I think it would have come up by now," Jason said as he stepped behind her and kissed her on the neck.

Loren's keys jangled in the lock, but stopped when she realized it was open. "Oh, it's you guys," she said as she peered inside. "I was afraid I'd left it unlocked."

"Nope. I'm just getting ready for the parents," Brooke said.

"When are they getting here?"

"Any minute."

Loren gave her roommate the once over. Gone were the all purple punk ensembles and heavy makeup. She was dressed in dark jeans and a loosely buttoned, pale pink shirt.

"Correct me if I'm wrong, but something seems different."

"I'm dressed to appease," Brooke explained.

"But don't worry," Jason said as he motioned to his girlfriend's shirt. "There's still some rebel there."

Brooke unfastened her top to flash one of Jason's TOOL shirts underneath.

"Where were *you* so early this morning?" Brooke asked Loren, her tone insinuating scandalous doings as she buttoned back up.

"The bookstore downtown."

"Oh really? Walking Braden to work after a night of passion?"

Loren shot her roommate a dismissive scowl. *"No,* but I *was* applying to that job he recommended me for."

"At R.K. Phillips?" Jason asked. "That would be a great place to work."

"I'm hoping I get it."

"If Braden recommended you, I'd bet you have a good shot," Jason said.

Brooke looked at the time and squeezed Jason's hand. "We probably better go downstairs and meet them."

Loren crossed her fingers as they headed out the door. "Have a good lunch you guys."

Brooke nodded her head nervously. "Thanks."

~

Campus was awash with parents and visitors.

As Brooke and Jason crossed the quad, they passed a very Brady family in the midst of an extremely disorganized football game. It was unclear who was on what side, but everyone in the large, ragtag group appeared to be having fun.

"There they are," Brooke said.

Jason did a doubletake, then he realized Brooke was pointing to the sidewalk in front of Brownie's, where an impeccably dressed blond-haired woman in her late-40s was marching toward them. A severe looking man in his early-50s was marching a few steps behind her. He scowled at the football-playing clan, sizing them up like a New Yorker who'd arrived at his weekend home to find hobos playing Frisbee with the hubcaps from his Audi.

Brooke was halfway to her mother by the time Jason realized she was no longer by his side. He hurried to catch up.

"There she is," her mother exclaimed as she gave Brooke a hug.

"You made it," Brooke said.

"We wouldn't have missed it, dear," her mother replied as she gave Jason a curious look.

"Mom, this is Jason. Jason, this is my mother."

"Cristina Winston," her mother offered as she put out her hand. "And this is my husband, Alex."

Alex looked vaguely in Jason's direction and gave a perfunctory nod.

"Brooke," he said gruffly.

"Dad."

Her father shot another look at the football family, who were now huddled together, exchanging pats on the back.

Cristina reached out and touched Brooke's hair, running her fingers under a lock and letting it fall free.

"You've changed your hair."

"Yeah, I thought I'd let it grow out a little and see how it looks natural."

"Hmm," Cristina murmured.

Brooke made eye contact with Jason.

"What do you say we get a bite to eat," Cristina suggested.

"Is that OK with you?" Brooke asked Jason.

"Sounds great," he replied, but Cristina and Alex had already turned and started for town.

Brooke hurried after them. "There's a nice place on The Ave called Ciao that you might want to try."

"I'll take a look at the menu," Cristina said. "It's sounds sort of…"

She trailed off without finishing the sentence.

~

The walk downtown was largely silent. Now and then Cristina commented on someone who passed by. Alex asked about a couple of buildings on the academic side – primarily questions about the donors they were named after – but the exchanges were all businesslike, almost curt.

The conversation picked up ever so slightly when they arrived at the restaurant and took a seat. Ciao was an Italian restaurant that Jason had taken Brooke to a few times.

"What's good here," Cristina asked as she looked over the options.

"They have great calzones if you… like that sort of thing…" Jason trailed off as he saw Cristina's lip curl.

"Calzones…" she muttered in quiet horror.

"Their salads are good too, Mom," Brooke offered.

"I'll probably get a salad," Cristina said to Alex, who was looking at the menu blankly. "I'm sure Tom and Janet will have some ridiculously big dinner later, so I might as well save my appetite."

"Are you going somewhere tonight?" Brooke asked.

"Your mother and I are eating with one of my clients in Rochester later," Alex explained.

"Oh, I thought you were staying in town tonight. We were thinking you might want to go to an event on campus with our friends and Jason's mother."

"I wish we could," Cristina said. "But we have to at least make an appearance. You know how important it is to keep the fund's investors happy."

Jason watched Brooke nod and look down at her menu.

"Yeah," she said. "That is important."

~

Hank studied the bartender at Lola's as he poured Bourbon into a shaker, slapped on the lid, and shook it briskly over his shoulder before straining it into a heavy glass.

"You're a fan of Manhattans," Hank observed.

Peter Merritt arched an eyebrow at his daughter's boyfriend. "This is my second."

"Oh, I'm not keeping count," Hank replied. "It just seems like an older cocktail. You don't see too many people ordering those these days."

Peter took his drink from the bartender and dropped a single on the bar.

"You're calling me *old* now, too?"

Hank studied Hannah's father's expression. "You're messing with me, aren't you?"

Peter put his hand on Hank's shoulder. "I'm messing with you," he confirmed as he took a swig of his drink.

They'd stuck around after their meal, shifting into the bar when the restaurant needed their table for the next seating. Hannah had excused herself and slipped away to the ladies room, giving Hank and her father a few minutes alone.

"Now I see where Hannah gets her dry humor," Hank observed.

"She can scare the hell out of you, can't she?"

She really can," Hank said as he looked over his shoulder and saw Hannah walking their way.

"What are you boys talking about?" she asked warily.

Peter shrugged. "Just guy talk."

They picked up their drinks and headed for a booth in the corner. Peter set his glass on the table as he sat down. Hannah picked it up and slipped a napkin underneath as she took the seat across from him.

"You've probably noticed my daughter is very detailed oriented."

"That's what you want in an architect," she said.

Judging by the speed of her reply, Hank guessed it was a defense she'd used in previous versions of this conversation.

"What about music production," Peter asked Hank. "Is that a field where details matter?"

"I sure hope not," Hank joked. "But I guess it really depends on the producer's intention."

"Like if he's trying to hide messages in there when you play it backwards?"

Hank smiled. "That and other stuff. The things you do or don't do play a huge part in the way things turn out. Do you know what I mean?"

Peter took another sip of his Manhattan, squeegeeing his upper lip with his lower teeth.

"Yeah, it's about making smart choices."

"Hank is one of the most pragmatic people I know," Hannah observed.

Hank laughed.

"Is she a sweet talker or what?" Peter observed. "Bet you only ever *dreamed* a girl would label you *pragmatic!*"

His smile faded as he saw his daughter shooting him daggers.

"I'm just teasing," he said. "The two of you seem to balance each other nicely."

"I hope so," Hank said as he met Hannah's gaze.

Peter polished off the rest of his drink and set the glass down with a *thunk*.

"Where to next?" he asked.

~

Brooke and Jason ate their calzones while her mother carried on a running commentary about her friends in the city. By the time the meal ended, Jason knew far more about a half-dozen residents of the Upper East Side, than he did about his new girlfriend's mother and father.

Though he'd brought cash with him for the meal, after observing Alex's parental indifference first hand, when the bill arrived, Jason took Brooke's advice and made no effort to reach for it. When her father eventually glanced at the ticket and dropped his credit card on the tray without a word, Jason still didn't say anything. Cathie Pepper had taught her son manners, but she'd also taught him self-respect, and it hadn't escaped his attention that Alex Winston had yet to say a single word to him. If the man was too self-absorbed to engage the boy who was sleeping with his daughter, Jason had no intention of groveling in thanks for a piece of folded pizza.

After the meal, save for Cristina's ongoing soliloquies, they walked back to the dorms in silence.

Jason's mother was sitting on the steps when they arrived.

"I was hoping I would run into you," Cathie said, getting to her feet when she saw them.

"Hey, Mom." Jason said

"Cathie," Brooke exclaimed. "Mom, Dad, this is Jason's mother, Cathie."

"Very nice to meet you," Cathie said, shaking Cristina and Alex's hands as she glanced at Jason and Brooke for guidance. "Will you be joining us for the show tonight?"

Cristina arched an eyebrow. "Show?"

"There's a comedian performing at the field house later," Brooke explained.

Her mother's nose crinkled. "I'm afraid we have to be heading out in a few minutes."

"Oh, I'm sorry to hear that," Cathie said, giving Jason a questioning look, which he met with an almost imperceptible shrug.

"I'll walk you to your car," Brooke told her parents.

"It was nice meeting you," Cristina said in Cathie and Jason's direction as they departed.

"And how did that go?" Cathie asked her son when they were alone.

"About how you think. Her parents are some cold fish."

"How is Brooke doing?"

"I think she's used to them, she seemed unfazed."

"What about in general?"

"I think things are going really well, actually."

"Good. She deserves it," Cathie said. She put her hand on his knee. "You both do."

Brooke emerged at the far end of the quad and started running back across the grass with a huge smile on her face.

"I am so sorry for my parents," she said when she reached them.

"Why do you say that?" Jason asked.

She flashed him a look that said *'Please.'*

"You seem happy," Cathie observed.

"I am," Brooke admitted. "There was no mention of a hospital bill. I think I'm in the clear."

Without a word, Cathie opened her arms and gave Brooke a hug.

"Let's go celebrate," Jason suggested.

~

They gathered at Brick's for a late meal after the show. Braden and Loren each came separately. Brooke and Jason brought Cathie. And Hank and Hannah arrived with Peter.

"I never thought that guy was funny on *Saturday Night Live*," Peter observed, "But as a standup, he's hilarious!"

They were seated at a bigger table than usual, a large corner booth in the back that curved around in a horseshoe shape. Braden and Loren were squeezed in next to each other near the end, with Hannah's father holding them in place like a bookend.

The waitress arrived with their drinks and started passing them around the table. Peter was drinking his beer before it had even touched the table. Braden watched the glass in Hannah's father's hands; when he glanced across the table at Jason's mother, he noticed she was watching the drink as well. Their eyes met briefly as Braden looked up.

"So let me get this straight," Peter said as he surveyed the table. "My lovely daughter is studying architecture, and she's dating Hank, who is studying business as well as music with Jason, who is dating Brooke. And Brooke is studying graphic design and rooming with Loren, who is in the writing program with Braden, only Loren and Braden aren't dating."

"You've got it," Hannah said. "Now can we please order some food? I'm starving."

"Any of you ever noticed what a taskmaster my daughter becomes when you go to a restaurant?"

"*Yes!*" Half the table replied in unison.

"See, honey, it's not just me," Peter said. "OK. So there's one part that's still confusing me."

"What's that?" Braden asked. He was beginning to detect the hint of a slur, and though he wasn't sure where this was going, he was hoping to get ahead of it.

Peter bobbed his head toward Braden and Loren. "Why *aren't* the two of you together? It seems like the perfect setup. You obviously have things in common. You could be one of those literary couples you always hear about. If nothing else, you could write some great books together."

"Why do we have to date to collaborate on a book?" Loren asked.

"I suppose you don't, but it would probably be more fun that way."

"Oh leave them alone," Hannah exclaimed.

"Fine, fine. I've said my piece. Let's get some food and another round of drinks."

~

"Well, *that* was awkward," Loren said.

"He was just having fun," Braden replied.

They were walking back along The Lookout. The other couples, each with their accompanying parent figure, had made their ways back to the dorms after the meal, but Braden and Loren somehow found themselves strolling the campus, just the two of them.

There was a knot in Loren's stomach.

"He's right you know," Braden said.

She took a deep breath. "How so?"

"We *should* write something together."

"You think?"

"Why not? We might enjoy it."

"Maybe we would."

"Just something fun that we could keep in our back pockets. What do you think?"

"Yeah. That might be fun," Loren admitted.

She wondered what Braden thought of the *rest* of Peter Merritt's comments, but opted to change the subject. "Brooke's parents sure sound like dicks."

"It makes you wonder why some people have kids, right? Cathie is sure nice though."

"She's a saint." Loren exhaled. "You don't have any other thoughts about Hannah's father?"

Braden hesitated, not entirely sure where this was going. Things were finally getting back to normal between the two of them, so he didn't want to take any chances.

"I think her father is a charming guy," he said with weary resignation. "I also thinking he's a functioning alcoholic, so we probably shouldn't put a whole lot of thought into *everything* he says."

3.

BRADEN WAS WORKING THE main floor with Cole. It was a typical Saturday morning in the store, with parents and kids filing past the front counter as story time began. As usual where toddlers were concerned, their visits to the children's section were brief, with little ones repeatedly fleeing the room, only to be nabbed by parents or nannies as they made a run for the front door. Having already seen a few near escapes, Braden was finding the experience slightly nerve-racking. Cole on the other hand was completely oblivious as he slipped into the back to grab fistfuls of Bugles corn chips, half of which he dropped on the floor as he absentmindedly stuffed them in his mouth.

Dan, the store's receiving clerk, walked out from the shipping room with a handful of new arrivals and set them on the shelving cart by the main counter. Dan was a big guy, a couple years out of school, who'd been active in a frat and played on his school's football team in college. Though he'd clearly gained some beer and pizza weight since entering the working world, he was a notorious nutritional scold.

"Do you have any idea much *saturated fat* is in those?" he asked Cole.

Cole shrugged and glanced down at his flat stomach. A Bugle crumb clung to the corner of his mouth.

Dan headed back to the shipping room, shaking his head in disgust.

Braden carried a stack of Dan Buckley's new book to the front table, spreading half the copies out with the hardcover new arrivals. The rest would have to go up in overstock. He was halfway up the ladder with the extra copies when he heard the door chime, and a familiar voice addressed Cole behind his back.

"Hi, I'm looking for Mary Ellen."

It was Loren.

"Just up those stairs," Cole said in his most mellifluous tone.

Braden placed the overstock titles on the highest shelf and climbed back down. By then, Loren had disappeared up the stairs, and Cole was running his fingers through his hair, primping for her return.

Save your energy, Braden thought to himself.

With any luck, Loren had the job. Braden wondered what it would be like working together. Now that the fallout from his ill-advised advance had finally blown over, he didn't want to risk doing anything to make things awkward between them again.

Braden heard Mary Ellen and Loren talking as they started down the stairs, and watched as Cole brushed the last of the Bugle dust from his shirt and hurried to the shelving cart. He *must* have thought Loren was cute if he was willing to do actual work in an effort to look busy for her.

Mary Ellen's mouth fell open as she emerged at the bottom of the stairs and saw Cole carrying a stack of books to the front table, but she closed it again when she too realized why he was suddenly behaving like such a worker bee. "Cole, can you man the info desk for a bit?"

"Sure, Mary Ellen," Cole replied.

Mary Ellen rolled her eyes as he left. "Now this guy I believe you know," she continued as she walked Loren over to the front counter where Braden was working. "Great news, McNutt, putting your thumb on the scale worked. Can you show Loren the ropes while I get some lunch?"

Braden smiled. "Absolutely."

"We'll finish up your paperwork when I get back," Mary Ellen told Loren as she slipped into the café.

Loren whispered to Braden conspiratorially once they were alone. "Was that Roxanne's son?"

"That was him."

"He didn't seem all *that* bad."

"Give it time." Braden muttered. "So… I haven't trained anyone before, but I can try to show you how the register works."

"Sounds good to me."

Braden picked up the nearest book and turned to the computer.

Loren reached over and put her hand on his shoulder. "Thanks again for recommending me, Braden."

"Of course," he said. "What are friends for?"

* * *

Cathie Pepper's house was a short walk from the bus stop, but Brooke was half frozen by the time they got there. Jason pulled the massive patchwork cap from his head and handed it to her.

"Here, put this on."

"All right," Brooke said as she eyed the oversized knitted hat warily – patchwork *anything* was not exactly her style – but she was freezing. The moment she pulled it over her head, a wave of warmth drifted over her. "Hey, this thing is *amazing.* Where did you get this?"

"My mother makes them every year," Jason said as he held up his hands to display a matching set of gloves. "They come as a pair."

"I might need to ask her for a set of my own," Brooke said through chattering teeth. "If this is what it's like now, I'll be dead by January."

"You'll be fine," Jason said. "Your blood will thicken up soon."

"Then I'll be dead long *before* January! A girl can't live with chunky blood, Jason!"

"How is it any colder here than in the city?"

"I don't know *how*, but it is. The city gets cold, but nothing like this!"

"Don't worry," Jason said as he rubbed her back. "We're just about there."

A short time later, they rounded a corner and stopped at the bottom of a set of stone steps. Brooke looked up and saw a two story brick house above the road. The roof sparkled with frost. Warm light glowed from the windows. And strings of white holiday lights framed the windows and crisscrossed playfully above the front porch."

"This is it," Jason said they started up the stairs.

"It looks so cozy. Are those Christmas lights?"

"Yeah, Mom usually puts up the first string on the day after Halloween. She *loves* Christmas and gets impatient. We hang the rest after Thanksgiving."

He unlocked the front door and led her inside. It was as warm indoors as it looked from the street. The front door opened into a foyer, with wood floors and a wide staircase that ascended to a landing, then disappeared around the corner. A long wooden bench sat against a bank of windows, with shoe cubbies tucked beneath.

"Mom! We're here!" Jason called as he hung their coats on a row of hooks to the side of the door.

The squeak of an oven door sounded from a distant corner of the house, followed by footsteps as Cathie hurried in to greet them.

"Brooke!" Cathie said as she gave her a hug. "I'm so glad you could make it."

"Thanks for having me."

"Good to see you, kiddo." Cathie said to Jason as she pulled him tight for a moment. "And on time no less."

"I love your house," Brooke said.

"Thank you," Cathie replied, starting back the way she'd come, as Jason and Brooke followed behind.

"It reminds me of something…"

"A schoolhouse?" Cathie suggested as they emerged in the kitchen.

"That's… it!" Brooke exclaimed. "But in a good way. It's just the wood, and the hooks, and-"

"It's everything." Cathie laughed. "Jeff, my husband, was an elementary school teacher. The look of the place is all him, and for better or worse, I guess you could say be brought his work home with him. I never had the heart to change anything, but I do feel like I should have tenure by now. You'll have to excuse me for talking and cooking, I'm not the most organized chef."

"It smells delicious, Mom."

"Wow," Cathie turned to Brooke with a broad smile. "For eighteen years his favorite question is *'Can't we order a pizza?'* but he brings you home and suddenly my cooking smells *delicious*."

"That's not true at all!" Jason protested.

"I'm kidding, he's a very appreciative kid. And he makes a great salad." Cathie motioned to the refrigerator. "Jason, would you mind making a salad?"

"Sure, insult me, then flatter me when you need help."

Cathie winked at Brooke as Jason set to work.

~

After dinner, Brooke excused herself and slipped off to the bathroom.

Cathie waited for the footsteps to grow quiet, then she turned to Jason. "So, how is she doing?"

"I think she's good," he said.

"Any slip ups? Red flags?"

He knocked on the table. "Nothing."

"You're sure? No unexplained periods when you can't reach her? No mugs filled with mystery drinks?"

"Nope. Nothing."

"It can happen all of a sudden you know. You have to be on the lookout."

"Don't worry, Mom. My eyes are open, but I trust her."

Cathie smiled. "I like her."

"I do too."

~

Fish oil and vitamin D.

No prescription medications. Certainly nothing illicit. Not that she was looking for them anyway. It was just a reflexive habit from years of popping open medicine cabinets upon entering new homes. Brooke hated that she'd done it, but she reminded herself that it was just muscle memory. She hadn't been the least bit inclined to mess around with *anything*, liquor or otherwise, since that ill-fated weekend. All she wanted was to be present. To go to classes. Work on her design. And be with Jason.

Just the thought of him gave her a funny little smile as she pictured him with his backpack strapped on like a parachute. Who would ever have thought she'd wind up with someone so square? And she didn't give a shit. Back in New York, with the folks she used to hang out with, she might have been self-conscious going out in public with him, but from the moment she'd awakened in the hospital to find him checking on her, any concerns about what other people thought had vanished from her mind. She no longer gave a shit.

Brooke closed the cabinet with a gentle *click* and headed down the hall toward the stairs. The wood floor creaked softly underfoot as she padded past a wall of photographs. There were several of Jason and Cathie standing next to a tall, painfully-thin man with a bushy-beard. That must have been Jason's father. Jason didn't appear to be older than ten in any of the pictures with the three of them. About halfway down the hall, the man with the beard disappeared, and the images were of just Cathie and Jason – at holiday parties, picnics, high school graduation – just the two of them. What had become of his father?

Brooke walked back to the first image. She stared at Jason's father's pale face, studying the deep lines around the eyes. Gazing down the row of photographs sequentially, he seemed to fade away.

When the smell of coffee wafted up from the first floor, Brooke realized she'd been gone longer than expected. She hurried down the stairs to the dining room.

"There she is," Jason observed as he set their mugs on the table. "Everything OK?"

Brooke looked at Jason and his mother as she took her seat.

These two people had saved her life.

"Yeah," she replied. "Everything is great."

~

Jason's dorm room was plastered with posters for hard rock bands. What was it about quiet guys and loud music? Maybe she didn't want to know.

They were lying in his bed, the warmth of his body pressed against her own.

"I was so cold on the way back," Brooke said

He held her tight. "Are you feeling better now?"

"I am."

She rolled over and kissed him.

"I had fun tonight. I love your mom."

"She likes you too."

"She's so different than my mother."

"Is she?"

"You *know* she is."

Jason didn't say anything, he just ran his hand over her shoulder blades.

"What do you think the others are up to tonight?" he asked.

"Hank and Hannah are probably doing what we're doing."

He smiled in the darkness. "*Exactly* what we're doing?"

"*Well*...maybe not that last part."

"What about earlier?"

"I don't know. Dinner? A movie? They're always together, so it's a safe bet neither of them was alone. They're pretty codependent."

"We're always together," Jason noted. "Are *we* codependent?"

Brooke grinned. "You might be."

"*Just* me?"

"I'm a hypocrite, but I'm not codependent."

Jason laughed. "Good to know. What about Braden and Loren? You think anything is happening there?"

"I haven't got a clue."

"I wish it would. We should try to get everyone together this week."

Brooke was quiet.

"Do you not want to?" Jason asked.

"Oh no, it's not that," Brooke said. "I was just thinking. You really like people, don't know?"

"Don't you?"

"Some people I guess, but you're different. You're a better person than I am."

"I don't think that's true at all."

"You haven't known me all that long."

"I still know you. You care about people."

"I hope I do."

They lay in the shadows, breathing and lost in their thoughts.

"My father would have liked you, too."

"I was just wondering about him." Brooke said, remembering that last photograph of the three of them. "I saw some pictures of you guys tonight."

"I have a lot of great memories of him from when I was little," Jason said. "But he got sick so fast-"

"I'm sorry."

"He went from this strong guy to… Well, you saw our house, every inch of that place is him, all the floors and cabinets, the stained woodwork. Mom says he was a teacher second and a frustrated carpenter first. He took that place from condemned to livable, then spent the next twelve years tinkering with it every chance he got until he couldn't lift a hammer anymore."

"How long ago was that?"

"Geez… probably eight years ago." Jason snapped his fingers. "He was gone like that."

Brooke kissed him on the cheek and pulled him closer.

"You might have noticed my mother has a bit of a protective mother hen thing going on now. That's why. She thinks things might have been different if she'd gotten my Dad to a see a doctor earlier. Now, as you know, if you have a medical situation, my mother won't let you out of her sight until she knows for a *fact* that you'll be OK."

"I can understand why."

* * *

Jason succeeded in getting everyone together the following weekend to watch the original *Star Wars* movies in his dorm room. They started *A New Hope* late, so by the time they got through *The Empire Strikes Back*, the audience was fading. Hannah nodded off before Lando's first appearance, awoke just as a one-handed Luke was rescued by the Millennium Falcon, and wanted Hank to take her home shortly afterward. Brooke was fast asleep by the time *Return of the Jedi*'s opening prologue crawled up the screen, and she didn't so much as flinch when the Jabba's pleasure barge exploded. By that point, the lucid audience was comprised of Jason, Braden, and Loren. And judging from the way her head kept slowly dipping forward, Loren was on the verge of passing out as well.

"You getting tired?" Braden whispered.

She stifled a yawn. "Yeah."

"Want me to walk you home?"

"That would be nice," she said.

They got up and quietly stepped over their sleeping friends, waving goodnight to Jason, who raised his hand in a silent farewell.

~

Bare branches creaked over the walkway outside.

Braden looked across the lawn to Valentine Hall, with Alan Grimwood's statue looming in the foreground. Keenly aware of how things had gone the last time they'd cut across the quad, tonight he opted to stay on the path and take the long way around.

Loren knew exactly what was happening. Braden was hoping to avoid disaster. She was too.

"Jason and Brooke seem like a good match," Braden said as they walked.

"They do, right?"

"You think she's serious about him?"

"Yeah, I think so," Loren replied as she gathered her thoughts. There was clearly something between the two of them, she just wasn't sure what it meant.

"He's *definitely* serious about her," Braden said. "I think it works."

Loren exhaled, her breath billowing in the chilled air. "I do too."

The conversation lagged until they reached the entrance to her building.

"What are you up to tomorrow?" Braden asked.

"Just catching up on assignments. Getting ready for the week."

"Same here."

Their eyes met.

Loren ticked through the pros and cons in her head as she closed her eyes and stepped toward him. Braden leaned forward. And at the last moment, Loren turn her head to the side, giving him an awkward half hug.

She didn't know why she'd done that.

Braden stood up straight. "I think I misread that again," he said apologetically.

"I… don't know that you did," Loren said. "I'm sorry. I don't want things to get weird between us again, but-"

Braden waited for her to finish, his lungs tightening as he inhaled the cold air.

"I think I need to do the single thing for once," Loren explained. "Just to see what that's like."

Braden nodded almost imperceptibly.

Loren tried to meet his eyes, but his gaze had dropped to the ground.

"Do you think we can keep things how they are now?" she asked. "I really don't want to stop speaking to each other again, cause that sucked."

"Sure we can."

Loren's eyes narrowed as she studied his expression.

She went in for another hug, squeezing Braden tight. She felt his hands on her back, then he pulled away.

"Have a good night, Loren," Braden said as he started toward his building.

Loren stood at the door, watching him go.

"Are you all right?" she called after him.

"I will be," he said.

Only Loren couldn't hear him. All she saw was Braden's back, his shoulders dropping forward, as he disappeared into the darkness.

4.

Well, *that* didn't sound good.

Brooke lowered the volume as the song Jason was introducing drowned out his voice and rattled her speakers. It was a strange feeling to hear your boyfriend on the radio. His taste in music was… inexplicable, but she loved him.

She hadn't told him that last part yet, but she'd said it in her head a hundred times. For some reason, it was an odd thing for her to come to terms with. She didn't think of herself as someone who fell in love that quickly, or ever. She certainly wouldn't have expected to feel that way about someone like Jason. And certainly not in her first few months at college. But what was that about anyway? Did she think she was too cool to fall for someone so normal? Then again… Jason wasn't *entirely* normal. He was pretty square, he just took it to such an extreme that in a funny way, it made him irresistible.

His music on the other hand was not.

Brooke flipped off the stereo and started going through her books. Now that she was back to school full time, getting a handle on workload and priorities was also something new for her. It was strange to give a shit how she did in her classes, and a little scary. Maybe *that* was why she'd always worked so hard to seem indifferent. Things were easier when you told yourself nothing mattered. Who cared if you passed or failed? Now she cared, if only for the fact that she couldn't imagine a life without Jason Pepper. A year ago, that thought would have made her sick to her stomach, now the idea of being without him had the same effect.

"No music?" Loren asked as she walked in the door.

Brooke gave her a sheepish look.

"Oh, are Jason and Hank on tonight?"

"I feel bad," Brooke admitted. "But I don't get their music."

Loren took off her backpack and coat and tossed them by her desk. "They're just…those guys."

"What do you mean, 'those guys'?"

"You know… like the guys back in high school who were into music you've never heard of, and they all knew everything about the same bands and stuff. There's usually someone named 'Tyler'."

"In the group or in the band?"

"Both." Loren laughed as she fell onto her bed. "I've actually heard them put on some good stuff at times, but yeah, I don't always get their music either. *They're* certainly in sync though."

"Yes they are."

Loren eyed the books spread out on Brooke's desk. "How are your classes going?"

"Pretty well. I'm still a little overwhelmed with the work, but I'm starting to get caught up. How are you?"

"*Tired,*" Loren replied.

"Did you work at the store tonight?"

"Yeah."

"Was Braden there?"

"Nope."

Brooke nodded. The way Loren popped the P in 'nope' confirmed what Jason figured. Whatever was or wasn't happening there had fizzled.

"What are you doing for Thanksgiving?" Brooke asked.

"I think I'll be here," Loren said. "I'm picking up some extras shifts at the store as the holidays get closer. Why?"

"Jason was wondering if anyone would be interested in going to his mother's for Thanksgiving."

"That might be nice."

"All right," Brooke said. "We'll start checking with the others."

~

"Carpe diem, Jason. *Carpe diem.*"

"OK, Robin Williams."

"I'm serious," Hank said as he pushed the WGRM microphone to the side.

They'd just introduced their next round of songs, which gave them thirty uninterrupted minutes to hash out what was quickly becoming their go-to topic of choice: starting their own label. Jason liked to look at it as something the two of them could do after college, or something they might ramp up in their senior year. Hank thought they should start now, while their financial responsibilities were minimal.

"Look at Microsoft, if Paul Allen had waited for Bill Gates to graduate from Harvard, they'd have been too late!"

"But we're not talking about software," Jason argued. "We're talking about *music.* There's no rush. I want to know what I'm doing first."

"All right, so this isn't Silicon Valley, but look at all the best success stories, they always involve people learning what they're doing *while* they're doing it. We could start our company while we're still in school and be the next Wozniak and Jobs."

"I would much rather be the next Herb Alpert and Jerry Moss."

"Then let's be them!" Hank exclaimed. "I *love* whipped cream and other delights."

"Whipped what?" Jason was briefly thrown, then The Tijuana Brass' iconic album cover flashed in his mind. "Oh right, well… I suppose it wouldn't hurt to start making plans…"

"Now we're talking!" Hank leaned back with a smile. "First things first. What would we call it?"

"Don't act like we haven't discussed that already," Jason exclaimed. "I told you, I've always wanted to name my label Cradle to the Groove Records."

"Right," Hank sighed. "You know, I have to be honest with you. I still don't get that."

"It's simple," Jason said. "Just think of a lifetime of music. Like listening to music from the cradle to the grave, only grave is groove, like a record groove."

Hank stared at him blanky. "You know, there's no reason we have to settle on a name right away. Why don't we come back to that?"

"OK," Jason conceded reluctantly. "But forgetting the name, what kind of music do you think we would put out?"

"That's easy," Hank said with a grin. *"Everything!"*

~

Although their selections inevitably put her on edge, Hannah had taken to setting an alarm to remind her to flip on the radio and catch the last 30 minutes of Hank and Jason's broadcasts while she finished her assignments. Hank liked to come to her place afterward, and it helped if she could describe something they'd played when he asked about the show. Fortunately, the radio recap portion of the evening was usually brief before they moved on to other things.

Letting Hank stay over every night was definitely cutting into the quality of the class work she was turning in, but in a funny way, Hannah realized she didn't care. Past relationships, no matter how serious, had always come second to academics. Throughout high school, AP courses, college prep work, and day to day assignments were given the highest priority, which her boyfriends hadn't always liked. But looking back on it now, Hannah realized she hadn't always liked *them*.

It was different with Hank. She was almost embarrassed at how anxiously she awaited that rap on her door each night.

Introducing him to her father was an important step. Some of the boys she'd dated in the past had *never* met him. Part of that was finding the right window of opportunity. Weekday afternoons, well before 5 were the safest bets. Any time later than that could get risky. And over the years, that window had narrowed.

Fortunately, the visit over parent's weekend had gone well. And though her father had been drinking, he never hit that mercurial tipping point. Her Dad liked Hank, as she knew he would, and Hank had nothing but good things to say as well, so she marked it up as a win.

The alarm went off, and Hannah flipped on the radio, turning the volume to the lowest intelligible setting as she hurried through the last twenty pages of reading.

* * *

"I think we should do it," Loren said.

Braden coughed on the cracker dust from his chili. "Do what?"

"I think we should write a book together. You mentioned it when we were here once, and I've been thinking it might be fun."

"What kind of book did you have in mind?"

"I don't know. I haven't thought that far ahead. I just wanted to see how you felt about the idea."

"I'd be down for that," Braden said.

"Great. I was trying to think of a way we could both work on it, something where we split the writing equally, Maybe traded chapters."

"Like an epistolary novel?"

Loren crinkled her nose. "I don't know. Those have always seemed sort of gimmicky to me."

"Me too actually. I suppose we could just write alternate chapters then rework them together." Braden pulled a notebook and pen from his backpack and set them on the table. "Or maybe we could tell the story from two points of view. Let one character narrate one chapter, and the other narrate the next."

"*That* could be fun," Loren said.

"Did you have a genre in mind?"

"I'd love to do a mystery."

"Let's go for it!" He scratched some notes in the notebook.

"What are you writing down?"

"I don't even know. Just warming up the engine." Braden scribbled a couple more lines, then read his notes aloud. "Mystery… Two narrators… Who are the narrators?"

"The hero – maybe a detective – and I don't know, the villain?"

"Are you thinking like a *Columbo* thing, where we know how the bad guy did it and see the detective cracking the case?"

"Maybe… What about partners?"

"Like a Nick and Nora thing?" Braden asked.

"Yeah! Like Nick and Nora; husband and wife detectives! We could have one chapter with him speaking, and the next with her. He can be sort of pompous and arrogant and get all the facts wrong, then she can come in and explain how things *really* are."

Braden laughed. "OK. So the guy is a blowhard dimwit. Are you thinking like a period setting?"

"That, or I suppose we could bring it up to modern times. It might be kind of fun to write a period mystery though. Maybe wait and see what we come up with storywise."

"And what did you have in mind for that?" Braden asked. "What kind of case are they dealing with?"

Loren gave him a comically serious look. "Well, *murder* of course!"

"Of course," Braden said as he slipped out of the booth. "I'm gonna get some more coffee. Do you want some?"

"Sure, why not," Loren replied as she spun the notebook around. "You get the coffee, I'll decide who dies."

***

"And classes are going well?" Loren's mother asked on the phone.

"Classes are fine. The quarter is wrapping up, so I'm turning in a bunch of papers and starting to prepare for finals-"

"Well, I'm sure you're on top of everything." Mary Beth cleared her throat. "I'm away on business for much of the month, but I'll be back a day or two before Thanksgiving. Should we be expecting you?"

Loren took a deep breath. "Actually, part of the reason I was calling was to let you know I won't be able to get back for Thanksgiving."

"Oh?"

"I'm a little short on money, and I'm just not sure it makes sense to go all that way for less than a week. This way I can pick up some extra shifts at the store as the holidays come up too."

"You know, we can send you the money. You don't have to pay for your travel expenses. You certainly don't have to be working in that store-"

"I know, Mom. But I *want* to work there. It's really the timing is all-"

"I see. Well, I expected this might happen."

The tone was familiar. Loren had heard the same thing when her brother and sister were cornered in similar situations. Although her mother frequently missed family gatherings, any time her children were unsure about making it home for a special occasion, the understanding Mary Beth demanded for her own absences was suddenly nowhere to be found.

"So, none of you will be home this year. That's fine."

"Where are Patrick and Julie going?" Loren asked.

"I don't recall." Her sentences were growing clipped.

"How is Dad doing?"

"Your father is fine."

"Is he there?" Loren asked. "I'd like to talk to him-"

"He's out."

"Well, please tell him I called. I haven't been able to get ahold of him."

"I'll let him know," Mary Beth said as the line went silent.

"Hello?" Loren asked, but her mother had hung up.

~

Most of the leaves had fallen now. The wind whistled through the brick buildings as Loren hurried toward the academic side. She wondered if Rick Austin had really been out when she called. In the past, she might have assumed he was just in another part of the house; in the garage working on a snowmobile, or out in the barn, tinkering with some home brew, but things had changed so much over the last few years, that the chances were just as good that he was down at the Brewery, or skiing at Purgatory with his current girlfriend.

Loren knew about her father's outside relationships. Actually, *outside* probably wasn't the right term for them these days, as there was really no longer an intimate connection between her parents. When she was younger, the dynamic between Loren's mother and father had been prickly, but by the time she was a teenager, her parents existed as two bordering nations – with their own rooms, their own friends, and their own worlds – but they were neighboring countries with a mutually beneficial trade agreement.

Aside from their kids – who were now scattered like shrapnel from a blast – Puzzlebox Brewing was the only thing Rick and Mary Beth Austin still had in common. Her father started the brewery years earlier to keep busy between ski seasons, and when it took off, he brought his wife in to handle the business side of things. Mary Beth had done a hell of a job, growing the business into something her husband could never dreamed of, and might never have wanted in the first place.

The curious thing about Puzzlebox was that the bigger it grew, the more vital it became to the heart of Durango, the farther apart it pushed the members of Loren's family. It wasn't that the brewery was operating on particularly tight margins, or that Loren and her siblings were jockeying for stakes in the family business, it was simply a case of financial support inevitably coming with unstated, continually-shifting expectations, ones that seemed to grow with the scale of the company. Even with the best of intentions, where family and money are concerned, there are always unseen tripwires. Seeing how her siblings had fared after they left home, Loren was determined never to fall into her parents' debt.

She almost never heard from her brother and sister anymore. And her relationship with her mother felt… stilted at best. Of all the members of her family, Loren and her father were the closest. She wished he'd been there to talk tonight.

Loren reached the library and walked around to The Lookout, crossing the stone platform and stopping at the railing where she could look down at The Falls. The rocky cliffs on either side of the cascading water were encased in ice and snow.

As far as Thanksgiving was concerned, it was true that she needed the money. But even if the trip was shorter, Loren really didn't want to go home this year. Truth be told, she was intrigued by the idea of spending the holidays in Grimwood.

Once again, she found herself thinking of Braden. Where would *he* be going for the holidays?

She closed her eyes, slowly inhaled the icy air, and turned to go. The sky was growing darker – the filtered gray of early winter – when she suddenly heard two hushed voices whispering sharply at her shoulder. She spun around, and caught a fleeting glimpse of two shadowy figures, one with its arm over the other's shoulder as they staggered around the back of the library.

Loren *knew* what they were, and wondered how long they'd been there. She clenched her fists, pressing her nails into her palms as she forced herself to follow behind. Her hair whipped around her face in the wind as she rounded the corner. The library towered above her, but the flares had vanished just as quickly as they had appeared.

* * *

"I saw two of them this time," Loren said as she and Braden were walking to class. Rock salt crunched on the sidewalk beneath their feet.

"Two what?" he asked.

"Flares."

Braden stopped and looked at her. "When was this?"

"Last night, behind the library."

"What were you doing out there?"

"Just walking and thinking…"

Braden studied her expression, but he didn't ask what she had been thinking about.

"Was your grandfather always interested in the afterlife?" Loren asked as they resumed walking.

"I don't really know. As long as I knew him he had an open mind about it, but he wasn't like F.W. Woolworth, there were no ornate carvings etched into the molding around his house or anything. It was just one of his things, if we were at an event and someone described seeing or experiencing something they couldn't explain, more often than not, Pops would talk about flares when we got home."

"What do you think it means if people repeatedly see them in the same place?"

"Something is out of balance on the other side? Perhaps unsettling moments reverberate through time, like history repeating itself."

"I'd be curious to know how often people see things on that part of campus."

"We should start keeping track of this stuff," Braden said. "See if we can find a pattern."

5.

"I THINK THIS IS good," Braden said as he held up one of the story outlines he and Loren had exchanged over the course of the week.

They were once again holed up in their customary booth at Brownie's, working on their book on a Friday night. They'd settled on their characters – James and Sara Tripp – husband and wife detectives, not unlike Dashiell Hammett's famous married couple from *The Thin Man*, only brought up to modern times and without the money or the dog. Whereas Nick and Nora tippled martinis and staggered through mysteries for amusement, the Tripps drank because they were tired, and they took on cases because they needed the cash.

"*Dead Men Don't?*" Loren asked when she saw the outline he was holding.

"Yeah, it's modern, but it has the feel of a classic cocktail class mystery. I'm not sure about the title though."

"Me either. I was thinking *Dead Men Don't Drink Gin*, since the victim dies from a poisoned martini. Then I thought I remembered something about certain parts of Juniper plants being poisonous, so I was thinking we might call it *Dead Men Don't Drink Juniper*, sort of play off the gin, maybe name the main suspect Juniper. Of course, then I started to wonder if I had my facts straight, so I dropped the last two words all together. We'd definitely want to research that part."

"That's what the library is for, right?"

"You don't want to consider any of the ideas you came up with?" Loren asked.

"If you want to be polite, we can, but yours is clearly the best."

"What about the one with the Rube Goldberg boobytrap? That was pretty clever."

Braden looked skeptical. "Let's save it for the follow up. It will be perfect for our sophomore slump."

Loren studied Braden's expression. "Are you sure you don't want to explore one of your ideas?"

"Positive."

"OK, then where do we go from here?"

"Well, we know who gets murdered and how, so the next thing is to figure out who did it and who else might be suspects, then we can hammer out the story scene by scene."

"Sounds good to me," Loren replied as she opened her notebook and took out a pen. "Who narrates the first chapter?"

"Lady's first?"

Loren set to work on the outline.

Before they knew it, the Friday night dinner rush had come and gone, and they'd worked out a fairly nice story framework.

"There you guys are!" Hank called over to them.

Braden looked up to see his roommate and Hannah walking to the table with their trays of food.

"I might have known the two of you would be down her working on your baby again," Hank said.

Loren crinkled her nose. "It's a book, not a baby."

"Careful," Braden told Loren. "Now that he knows you don't like it, that's all he'll call it."

Hank set his tray on the table. "You guys mind if we join you, or are you still working?"

Loren exchanged looks will Braden and put down the pen. "I guess we're at a good stopping point."

"Your roommate and Jason are on their way here, too," Hank told Loren. "We're going to that big hullabaloo downtown if you want to join us, even Hannah is going."

"Yep, even *I'm* going, if you can believe it," Hannah joked as she slid into the booth. "Sorry to crowd you, Loren."

"What's the event?" Braden asked.

"The Powwow," Jason said from behind them as he and Brooke arrived. "You guys should join us. It's a lot of fun."

"What is it?" Loren asked.

"It's a sort of block party The Dinosaur Bar-B-Que on Greenwood throws every year before Thanksgiving break. They have bands and beer and barbecue of course. It's a huge event, anyone with a college ID gets in free. You just pay for your drinks," Jason explained as he and Brooke sat down. "It's a blast."

"It sounds like fun," Loren said. It also sounded like a haven for underage drinking. She wasn't sure if she should be the one to raise an awkward question, but she wondered if Brooke was comfortable with the idea.

"If you're worrying about me, don't," Brooke said, as if reading Loren's mind. "We've been back to The Shack a couple of times now, and I haven't been tempted to pickle myself. Turns out there's this great stuff called Diet Coke, which hops you up, but doesn't leave you hung over for 36 hours afterwards."

"So, 'Powwow,' is that a play on the Indians and the first Thanksgiving?" Hannah asked. "That seems a bit… old school?"

"It's not exactly PC," Brooke said.

"Yes, the name is a somewhat problematic," Hank said. "But I think it's possible to go to The Powwow without condoning rampant racism."

"Plus, they have this fantastic firewater punch that you won't want to miss," Jason interrupted.

Hannah smacked her forehead.

"OK, so maybe it's not a shining example of progressive thinking," Hank conceded, "But I'd still like to go."

~

The Dinosaur sat on a corner lot one block removed from The Avenue's main stretch. From the looks of the place, the property had once been a lumber yard, with corrugated metal buildings, heavy beamed construction, and weathered wood siding. The rustic elements had clearly provided inspiration for the overall design, as rusted metal awnings covered the long picnics tables surrounding the building's open courtyard. The place was swarming with college kids, who were drinking and talking while a rockabilly band played onstage.

As they made their way through the crowd, Brooke noticed a familiar-looking girl with black hair and red streaks glancing her way: Miranda. Her former cohort surveyed Brooke's new circle of friends and shot her a disapproving smirk as she strolled past.

Jason caught the exchange. "Was that-?"

"Yeah, that's one of them," Brooke said as she set a hand on his shoulder and encouraged him to keep moving.

"Where is this firewater?" Hannah asked Jason.

"Follow me."

The band was winding down as the group reached the center of the action. No one seemed to be in charge, but an enormous metal trough was flowing with some kind of deep red punch. Tin cups were stacked in teetering towers alongside.

"Is that it?" Hank asked.

"That's it," Jason said.

"What's in it?" Braden asked dubiously.

Jason handed him a metal cup. "Try it."

"Are you having some?" Braden asked Loren.

She looked at Brooke. "Are you sure you don't mind?"

"Trust me," Brooke told her, "I've had *more* than my fair share over the years."

"OK then. Sock it to me," Loren said to Hank as he began filling cups and handing them out.

Hannah was the first to take a sip. She brought a hand to her throat. "Oh man, this stuff burns."

Braden was next. He grimaced and sputtered on his first sip.

Hank, who was watching all of this skeptically, looked from Braden to Hannah, then he took a gulp. He stood in silence for a moment, his face growing redder and redder, until his jaw dropped open and he gasped for air. "*That* is one *rough* drink."

"It *is* called firewater," Jason said as he took a small sip.

Loren was the last to try it. She brought the cup to her lips, hesitated, then downed it in one long gulp. "Yum," she sighed, wiping her mouth on her sleeve as she immediately went back for a refill.

When she turned back around, the entire gang was staring at her in disbelief.

"My family owns a brewery," she said with a shrug. Then she pointed down the line from Brooke to Hank. "I'm gonna go get Brooke a Diet Coke. Any of you turkeys want me to bring you back a Shirley Temple?"

"Jesus," Hannah said as she choked down another sip of firewater and watched Loren head to the bar. "I thought she was the *nice* one, but you give her one drink and she starts taking potshots."

"Speaking of turkeys," Jason said. "I've been meaning to talk to you guys about Thanksgiving. If any of you will be in town, my Mom says you're all invited to come to our place for the holiday."

"I'll be in Albany," Hank said. "Otherwise I'd love to go."

"Same here," Hannah added. "But I already have my tickets for Chicago."

"I'll be there," Brooke said. "I don't know if that's a warning or a selling point for any of you."

"Be where?" Loren asked when she returned with Brooke's soda.

"Thanksgiving at Jason's house," Braden replied.

"Oh, that would be nice," Loren said to Jason. "I'd love to come if you have room."

"You're the only people invited, so there's *plenty* of room if you can make it."

"Then count me in. I figured I'd have to settle for a turkey sandwich in my dorm."

"The more the merrier," Jason said.

"I'll probably be in town too," Braden said. "I was thinking I might take some extra shifts at the bookstore over the break."

"I'm doing the same thing," Loren said.

"That place gets crazy over the holidays," Jason noted. "You guys can probably make some good money."

"I need to check that place out," Hannah said woozily. "I love books."

Loren and Braden exchanged looks. The firewater was beginning to do its thing.

~

Everyone relaxed as the night wore on. Even Brooke, who had never been comfortable at a party without a drink in her hand, was having a good time as she and Jason danced together. And the Dinosaur kept rolling out fresh platters of Bar-B-Que , baked beans, and chili; the hot food, combined with the heat from the smoking pits, kept the crowd warm, even as the temperatures tipped downward.

Hannah, comfortably soused, wrapped her arms around Hank's shoulders, gently kissing him behind the ear. His expression was a mix or wariness and amusement.

Loren watched from the sidelines, observing Braden from the corner of her eye. Once or twice, she caught him doing the same thing, but neither of them wanted to risk rocking the boat.

The band, a group called the Dusty 45s, wrapped their set with a blaring bullfighter's call to battle, the front man playing a flaming trumpet as the crowd went into a frenzy.

The gang regrouped as the band's final number came to a crashing conclusion. Hank and Braden headed back for more food, while Loren and Brooke set off in search of water. Just Jason and Hannah remained as The Powwow briefly grew quiet.

"This is great!" Hannah yelled, loud enough to be heard over the din of the music… assuming the band was still playing. Instead, her exuberant exclamation drew a series of blinking stares from people nearby.

Jason laughed and wiped the sweat from his forehead. "I'm glad you're enjoying it," he replied as he looked over and saw Miranda standing just a few feet away, flirting with a muscular guy in a black leather coat. "Oh, great-"

"What?" Hannah asked.

Jason sighed. He knew he shouldn't say anything. "I just saw one of the people Brooke was hanging out with at the start of the year."

"The *assholes* who left her passed out in that club?" Hannah exclaimed as she whipped her head around.

Miranda looked their way, then went back to her conversation.

"It's nothing," Jason said reassuringly. "Brooke wouldn't want me saying anything."

Hannah downed the last of her firewater and started forward. "She could have choked to death if you hadn't found her."

Miranda – who had clearly taken notice of them now, not to mention the daggers Hannah was shooting her way – held her hands up and shrugged her arms questioningly.

Hannah mimicked the move.

"What's your problem?" Miranda shouted.

"Can we try to keep things calm here?" Jason said.

"*You're* my problem, smokey eye!" Hannah hollered back.

"Bitch, I don't even *know* you!" Miranda growled as she hurried forward, quickly closing the gap between them.

"Who are you calling a bitch, *bitch!*" Hannah yelled as she stepped forward, and with no warning, slapped Miranda across the face.

Miranda stumbled backward, caught her balance, and came back at Hannah fast.

From the back table, Braden saw the fists begin to fly. "Uh, Hank?"

Hank choked on his beer when he saw what was happening.

The guy in the leather jacket bolted forward, lunging for Jason, who dropped his head, grabbing ahold of his would-be attacker's waist and hanging on tight.

"What the hell is happening?!" Loren yelled as she and Brooke returned.

Brooke's jaw dropped as she watched Miranda lunge for Hannah, both of them tumbling to the ground in a blur of flailing arms and legs.

Meanwhile, the guy in the leather jacket spun around in circles as Jason held on tight.

Brooke rushed into the fray, with Braden and Hank close behind.

Hank caught up first, clenching Jason's wrists in his hands. Braden looked around, perplexed at the strategy, and grabbed ahold of the pockets of the guy's leather coat. Then *all* of them were whirling around in an awkward, off-balance cyclone.

Meanwhile, Miranda clenched Hannah's curly red hair in her fingers, pushing her head to the ground until Loren shoved her way through the crowd of confused onlookers and leapt onto Miranda's back, flailing her feet until the guys' tussle collided with the girls' spectacular skirmish, and the whole lot of them went down in a dogpile.

Jason was the first to extricate himself from the mess, quickly pulling the leather jacket over his opponent's head as his friends disentangled their arms and legs. They wiped the dust from their clothes as Miranda and her companion grumbled and groaned their ways to sitting positions.

Miranda looked at Brooke. Brooke looked at Miranda. Neither of them seemed to know what to say.

"You folks are gonna have to leave," a deep voice bellowed behind them.

The group turned to see three big guys in Dinosaur BBQ shirts. Judging from their expressions, and the size of their arms, they weren't messing around.

Moments later, the gang was standing on the corner of 78th and The Avenue.

Hank was the first to break the silence. "Anyone up for a bite to eat?" He pointed across the street to Red Tomato. "I can get us a pie on the house."

Bloodied and bruised and aimless, the six of them looked around the group.

"Sure." Hannah laughed as she rubbed her bruised arm. "Why the hell not?"

~

Steam from the open pizza box swirled in the night air as Brooke extricated one last slice and fell back on the bleachers. The group was scattered in the stands looking out over Grimwood's darkened sports fields. Aside from the sound of a single train whistle in the distance, the town was silent.

Brooke took a bite of her pizza and smiled. "I'd just like to say that I am shocked and appalled by the way you all behaved tonight, and I wouldn't bet a dime on any of you in a street fight, but for the record, I really appreciate it."

"What do you mean by that street fight crack?" Hank asked.

Brooke laughed. "I mean you guys are *ugly* fighters."

"Hey!" Jason countered. "I was good!"

"You weren't bad," Braden conceded. "But there *was* a sort of Three Stooges quality to the whole spinning our opponents around in circles technique."

"Whatever," Hannah said dismissively. "That bitch and her boy toy had it coming."

"Maybe *she* did," Loren offered. "But I feel kind of bad for jumping him like that."

"He jumped first! No one forced him to go after Jason!"

"You hit his date in the face!" Brooke exclaimed.

"I'm not really sure they were on a date," Hannah said. "He was probably just some mimbo who caught her eye, but… OK, point taken. Give me some credit though, warranted or not, I think I got a few good hits in."

"You did," Brooke said. "But guys, can you all do something for me?" She looked around at her friends' faces. "Can you promise me this is the last time we ever have to talk about any of those people again? I'd just assume forget them if I can."

"Of course," Jason said.

"Yeah," Hank added. "We can do that."

Hannah was a little less enthusiastic "I suppose so. But I'm telling you, if any of those losers start giving you trouble again, all bets are off."

"Understood," Brooke said as she stood and stretched. "Now, if you don't mind, I need to go to sleep."

Jason raised a slice of pizza in a toast. "To sleep!" he said as his friends – some of them in more pain than others – got to their feet and started down the bleachers.

* * *

"I'm working on it now," Loren said as she shifted the phone receiver to her shoulder and studied her computer screen. "How is yours coming?"

"I turned it in this morning," Braden said.

"You brat. Why are you calling me then, to gloat?"

"I don't know," Braden replied. "Just seeing if you're around."

They'd taken to talking on the phone occasionally. Sometimes the calls were related to their book idea or an assignment, but not always. With exams out of the way, all that remained were their final papers for The Novel.

"Is Hank still around?" Loren asked as she stood and stretched.

"Nah. He drove Hannah to the airport this morning and headed to Albany."

"So, you're baching it."

"Baching it?" Braden asked.

"You know, like a bachelor, you have the place to yourself."

"I always have the place to myself," Braden said.

"Yeah, I guess I do too."

"Gets sort of old, doesn't it?"

"Sometimes."

Loren looked around her empty dorm. The truth was, she loved having the room to herself most of the time.

"You have any shifts at the store this week?" Braden asked.

"I was there last night. I'm there most of Friday and Saturday, too. You?"

"I still need to check my schedule, but I told Mary Ellen I'd be in town. Is it getting busy?"

"A little," Loren said. "Cole told me the rush really starts the day after Thanksgiving."

"You worked a shift with Cole?" Braden asked. "How was that?"

"It was OK. Jan was showing me a few things on the main register, so he was up at the information desk. I barely saw him."

"Consider yourself lucky, my friend," Braden said. "I'm sure Jan helped with shelving, too. Cole just hangs out in back."

"That sounds annoying," Loren said as she opened Brooke's fridge and poked through the sodas. "I suppose that's one of the perks of your Mom owning the place."

"I guess so." Braden's voice brightened. "Maybe we'll have some shifts together once you're trained."

"That would be fun," she said as she looked out over the quiet quad.

"Hey, do you know what time dinner starts at Jason's place?"

"I think around five, but I'll check with Brooke."

"Think I could walk over with you guys?" Braden asked.

"Of course. We'll wait for you."

~

Despite Brooke's protests, Braden carried her bag as the three of them trudged down the street from the bus stop.

"So you're staying at Jason's all week?" he asked.

"Yeah. I figure I might as well seize the opportunity to eat as much home cooking as possible."

"That does sound like a nice change of pace," Loren said. "Actually, is Brownie's even open this week?"

"You know, I hadn't even thought about that," Braden replied. "It *did* look pretty dark as we were heading out."

Brooke studied the two of them, her mouth hooked in a bemused half-grin. "Neither one of you thought to see if you'd have a place to eat on campus for the next week? What did you guys have for breakfast?"

"I took one of your pop tarts," Loren admitted.

"I guess I forgot about breakfast," Braden said.

"What about lunch?"

Braden snapped his fingers. "I grabbed some Chex mix from the machines."

"I… borrowed a bag of your microwave popcorn," Loren said sheepishly. "And one of your sodas."

"What the hell, Loren? OK, first of all, I think we need to start splitting the cost of my food runs. And second, what's with you guys? Is this some sort of Edgar Allan Poe malnourishment regimen the two of you are on? You need to eat more than snack foods. Your diets are like ninety percent sodium."

"I just forget about it sometimes," Braden said.

"I cannot imagine how someone can forget to eat!" Brooke exclaimed.

"You're sure we shouldn't have brought something?" Braden asked.

Brooke shook her head as they rounded the corner and stopped in front of Jason's house. "Cathie said not to. And if I've learned one thing by now, it's not to mess with Cathie Pepper's hospitality, she doesn't stand for it."

"She'd be upset if we brought an *appetizer?*"

"Look, I'm just telling you the rules," Brooke said as she led the way up the front steps. "I didn't say they make sense."

Jason met them at the front door.

"You made it," he said as he gave Brooke a quick kiss and ushered them inside. "How are you guys doing?"

The smell of dinner enveloped them as they pulled off their coats and shoes.

"Your house is so cozy," Loren said to Jason.

"Thanks."

"Didn't I say it was nice," Brooke confirmed. "It's exactly the kind of place you want to go to for Thanksgiving dinner."

"Then our timing is impeccable," Braden observed as Jason led them down the hall.

They emerged in the living room, where Cathie Pepper was setting a tray of appetizers on the coffee table. She looked up as they entered. "Happy Thanksgiving, everyone."

"Thank you for having us," Loren said.

"I'm glad you could make it," Cathie replied as she took a seat in a big leather chair, watching as Jason and Brooke sat close to one another on the couch, and Braden and Loren took a seat on the sofa across from them.

Braden reached for an appetizer, taking a bite as Cathie

pulled her feet up on the chair so she was seated cross-legged. She turned to Loren and Braden. "Now, before I ask how the first quarter went for everyone, tell me…how long have the two of you been together?"

Braden choked on his cracker.

Loren – slightly flustered – mumbled, "Oh, we're not dating actually."

Cathie look at them for a moment and blinked. "Why the hell *not?*"

~

Loren was still mulling Cathie Pepper's question as they sat around the table eating dinner.

"So, how did everyone's first quarter at Grimwood go?" Cathie asked.

"Well, it started out a little bumpy, as you all know," Brooke said. "But I think it ended pretty well."

"Same here," Braden agreed. "Maybe a few things I would like to have done differently."

Loren took a bite of her food, wondering what he meant.

"How about you, Loren?"

Loren looked up questioningly.

"Are you happy at Grimwood?" Cathie asked.

"Oh, yeah. It's been great."

"It certainly seems like you've all formed a good group of friends. What are the others up to, Hank and…?"

"Hannah." Brooke replied. "She's back in Chicago with her father."

"And Hank is with his family in Albany," Jason said.

"So, as the few stragglers in town for the break, what are you all planning to do with your free time?" Cathie asked.

"Work mostly," Loren replied. "Maybe try to make some headway on a project Braden and I have been doing together."

"What kind of project?"

"Just a little book idea we have," Braden replied.

"Braden and Loren are enrolled in The Writing Center," Jason explained.

"Oh, that's a good program."

"And they both work at the bookstore," he added.

"So, what kept the two of you in town this week?" Cathie asked.

"I'm from Colorado," Loren said. "So I didn't really think it made much sense to trek out there, then turn right around and come back. This way I can save up a little extra money." She looked at her roommate, "And since Brooke is staying with you guys, I have the dorm all to myself for a week."

Brooke laughed. "Not that you don't have it to yourself all the time anyway!" No sooner had she said it, then she caught herself.

Jason shot Brooke a look in the awkward silence.

"Oh then…" Cathie said. "Braden, where are you from?"

"Huntington, Long Island."

"Do you have much family there?"

"Umm, no…" he said with a hollow half smile, like the realization had just struck him as he said it. "Not anymore."

"Braden is staying on campus this week too," Loren interjected. "We were just wondering whether or not the dining hall will be open over the break."

"I'm guessing it won't be," Cathie said. "But if you have fridges in your rooms, I can send you home with a ton of food tonight. And you're more than welcome to come here for as many meals as you like."

"That's really nice of you," Loren said. "We may take you up on that."

"Seriously, guys, you should," Jason said. "We don't have anything planned for the weekend. We're just hanging out and putting up the tree and things tomorrow."

"We are?" Brooke asked.

Jason turned to her. "Sure. We always put everything up the day after Thanksgiving."

"Well, we don't *have* to," Cathie said. "Maybe Brooke isn't into that."

"No." Brooke squeezed Jason's arm. "That sounds like fun."

~

"She really likes my son, doesn't she?" Cathie said to Loren when the two of them were alone in the kitchen, wrapping things up.

"She *loves* your son," Loren assured her.

"I'm glad. They both deserve a little happiness."

Loren studied Cathie's eyes as she packed up two sets of leftovers, one for her, the other for Braden.

They could hear Jason and Brooke laughing at a story Braden was telling in the next room.

"That boy is crazy about you you know," Cathie said after a moment.

"I know," Loren said softly.

"And you *obviously* care for him," Cathie observed as she turned and handed Loren the packages of food. "If the feelings are mutual, and you have any interest in pursuing things with him, don't wait too long. You never know what life has planned for us."

~

The bus sailed past the stop up ahead just as Loren and Braden trudged around the corner with their leftovers.

"Ah shit," Loren sighed as she watched the tail lights slip into the darkness.

"Was that the last one tonight?" Braden asked.

"I'm pretty sure it was."

"Then I guess we're trekking it back to campus," Braden replied.

A frigid blast of wind shot needles of cold through the seams in their clothing.

"All right," Loren said, psyching herself up for the long walk. "I suppose we can do this-"

Another gust of air rushed past them, blowing Loren's hair in her face as she tried to speak.

"Does it feel like the weather is rubbing salt in our wounds?!" she asked.

Braden smiled and brushed the hair from her eyes with a gloved hand. "A little bit, yeah."

The two of them grew quiet as they started on their way.

Loren listened to Braden's steady breathing as they walked along the darkened sidewalks, and wondered if this a welcome change from the solitary holidays he'd lived through over the last couple of years. She felt the sudden urge to stop and hug him tight.

Braden glanced at her from the corner of his eye. "What?"

"I was just thinking about something Cathie said." Loren shook her head. "Think she sent us home with enough food?"

Braden hoisted his bag with an appreciative groan. "Yeah, but I do wish you'd angled for more pie."

"Braden, she gave us each enough turkey and stuffing to last a month."

"I know," he said. "But the pie was… scrumptious. That was the Sophia Loren of pumpkin pies."

"I think Sophia Loren is more of a savory meat pie," Loren said.

"Then that was the Myrna Loy of pies. I wish that pie had a little scrunchy nose I could nibble on before bed-"

"OK. I get it. You liked the pie."

They walked the next half a block in silence. Loren wondered if he was thinking of the two of them-

"You know," Braden said after a while. "I think Sophia Lauren would be an onion tartlet,"

"Can we talk about something else?"

"Like what?"

Loren took a deep breath. "What are your plans for the rest of the night?"

"I don't have any."

"Would you like to hang out and watch a movie or something?"

"What did you want to watch?"

She thought for a moment. "Ever seen *Wonder Boys?*"

"I have."

"Do you like it?"

"Very much."

"Then, would you like to watch that?"

"Sure."

They crossed at the intersection of 78th and The Ave, passing Lola's, and heading across the university's moonlit sports fields. At one point, Braden instinctively took hold of Loren's forearm, steadying her as they crossed a pathway glazed with ice; Loren's eyes went to Braden's hand, then to his face, but he seemed unaware of having done it.

Loren's heart raced as they climbed the hill at the end of the field and stepped into the shadowy woods where she had once seen Grimwood's flare.

"I like the way Cathie and Jason still talk about his father," Braden said in the darkness.

"What made you think of that?"

"I don't know. I just remembered a line my grandfather used to quote from *Carousel*, something like 'as long as one person remembers you, it isn't over.' We should talk about the people that matter to us, even when they're gone."

"You do that," Loren said. "The first night we hung out, you told me about your grandfather and Jeremy."

"I really know how to sweet talk the ladies, don't I?"

"I thought it was sweet."

"I don't normally do that…" Braden said. "For some reason I bring that stuff up with you."

"I'm glad you do."

She reach down and squeezed his hand.

It was beginning to flurry when they stepped out of the woods. Loren steered them well away from Alan Grimwood's statue as they crossed the quad en route to Valentine Hall.

~

Snow was whipping past the window as the movie entered its second half. Braden was stretched out on Brooke's side of the room, watching the TV at the foot of her bed. Loren was lying on her own bed, sleepily playing with her hair as she watched. Braden sat up and looked out the window to see if Eldredge Hall was still visible through the falling snow. He could just make out the glow from a handful of dorm windows. He dreaded the idea of going back out into the cold, but the longer he waited, the more miserable he imagined the trip across the quad would be.

He settled back on the bed and studied Loren's expression. She was caught up in the movie.

"I ought to head back soon," he said.

"You don't have to go," she replied, meeting his gaze with her sleepy blue eyes.

Braden felt slightly more alert.

"Stay and watch the movie. Brooke certainly isn't coming back tonight. You can sleep on her bed."

"You know, maybe I'll do that."

He shifted on the bed, propping the pillows up against the cold of the cinder block wall behind him. Hot water burbled in the radiator beneath the window. Eventually, as a cloud of manuscript pages whirled on the screen before them, Braden drifted off to sleep.

~

The television was turned off the first time Braden awoke and tried to orient himself. He looked over at Loren's sleeping face, studied the gentle crease at the bridge of her nose, her loose, open hands, the fingertips naturally curling inward, then he closed his eyes, shifted the weight of his head on the pillow, and fell back to sleep.

~

Braden woke again early the next morning as a sliver of light slipped between the curtains in Loren's room. He reached for his jacket and shoes, retrieved his bag of leftovers from Brooke's fridge, and crept to the door as quietly as possible. Slowly, painstakingly, he turned the knob until the door creaked open. He studied Loren's sleeping outline, just for a moment, then he slipped out into the hall and pulled the door closed behind him.

* * *

Brooke lay in Jason's bed – the duvet pulled up to her chin – peering at the steam billowing through the half-open bathroom door. She hadn't heard Jason get up, but at some point, the sounds of running water, and the wafting aromas of breakfast roused her from her dreams. She lay on her back, listening to the shower. Eventually, the water was shut off with a squeak, and after a few minutes, Jason emerged from the bathroom wearing jeans and a Led Zeppelin T-shirt.

He smiled when he saw she was awake. "How did you sleep?"

"Great."

Brooke rubbed the sleep from her eyes and looked around the room. Her gaze settled on a green transistor radio sitting on the nightstand. Three anthropomorphic, martial arts-practicing tortoises were leaping across its face.

"Nice *Ninja Turtles* radio. Where did you get that?"

"You like it? My father gave me that when he saw how much I liked music as a kid."

"What kind of music?"

"Everything," Jason said matter-of-factly.

Brooke smiled sleepily. "That sounds about right."

"I'm gonna grab a bite to eat, then get started on the lights." Jason leaned down and kissed her before he left.

"…I'll be down soon," she said sleepily.

Eventually, she managed to get dressed and pad down the upstairs hallway, once more taking note of the framed pictures of Cathie, Jason, and Jeff Pepper that lined the walls.

A coffee carafe sat on the counter beside a plate of cinnamon rolls. Brooke poured a mug of coffee as she listened to the muffled sounds of Jason and Cathie Pepper discussing their illumination strategy outside.

~

Damn was it cold.

Brooke pulled her hat down over her ears as she rounded the front corner of the house and found Jason standing atop a ladder by the front porch, talking to Cathie.

"Hey, you're up!" he exclaimed.

"How did you sleep?" Cathie asked.

"Like a rock. Thank you for breakfast, it was delicious."

"Glad to hear it."

Brooke surveyed the tangled bundles of lights spread out on the porch. "So, where do we start?"

Jason laughed. "*That* is the age old question."

"Just so you know," Cathie said as she patted Brooke on the back. "I realize this isn't the most fun way to spend the day after Thanksgiving. If you don't feel like fumbling around in the cold all day, I *completely* understand!"

"No, I'd like to help," Brooke said. "It looks like fun."

"Oh it is. For the first fifteen minutes. Then agitation sets in."

"We were just trying to remember which colors go where," Jason said.

"We have the same debate every year. Jason always tells me where everything goes. I second guess him. Then I see everything set up and admit he was right."

"I think the red ones go along the top of the porch, with the green running along the bottom," Jason explained as he grabbed a coil of lights and started up the ladder.

"Which means I need to dig out the green lights and get them untangled."

"What can I do?" Brooke asked.

Before either of them could answer, two quick honks sounded from the street, and the three of them turned to see a station wagon with wooden side panels cruise past the house. Brooke caught sight of a girl in the passenger seat, who waved and flashed a peace sign as the car drove away.

Neither Jason nor Cathie waved. They both seemed caught off guard. Jason picked up the lights, shaking his head almost imperceptibly as he returned to the top of the ladder. Cathie Pepper's mouth went flat. Then she blinked and turned to Brooke.

"You can help me if you like," she said with a forced smile.

"Sure," Brooke answered uncertainly as she glanced up at Jason, who appeared to be deep in his own thoughts as he began clipping lights in place.

Brooke followed Cathie around the side of the house to the open garage door in back. "Who was that?" she asked once they were inside.

"That was Jason's ex-girlfriend… *Susie.*"

A knot of jealousy formed in Brooke's stomach. "Oh."

Cathie moved a couple of boxes aside, visibly agitated as she dug out two strings of green lights. She handed one to Brooke to untangle, and set to work on the other herself.

"What do you suppose is going through the head of a girl like that? Flashing a peace sign to the guy you left hanging out to dry?" Cathie looked up, realizing she was ranting. "I'm sorry. Did Jason ever tell you about her?"

"Not a word."

"They were together the last two years of high school. The initial reason Jason settled on Grimwood was because Susie decided to go there when her first choice school turned her down."

"So, what happened?"

"Two weeks before the start of classes, the Rhode Island School of Design called Susie to say a spot had opened up at the last minute if she still wanted to enroll. And she took it. Not only that, but the very same day she told Jason about RISD, she said she wanted to go to school with no commitments and broke it off with him."

"That's cold."

"That's one word for it," Cathie agreed. "Of course, Jason being Jason, he had no hard feelings. He just rolled with the punches." Cathie paused to wrestle with the tangle of lights. "That's the thing about being a parent. You love your kid more than you can possibly imagine, and you commit yourself to protecting them, but sooner or later someone is going to hurt them, and you might not even know when it happens. But God help the person you catch red-handed. I could *never* let that girl off the hook for what she did… He *really* never told you any of this?"

Brooke shook her head. "Nothing."

"That's what makes my son such a good person. Me, I'd tell *everyone*, but he just makes the most of it, and finds someone a hundred times better."

Brooke smiled, the flash of jealously replaced by a protective jolt of adrenaline.

Jason was coming down from the ladder when Brooke walked back to the front of the house.

He looked at her curiously as she got closer. "You all right?"

Brooke stepped forward to hug him. "I love you," she said.

Her words appeared to catch him off guard.

"I love you, too…"

* * *

Loren was working that day, but Mary Ellen hadn't put Braden on the schedule, which was actually a relief, as it gave him a chance to catch up on some sleep after he got back to his dorm.

He finally pulled himself out of bed around noon and micro-waved the first batch of Cathie Pepper's Thanksgiving leftovers as he drank a mug of instant coffee.

Braden sat down at his desk and spread out the materials he and Loren had brainstormed for their book. They'd expanded their idea and worked out the method and motive behind the inciting murder. The tool of the killing was a concentrated poison delivered in an ice cold martini.

With the bulk of the characters and plot in place, they were working backwards from the conclusion, breaking down the con-text of the chapters as told from the alternating perspectives of the husband and wife detectives. This part of the process didn't come naturally to Braden – Loren had much more of a knack for it – but the day passed quickly as he sorted through their sketchy notes and decisions.

Late that night, after a day of solitude, Braden was startled when the dorm phone rang. He picked up the receiver warily. "Hello?

"Hi," Loren said in a bright voice.

"Hey."

"I hope you don't mind me calling you so late?"

"Of course not.

"I didn't get out of work until late. The store was *crazy* today. Once I got back here, I just wanted to eat and relax, but I couldn't stop thinking about the book."

"Which book?"

"*Our* book of course. I think we should stick with the shorter title."

"Just *Dead Men Don't?* Don't what?"

Loren laughed. "I don't know. But hopefully people will pick up the book to find out."

"Sounds good to me."

"Listen, are you working tomorrow morning?" Loren asked.

"Yeah. I'm scheduled for 10."

"I'm due there at 8:30," Loren replied. "Would you want to go for a bite to eat and hang out after we finish our shifts? Maybe see what else we can get done for the book?"

They were entering the danger zone again.

"Sure," Braden said. "That sounds good."

"OK, then I'll see you at 10."

"See you then."

~

Loren smiled at him from behind the register as he walked in.

The store was busier than Braden had ever seen it, with customers lined up at the front registers and milling about on the sales floor. If it was this hectic two days after Thanksgiving, he couldn't imagine what it would be like in a few weeks.

Dan was restocking the new releases on the front table, but looked up as Braden started for the stairs. "You working the info desk?"

"I am."

"I just put a bunch of special orders behind the counter. If you guys have a chance, can you call a few of them and let them know their orders are in? Cole didn't contact *anyone* last night, and I'm running out of places to put stuff."

"Will do," Braden said.

Upstairs was just as busy as down. Virginia, a pragmatic high school girl with brunette hair and razor straight bangs, was running the register. She was hardworking, with a dry sense of humor.

"Thank God," Virginia said when she saw him. "I'm supposed to go for an early lunch."

"Anything I should know?"

"Just remember to breathe. It's crazy today. When I get back I'll start calling people about those special orders."

"Yeah. Dan was just telling me someone dropped the ball on that last night."

Virginia rolled her eyes as she reached under the counter to retrieve her purse. "Yeah, not the most helpful. I'll be back in an hour."

Braden turned to the counter, where a little white haired woman was standing at the front of the line.

"Who moved my cheese?" she whispered.

"Excuse me?"

"Who *moved* my *cheese?*" she eked out.

Braden looked around. "I… don't know…"

"She means the career book!" the customer behind her snapped.

"Oh, of course, sorry. It's in the business section behind you," Braden said.

The white haired woman turned and left without another word.

Holiday shopping was in full swing, and for the rest of the day, Braden barely had a moment of downtime. It wasn't until 6 o'clock, when he and Loren were both done with their shifts, that either of them had a chance to talk.

"Where do you feel like going?" he asked Loren as they pulled on their coats and headed downstairs.

"Well, I can't believe I'm saying this, but it feels strange to go this long without eating at Brick's."

Dan was restocking the bestsellers by the front door and looked up in horror as he overheard their conversation. "Do you have *any* idea what that stuff does to your body?"

"Umm…good things? Braden asked.

"If you think arteriosclerosis, diabetes, and fatty liver are good, then yeah, sure. Chow down," Dan sputtered. Then he saw Braden's barely suppressed grin. "Oh, never mind, you'll see, mark my words. You'll see."

"I'm just kidding with you," Braden replied. "Thank you for caring."

But the receiving guy was too irritated to respond, waving them away as he went back to what he was doing.

~

"Would you tell me about Jeremy?"

Loren and Braden were seated in the gang's usual booth. Two decimated Brick Plates sat on the table between them.

"What made you think of Jeremy?" he asked.

"I was remembering that line from *Carousel* you quoted the other night. You mention him every so often, so I was curious to know what he was like."

Braden took a sip of his drink as he considered where to start.

"Ever have a friend who protected you?"

"Like in fights?" Loren asked.

"Yeah."

"Not really. Although, I suspect if it came to it, Hannah would have my back."

"Jeremy used to protect me. It's not like I used to get into brawls or anything, but in elementary school, some of the other kids used to gang up on me at recess. Or they did, until Jeremy put a stop to it. He was never the biggest guy – even in high school – but he was *tough* and he was loyal. You know those friends you make in grade school who are nice to your face, but throw you under the bus in middle and high school if they see a chance to make inroads with a more popular group?"

"Oh yeah."

"Not Jeremy. He was cool, I mean, he was an athlete, girls liked him, everyone liked him, but he cut his own path. He was a football player, but he was also an art nerd. He was popular, but then his best friend was… well, me."

"So you were close."

"He was like my brother. I don't know how I would have gotten through last year without him." Braden paused and picked at his food. "Anyway… Jeremy dying really freaked me out. I mean, Pops was one thing, but Jeremy was young, and he seemed to be completely healthy. That's the scariest, when there's no warning. You're here one day, and the next you're gone."

"Did he have any siblings?"

"He didn't. Can you imagine what that's like for his parents? The quiet must echo. That's all I could think about for months. Once they're gone, will anyone remember the great kid they raised?"

"You will," Loren said.

"What about when I'm gone?"

"Then I will."

"All through the spring I was in this sort of daze, just thinking 'what is the point of all this?' You know how Robinson Crusoe leaves his mark on the tree, so no matter what happens, someone, at some point, might realize he was there? That's what I was thinking all the time…"

"So you started writing."

He looked at her for a beat. "How did you know that?"

"You're a *writer* Braden. That's what you do."

"You're right. I did."

"So what did you write?"

"A little bit of everything, most of it totally sucks, but it got me out of my head. And I started to make some headway on…"

"On what?"

"It sounds pretentious to say it out loud, but… a novel."

"Oh *really?* So you've actually written one book already."

"I'm not quite done with it, but yeah. I mean, I've written some rough drafts of other things that I just stashed in the back of a drawer, but this one feels different. Like it's something… bigger. I hope so anyway.."

"So, you're really working on *two* books now."

"I guess I am," Braden admitted. "But *Dead Men Don't* is the priority."

"Well of course. That's the one we'll be remembered for, right?"

"Without a doubt."

"You know, I have to be honest with you," Loren said as she fished a piece of macaroni salad from his plate. "I'm not always the best at seeing things through. I have a habit of finding distractions."

"Writers are notorious for that."

"Yeah, but I don't mean in the usual sense. Like staying away from the keyboard until the house is clean, I mean like never going back."

"What sidetracks you?"

"Life. Boyfriends. Generalized angst."

"Well, first of all, I don't see how any of those things are bad. Maybe the boyfriends, but you need experience to draw from, right? What did you submit when you were applying to The Writing Center?"

"Essays. A few short stories. I write a lot of short stories."

"Some people think you should never write a novel *until* you've mastered the short story."

"I certainly wouldn't claim to have *mastered* the short story, but thank you. Do you like writing them?"

"Not really, but I tend to write long. Probably because I don't have a life or a girlfriend."

Loren gave him a dubious look.

"OK, let's be realistic for a minute," Braden said. "We're both young. Let's not get ahead of ourselves with self-imposed pressure. How old are you?"

"Seventeen."

"You're younger than me?! When is your birthday?"

"January first."

"Huh. New Year's Day. What's that like?"

"It's not the best…" Loren admitted. "It gets overlooked a lot."

Their waitress dropped the bill on their table. Loren flipped it over and set a twenty on top. "I'm getting this by the way."

"Why?"

"Just because I want to," she said. "What do you say we finish that outline this week? Think we can do it?"

"I don't see why not."

* * *

The night before the rest of the gang was set to return for Winter quarter, Braden was seated at his desk, typing up the last scene of their outline, while Loren sat cross-legged out on Hank's bed, considering the half-finished bottle of Genesee she'd snagged from the fridge.

"Is your roommate going to be mad we drank all his beer?"

"Maybe. I suppose we could replace it for him, if either of us had a way to get more."

"How does *he* get it anyway?"

"That I have yet to figure out." Braden finished what he was typing and spun around in his chair. "Done."

"Seriously?" Loren asked.

"Seriously. Now the real work begins."

They clinked their bottles together and sat for a moment, absorbed in their thoughts.

Loren looked at him. It had been a nice break. They'd managed to avoid any awkwardness for the most part. Hanging out felt so natural.

"It will be kind of strange to have everyone back tomorrow," Loren said. "Any idea when your roommate gets in."

"I assume late, but I haven't heard from him."

"When do you want to start the actual writing?"

"Soon. I don't want to lose momentum."

"We won't let that happen," Loren said as she got to her feet. "You heading back?"

"Yeah. I want to get things organized while I still have the dorm to myself."

Braden looked around the room, which was strewn with pizza boxes and empty beer bottles. "Geez, you think I ought to do that here?"

"Yeah, you might want to get rid of some of the evidence." Loren opened the door and stepped out into the corridor. "Braden?"

"Yeah?"

"Did Jeremy ever flare?"

"No."

"Do you think that meant it was his time?"

Braden was quiet for a moment. "I hope so."

~

The frozen grass crunched underfoot as Loren crossed the empty quad.

Why did she always have a sense of sadness when she left Braden? Was *that* what kept her from wanting to get involved with him? Or was it a sign that she should be staying there with him? When they were together it seemed so natural and comfortable, but something always made her keep a slight distance. Even as she felt she knew him – probably better than she knew any of her other friends – something about Braden remained a mystery. It was as if he'd appeared on campus fully formed, yet so much about him seemed unclear.

His grandfather was gone.

He had a father he never saw. And what about his mother?

Then of course there was Jeremy.

She'd felt the urge to touch him at the door. To step forward and put her arms around him, but again, something had held her back.

Did the other person always have to make the first move before she took the leap?

~

Braden lay awake, dreading the long stretch of night before him. He hoped he would sleep, but he was anticipating a restless night, watching the shadows creep across the ceiling.

He wasn't looking forward to classes. Or returning to the grind.

It would be good to see his friends, but the last week had been nicer than he could have hoped for, even with the occasional ache in his chest.

But why had Loren mentioned Jeremy before she left?

He'd just been thinking of him as well.

It was another of those funny instances where what was on his mind was also on hers.

Life felt short…

It always did at night.

6.

THE TENTH FLOOR WAS buzzing with activity as Hank stepped off the elevator and made his way to his dorm. He opened the door to find his roommate crouched on the floor, knotting the drawstrings on a black garbage bag.

Braden looked up, a guilty expression crossing his face. "You're back!"

"I am," Hank replied as he dropped his duffel on his bed and pulled out a 6-pack of Genesee.

"How was Albany?"

"Albany was living the dream. Same as always."

"Is Hannah back?" Braden asked as he hoisted the unwieldy bundle of trash over his shoulder.

"She hopped out on the way up. She's waiting for me in her room." Hank said as he eyed the garbage bag in Braden's hands, instinctively following the sound of clinking beer bottles. "Brady, did you happen to drink some of my beer while I was gone?"

"I might have had a few..."

Hank opened the fridge to reveal the barren shelves. "Correction. Did you happen to drink *all* of my beer."

"I didn't drink *everything*, there are a still couple Labatts in there-"

"I see *a* Labatt," Hank said as he slipped the 6-pack into the spacious interior. "I think we need to discuss our system for procuring and *financing* our beer soon."

"Fair enough-"

"But not now," Hank said as he extracted two Genesees and headed for the door. "I've gotta get downstairs and… catch up with Hannah before dinner."

"OK." Braden knew better than to solicit clarification.

"Is everyone heading to Brownie's at five?"

"That's the plan."

Hank checked his watch. "We'll meet you guys there. But we *may* be a little bit late."

***

"They could probably use some help getting holiday decorations down from the attic," Mary Ellen told Braden as he entered the back office.

"Who?"

"Your girlfriend and Cole."

"Loren? She's not my girlfriend."

"No?" Mary Ellen arched an eyebrow. "You knew who I was talking about though."

Braden wasn't sure how to respond to that, so he continued into the back, where he found a ladder set up beneath the open attic door. Along with the clattering sounds of boxes being moved around up above, he could hear a couple of muffled exchanges, along with some quiet laughter. After a moment's hesitation, Braden climbed the ladder and poked his head through the opening.

"You guys need a hand?"

Cole and Loren turned to look at him from the far end of the attic. Cole was wearing a small wreath on his head.

"Hey, Braden," Loren said with a smile. "Yeah, we could definitely use some help."

"What's up, man?" Cole said as he plucked the wreath from his head.

Braden gave him a dubious nod, then he climbed up and looked around. They'd pulled out a dozen boxes of ornaments and artificial greenery.

"We're late getting the last of the ornaments up this year," Cole explained.

"That's better than putting everything out right after Halloween I suppose."

"That's exactly what *I* told him!" Loren exclaimed.

"Great minds," Braden replied, his eyes narrowing as he watched Cole like a hawk. He picked up a box and headed for the ladder. "What do you say we take this shit downstairs and get the two of you out of this attic?"

~

Braden manned the front register while Loren and Cole wrapped garland around the stair banisters.

His schedule was barely overlapping with Loren's this quarter. They didn't have any of the same classes together, and aside from today, they hadn't crossed paths at the bookstore in over a week. The periods that passed without seeing her were interminable.

His chest ached at the sound of Loren's laughter as she worked. He wasn't sure what was happening, but he suspected it was going to hurt.

~

Loren rolled her sandwich crumbs up in the DiBella's wrapper and looked at the back of the reader's copy she'd snagged on her way to the break room. She was reading the author blurbs when she heard footsteps behind her and looked up to see Braden carrying a matching sandwich.

"Hey," she said, lifting her crumpled DiBella's wrapper so he could see. "Great minds."

"Oh… yeah."

Braden flashed a tight smile and sat down to eat.

"How was your first week back?" she asked.

"It flew."

"Mine too," Loren said. "Everyone says the Winter quarter is weird, since we only have a few weeks of classes before we scatter again for the holidays. Now I know what they mean."

"How are you liking Gridley's class?"

"It's *good*. I've never been all that into poetry, but she just might turn me around. What about you?"

"I think it's great so far."

"Sucks we're not in the same session though, doesn't it?"

"Yeah it does."

Braden chewed a bite as he felt around for a topic. "How has the little prince been today?" he asked.

"Who?"

"Cole."

"You know… he's actually a really nice guy."

"Is he? How old do you think he is anyway?"

"I don't know. Twenty? Twenty-one? Did you know he studies at Grimwood?"

"Oh yeah? What's his major?"

Loren straightened at the tone in his voice.

"He takes art courses."

"Is that his *major*, or does he just take a bunch of art classes?"

"Gee, Braden. I don't know," Loren crumpled up her wrapper and tossed it in the trash. "What difference does it make?"

"It doesn't. I'm sorry," he said when he felt the tension rising. "I was just asking."

Loren gave him a sideways look. "Is that what you were doing?" she asked as she headed out the door.

~

When he checked the schedule after lunch, Braden was happy to see Cole's shift was just about over. As a bonus, he and Loren were both scheduled to work the main counter until closing. Perhaps he could smooth things over after his stupid comments earlier. For the first time all day, the sinking feeling in his stomach began to subside.

Braden came downstairs to find Loren working the second register while Cole chatted up an attractive young woman at register one.

"These are like Ayn Randian fever dreams," Cole said as he slipped her books into a bag. "I'm stoked to hear what you think."

Braden rolled his eyes.

The young woman left and Cole slid the register drawer shut with a *clunk*.

"It's all yours, man," Cole said as he started for the stairs. "Later, Loren."

"Have a good night, Cole."

"Later," Braden mumbled. He waited until Cole had disappeared up the stairs, then he looked at Loren.

"Yes?" she asked, sensing his gaze but refusing to turn his way.

Finally, when Braden still didn't respond, Loren relented and turned to face him.

"*What?*" she asked.

"Ayn Randian... *fever dreams,*" Braden blurted out. "I just have to ask..."

"I knew this was coming." Loren said. "Go ahead..."

"Do you think that guy has *ever* read anything by Ayn Rand?"

"Probably not," she said, a weary twinkle in her eye.

"Thank you!"

"Can we start over?" Loren asked. "For some reason I feel like we're bickering."

"Yeah, it sort of feels that way, doesn't it?"

"I don't know why either. There's no reason for it," she said. "But just for the record, I don't think Cole is quite the moron you think he is."

"I never said 'moron,' but would 'pseudo-intellectual' be out of line?"

Now it was Loren's turn to roll her eyes. "Oh look, books!" she with exaggerated enthusiasm as she approached the shelving cart. "What do you say we table this discussion and put some of these away?"

"All right. I get the message," Braden said as he took a handful of titles off the cart and set to work shelving them.

Now and then they would stop to comment on a book, or hold up a title they thought the other might find interesting. Eventually, the light outside began to fade, and the pace of the evening slowed even further.

"What are your thoughts on this one?" Loren asked as she held up a copy of *The Cobbler of Venice.*

"Oh, you mean sepia-toned beach accessories?"

Loren laughed. "I knew you'd hate it."

"Come on," Braden said. "Those books are like a genre all their own. *The Arsonist's Daughter. The Wall-Plasterer of Kabul.*"

"Maybe we should title our mystery *The Distiller's Apprentice*," Loren suggested.

A pained expression crossed Braden's face. "That's actually not a bad idea. What would the cover be?"

"A blurry close-up of an old apothecary bottle. With a little skull and cross-bones etched into the glass. And the title would have to be in really thin, white text that you can barely read."

"And we'd need an exotic locale in the title," Braden said. "Something in the news, but exotic sounding, like it *might* have been a glamorous vacation spot fifty years ago."

"*The Distiller's Apprentice of Yemen*."

"Are people allowed to distill anything in Yemen?" Braden wondered.

"We're talking about *poison* Braden, I don't think the killer is all that concerned with the regional rule of law."

"That's true. Still, I'd have to see the book next to a Ferragamo scarf or something. Just to be sure it pairs well."

"Ferragam-what?" Loren asked.

"Obscenely over-priced scarves. They're like rich-person catnip."

"Remind me to never let you two see my bookshelves," a voice murmured from one of the alcoves. They turned around to see a man in an emerald green shirt and slacks step out from the classics section.

"Professor Price," Braden said. "How are you?"

"I'm fine, Mr. McNutt," Price said. "Good evening, Ms. Austin."

"We were just joking around," Loren said. "I hope you don't think-"

Price waived them off. "Please, I'd be worried about Writing Center students who *didn't* have strong opinions about books. I didn't realize the two of you were working here. There's nothing like bookselling to instill a degree of contempt for certain aspects of the publishing business."

Braden smiled, suddenly reminded of some of Pops' more biting comments about the world of big books.

Price studied them for a moment. "It sounds like the two of you are working on something together."

"We're trying." Loren said.

"Writing is a lonely vocation, Price said. "It's nice if you can find a good collaborator."

Braden made fleeting eye contact with Loren.

"Can we help you find anything professor?" Braden asked.

"Oh… I'm just browsing, thanks."

Loren headed back to the counter. "Let us know if you need anything."

"Thank you," Price said with a warm smile, as he drifted toward the other side of the store.

Braden returned to his register and whispered to Loren. "Have you ever noticed he always wears a little bit of green?"

"Now that you mention it, yeah. What do you suppose that's about?"

"I have no idea," Braden replied.

* * *

Snow flurries swirled in the air as Brooke and Jason walked to the Alumni Union to get dinner.

"Listen, I know we were planning to hang out later," Jason said. "But Hank and I really need to get some work done on our mixing assignment. Would you mind if I met up with him after this?"

"That's fine with me," Brooke said. "I could stand to catch up on some work myself."

"You're welcome to hang out at my place if you want."

"I was planning on it either way," she said with a smile.

"Good."

Brooke sighed as they ducked inside from the cold and headed down the stairs to Spike's.

"What's on your mind," Jason asked.

"I really don't want to go to the city next week."

"Then don't go. Stay in Grimwood with me."

"Do you think I could?"

"Are you kidding?" Jason exclaimed. "My mother would *love* to have you stay with us again."

"All right," Brooke said as she contemplated the least explosive way to bring the idea up with her mother. "Let me see if I can do it. I'd love to be with you for Christmas."

* * *

It was the last day of classes before the holiday break, and Loren was working another evening shift at the store. Had she been traveling home to Colorado as originally planned, she would have been worried about getting everything turned in before she left, but as of now, she was staying in Grimwood for the break, her Christmas plans having unraveled over the course of the last week.

Word from back home was that her parents had shifted from an extended stretch of mutual apathy, to a rare period of all-out war, with her mother calling her father out on his various indiscretions, and her father suggesting hypocrisy in his wife's vehement indignation. That at least was the word from her sister when Julie called Loren's dorm earlier in the week to say that neither she nor Patrick would be in town for the holidays, and she wasn't even sure if their parents would be around either, let alone marking the occasion.

Loren was surprisingly relieved to be spending another holiday in Grimwood, but there were still logistical questions that needed to be answered. Like, where she would stay? Was campus even accessible? She seemed to remember hearing the heat in the dorms would be kept just a hair above freezing over the break. She wondered where that would leave her.

Maybe Cathie Pepper would put her up.

Would Braden be in town?

Cole Phillips came around the corner as Loren slipped into the back to wrap a purchase for an older gentleman.

"Hi, Loren," Cole said as he joined her in the narrow back room.

"How's it going?" Loren asked.

"I'm hanging in there."

He opened the door to the basement and headed down the steps.

Loren carefully wrapped the book in festive green and red paper, and was just starting back to the counter when she felt a hand on her shoulder.

"Sorry. Coming through again," Cole said as he passed behind her with a bundle of shopping bags in his arms.

Loren felt her cheeks flush unexpectedly.

"Need one?"

"I do actually," she replied as she took a bag and slipped the wrapped book inside. "Thank you."

"No problem."

Her stomach tightened.

Shit. She hadn't seen that coming.

"Hey, Loren," Mary Ellen hollered as she hustled past the registers. "If you're looking to pick up some more hours, a bunch of holiday shifts just opened up."

"I'll take them," Loren said as she watched Cole slip around the corner.

~

"It looks like I'll be going home for the holidays after all," Braden announced.

"You are?" Loren asked. She caught Hank casting an eye toward her side of the booth at Brick's.

"My father called last night and said he'll be coming back to take care of some things. He thought Christmas at home might be fun."

Loren wanted to say *'Christmas at home should be non-negotiable,'* but given her own situation, she realized the hypocrisy of such a comment.

"That's great, Braden, " Jason said. "My mom says you and Loren are welcome to stay with us if either of you need a place over the break. Loren, if you're interested, the invitation still stands."

"Thanks," she replied, adrift in her thoughts. "I may take you up on that."

"Seriously, Loren," Brooke added from across the table. "You should come."

"What about the rest of you?" Jason inquired. "Hank, Hannah?"

"We're both headed home again," Hank said. "I'm taking Hannah to the airport in the morning, then driving back to Albany."

"I'll be in Chicago until classes start up again in January," Hannah added.

"Which means *I'll* once again be watching The Three Stooges marathon by myself on New Year's," Hank observed.

"Are you going to order some food?" Braden asked Loren as the rest of the table continued to talk.

She'd lost her appetite, but picked up the menu anyway. "Yeah, I guess I ought to. What's everyone having?"

"We've gone with a dead man walking theme," Braden explained. "Brick Plates and milkshakes for the table."

"Dead man walking, huh?"

"If the executioner doesn't get you, the last meal will."

"I suppose I'll follow suit."

"You OK?" he asked.

"I'm fine," Loren replied. "Just tired."

Jason raised his milkshake as the first of the food arrived. "As the resident townie in the group, I know I'm supposed to be resentful of all of you outsiders for coming to Grimwood and making it your own, but I just wanted to say how happy I am to have gotten to know all of you. And while I'm sorry we won't all be together as the year draws to a close, hopefully this is just the first of many celebrations to come."

"Here here!" Hank agreed as the group clinked their glasses together.

Loren looked around the table. Who could have predicted any of these friendships just a few months earlier? She looked out the window at the falling snow, then turned to see Braden watching her with a half-smile.

"Have a good Christmas, Loren."

"You too," she replied quietly.

7.

POPS' CAR WAS STILL broken, so Olga drove Braden into town the day before Christmas Eve. His grandfather's longtime housekeeper and cook was in her late-70s and had mostly retired since Braden left for school, but she was still stopping by the house once a week to keep the place in working order. David McNutt, Braden's father, continued to pay her salary into retirement, so when she heard the two of them would be home for the holidays, she informed them she'd be moving back in for the duration of their visit; news that came as a relief to Braden. The house wouldn't feel so empty, and Olga was like family.

"I told you, I have all the basics back at the house," Olga said as they pulled up to the IGA.

"I know," Braden replied as he climbed out of the car. "I just need to grab a few essentials."

The old store seemed smaller than ever as he made his way down the aisles, picking out Pepperidge Farm goldfish and an Entenmann's crumb coffee cake. It was sleeting when he got back to the car. Olga glanced down at the open grocery bag and smiled as she recognized Pops' old staples.

After stopping at Dairy Barn for eggnog, and *Just Kids Nostalgia*, a comic book shop and pop culture haven chockablock with gift items perfect for eternal children like David McNutt, they headed home.

There were no lights on in the windows of Pops' big old house as Olga parked her car by the back door. And there was no sign of David McNutt when they went inside.

Braden and Olga ate dinner at the kitchen table as he told her how things were going at Grimwood. Neither of them was holding their breath for the phone to ring. They'd been to this rodeo many times before.

After dinner, Braden climbed the stairs to his grandfather's office. He flipped on the light, eased into Pops' old leather desk chair, and wondered what Loren was doing.

He should have stayed in Grimwood.

After a moment's hesitation, he picked up the phone and called Loren's dorm. Though he knew she wouldn't answer, it was soothing to hear the phone ring and picture the bell chiming in that far away room.

Braden briefly considered calling Jason's house to see if Loren had ended up staying there, but that made him nervous. He knew his feelings were obvious to all of their friends, but he didn't feel like opening himself up quite so clearly. His father's silence was already drawing a mix of hard feelings to the surface. Why make himself feel any worse?

He glanced out the window, peering across the snowy lawn that stretched down to Long Island Sound. If Jeremy were around, they would surely have hung out tonight. Braden could imagine just what his departed friend would have said about first David McNutt…

"The hell with him."

…and then Loren.

"Call her, man! Tell her how you feel."

But hadn't he done just that?

Jeremy would have argued no. He obviously hadn't laid it out there clearly enough, because here he was, alone in a house, spending the holidays with memories, while the one person he most wanted to be with could very well be alone on Christmas as well, and if he'd played his cards right, who knows what could have happened.

~

Olga took a call from David McNutt early the next morning. After wrapping up business in the city the day before, Braden's father had caught a flight to London in order to beat the incoming snowstorm. He knew it was a last minute change of plans, but he was scheduled to join an expedition in Cape Town in a few days, and he couldn't risk getting stuck in New York and missing his flight out on the 26th. Olga jotted a summary of David's excuse on a piece of paper and set it on the kitchen table, where Braden found it later that morning and dropped it in the trash on his way to the coffeemaker.

After he'd eaten, Braden slipped into the front room, gathered up his courage, and called the bookstore.

"R.K. Phillips," a distracted voice said over the sounds of a crowd.

"Good morning," Braden replied, unsure who had answered. "I was wondering if Loren is working today."

"Braden! *This* is Loren. Did you forget me already?"

"Oh, hey! I didn't recognize you over the noise."

"Yeah. It's crazy here this morning." Loren's clipped voice was nearly washed out by the background noise. "I think half the town waited until Christmas Eve to finish their shopping. How is home?"

"Oh, you know, same as always I guess."

"I bet it's nice."

Braden fumbled for an answer, embarrassed to have once more fallen for his father's bullshit.

"Are you staying at Jason's?" he asked finally.

He could hear her tearing off a sheet of giftwrap, and pictured her wrapping presents in the small area just out of view behind the register.

"I'm not sure. I might stop by later."

The answer didn't sync with the question.

"So where are you staying?" he asked.

There was some commotion on the line as another employee could be heard shoving past her.

"Are you there?" Braden asked after a moment.

"…Yeah, I'm here." Loren seemed distracted.

"It sounds like I ought to let you go." Braden said. "I just wanted to wish you Merry Christmas."

"Merry Christmas, Braden."

He could still hear the sounds of the store coming through the handset before the call disconnected.

8.

Loren's birthday came and went on New Year's Day, but Braden didn't call. Their halting conversation on Christmas Eve had provided all the awkwardness he could handle for a while. Instead, he spent the remainder of his time at home looking through his notebooks and fleshing out old story ideas. By the end of the break, he'd managed to produce a loose outline for another novel. Something told him an extra project might not be a bad idea if he needed a distraction in the new year.

He was relieved to return to Grimwood a few days later, but increasingly anxious about seeing Loren again. Other than Hank and Hannah, who he couldn't help but run into at the dorm, Braden didn't see any of his other friends until the first weekend back, when he was working an early Saturday morning shift at the store.

Braden was adding up his cash drawer when Loren walked in the door. If he'd secretly hoped to get over her during the time away, the twinge in his chest cured him of any such illusions.

Loren smiled when she spotted him at the register. "You're back!" she said as she slipped behind the counter to give him a hug. "Happy New Year."

"Happy New Year to you," Braden replied. "And happy *birthday*. I'm sorry I missed it, but I hope you had a good time."

"It was good," Loren replied. "Quiet, but nice. How was your break?"

"Let's just say I'm glad to be back."

Loren nodded and let the topic drop. "How was your first week back?"

"Busy."

"Same. And I've still got so much left to do before Monday."

"Are you working tomorrow?" Braden asked.

No, you?"

"I'll be back here bright and early tomorrow morning."

The morning passed quickly as they talked books and worked their way through the glut of incoming titles. Eventually they finished shelving everything Dan had hauled out from receiving. Braden was just stepping back to complement their handiwork, when Cole came down the stairs and stole his line.

"Look at that cart!" Cole announced. "*Nice job* guys."

"Impressive, right?" Loren said cheerfully.

"Braden, good to see you."

"Hey, Cole."

Braden watched as Cole slipped off his jacket and disappeared in the back. He returned a moment later, brushing a mop of black hair back behind his ears. There was something different about him, but it took Braden a moment to figure out exactly what it was. Then it hit him. Cole had shaved off his straggly goatee, and though Braden hated to admit it, the change was a positive one. The guy no longer reminded him of a seventeen year-old Jack Kerouac wannabe. He now resembled the child of well-to-do parents that he was. Unfortunately, he also looked a hell of a lot older.

"Are you working down here?" Loren asked Cole.

"That's what Mary Ellen says." He turned to Braden. "Oh, she also said you can take your break now if you're ready."

Braden glanced at his watch. A break sounded good. "I'm gonna get some coffee. Either of you want anything?"

"I'd love a medium drip with cream," Loren said as she reached into her pocket for cash.

"Don't worry about it, I've got this." Braden said. "Cole, what about you? My treat."

"A latte would be great," Cole said.

Braden headed for the café in the back of the store as he heard Loren and Cole exchanging small talk.

The sales floor was quiet when Braden returned a few minutes later. Neither Loren nor Cole was visible behind the counter. Braden was just bringing the carrier with their drinks into the back room when he stopped short.

His timing could not have been worse.

Loren's back was pressed up against the giftwrapping counter, her hands resting on Cole's shoulders as she kissed him deeply.

Neither of them could see Braden as he stood in the doorway, gutted.

He retreated quickly, the wooden floor creaking gently underfoot as the pieces fell together in his head.

Braden took his coffee, leaving the carrier with their drinks on the counter before he headed out the front door into the bitter cold.

The moment Loren and Cole slipped back out to the registers and saw their drinks abandoned on the counter, Loren knew what had happened.

Braden had seen them.

~

Why Jason Pepper was wearing his book bag on a Sunday, Braden would never know, but there he was, first thing that morning, bounding up the bookstore's steps on his way to the information desk.

"Braden!" Jason said as he reached the second floor. "Just the person I was looking for." He pulled a hardbound copy of *Revenant* from a shopping bag and set it on the counter. "I got this for my mother for Christmas, but it turns out she already has a copy. I'm hoping you can suggest something else."

"Yeah, I guess it's a safe bet that anyone who grew up here will have a copy of that one," Braden said. "Do you know if she has any other Alan Grimwood books?"

"Can you tell me some of the titles?" Jason asked.

"Does *Black Robes* sound familiar?"

"Yeah, I'm pretty sure she has that one. She's not so wild about it actually."

"I suppose I can see why, but that's a shame." Braden said as he clicked through the inventory. "I have one other title she might like. It's not completed, but every *Revenant* fan should read *Doppelganger,* if only to see where Alan Grimwood was going."

"That one I'm sure she doesn't have. Do you have any copies?"

Braden was already halfway to the local authors section. "She should find this one interesting," he said as he snatched up the last copy and handed it to his friend.

Jason studied the image on the cover – an out of focus figure walking in a snowstorm – then he handed it back to Braden. "I'm sure she'll love it. Thanks."

Braden sorted out the gift exchange as Jason waited.

"Thanks, man," Jason said when Braden handed the book back to him. He inhaled deeply. "Hey, do you have a minute?"

"Sure" Braden replied as he met Jason's gaze.

"I know we don't really know each other all that well outside of the group, but there's something I wanted to talk to you about."

"OK."

Braden had a funny idea he knew what the topic might be.

"I don't want to embarrass you or anything, because believe me, I can relate, but Brooke has filled me in a little, and I think we all sort of know how you feel about… Loren."

Braden forced an uncomfortable smile.

"So I figure it's better that one of us tell you now, before you bump into them somewhere. The thing is… Loren didn't spend any of the Christmas break at my mom's place. She stopped by once, but she was with some guy she works with here at the store. Apparently she stayed with him over the break. Brooke says it just started, but it sounds like they're pretty hot and heavy."

The bottom dropped out of Braden's stomach.

"Well… Thanks, Jason." He cleared his throat. "I sort of had a feeling. It just wasn't meant to be."

"Like I said, I hate to even bring it up, but I know that if it was me, I'd want to know so I wouldn't get caught off guard."

"Yeah, that would really suck," Braden said as his mind flashed to Loren and Cole in the back room the day before. "I appreciate the heads up."

"Hopefully you won't shoot the messenger-"

"Of course not. Don't give it a moment's thought. This is… good to know."

Jason picked up his book and started for the stairs. He paused at the top, "I hope you'll both keep hanging out with all of us."

"I'm sure we will," Braden said. "Hey, Jason?"

"Yeah?"

"How are you and Brooke doing?"

"We're great," Jason said, a smile spreading across his face. "That was the best Christmas of my life."

At least it had been for someone.

"I'm glad to hear it," Braden said. "You guys deserve it."

~

Loren was spending less and less time at the dorm these days, which was nice for Brooke, since she could now have Jason stay overnight at *her* place from time to time. It wasn't that his room was bad, it was just that Jason was… very much a boy. Which was to say that while she liked getting into his shorts, there was something less appealing in waking the next morning to find worn boxers resting from the bedpost mere inches from her face. It would be one thing if they were from the night before, but at the rate Jason did laundry, they could just as easily have been there since the first week of classes. Neither Brooke nor Loren could be accused of maintaining June Cleaver level hygiene, but they did keep their place up to at least *some* level of cleanliness. Plus, they had a TV, so it was an all-around win. Even the most libidinous couple needed to watch a movie now and then.

Jason paused *Manhattan Murder Mystery* and turned to her. "I stopped by the store today to give Braden the heads up about Loren."

"You probably didn't have to do that," Brooke said. "She thinks he might have seen them at work Saturday."

"Seen them doing what?"

"Just sneaking a kiss. I guess Braden avoided her for the rest of their shift."

"Well, *that* sucks." Jason muttered. "That's exactly what I was trying to keep from happening."

Brooke rubbed his chest. "It was nice of you to try at least. I didn't realize you guys were all that tight. You don't seem to talk much when we go out."

"It's a guy thing, Brooke. You wouldn't understand. We speak telepathically."

Brooke rolled her eyes. "Sure, if grunting is telepathic."

"That does suck though. Is she sure he saw?"

"Pretty sure. She was upset about it when she came back from work."

"But, didn't she go over to Cole's Saturday night *and* last night."

Brooke shrugged. "Worrying about Braden's feelings doesn't mean she can't have what *she* wants."

Jason studied her expression in the blue light. "I never knew girls were such mercenaries."

"Wake up and smell the white musk, buddy. We'll eat you alive."

~

It was strange to feel like she couldn't talk to Braden about their courses anymore. Having different sessions was one thing, but up until the holiday break, Loren had always felt free to pick up the phone and see what he thought about whatever assignments they were both working on that night.

Now it felt like something had been taken from her, and she was alternately upset and pissed off about it.

Why the hell should *she* be feeling guilty? She had every right to date whoever she wanted.

"Braden thinks he's a moron," she'd told Brooke after work on Saturday, "but Cole is actually a nice guy."

"That doesn't matter though," Brooke replied

"Why not? If he got to know him, he might like him."

"Look, Loren. That might make *you* feel better, but believe me, if a guy has the slightest interest in a girl, the *last* thing he wants to hear about is how nice the guy she's seeing is." When

Loren didn't say anything, Brooke elaborated. "If Braden were dating some girl, would you want to hear glowing character references about *her?*"

Of course not.

But why was that?

And what had changed her whole 'no relationship' stance? Was it loneliness at the holidays? Was it the fact that Braden was so up front about how he felt that it turned her off?

Was Cole just a fling? A space filler before something serious?

She'd spent the better part of the day in the Alumni Union, drinking coffee and catching up on the reading for Professor Gridley's class. Yet, if she was being completely honest, she'd spent half that time wrestling with her feelings. Ultimately, the best she came up with was that she was having fun. There was no reason to be taking everything so seriously. She was a freshman in college. There were no stakes. What happened happened. If she and Braden couldn't get past this, then maybe they weren't meant to be friends.

Even still, as the light faded and she headed out for the evening, Loren decided that a night in the dorms, in her own bed, might not be such a bad idea.

For the first time in a long while, it wasn't snowing. It was crisp and clear. The cold was intense, slicing through the layers of her clothing as Loren passed a handful of students on the walk back to the residential side. It wasn't until she cut through the woods that surrounded the dining hall that Loren sensed she was going to see him. She didn't know where or why, but something in the air told her what would happen if she turned now and kept her wits about her.

And then there he was.

Standing alone in the clearing. The familiar figure of Alan Grimwood.

A warm sensation bloomed in her stomach as she watched him. Then he was gone. And before Loren knew what she was doing, she had turned towards town, once again headed for Cole Phillips' apartment.

9.

"Wʜᴀᴛ ᴛʜᴇ ʜᴇʟʟ ɪs that stuff?" Hannah whispered. "That cannot be healthy."

They were standing at the counter of The White Russian, watching the attendant spray disinfectant into three pairs of red and blue bowling shoes, which he then scooped up and dropped on the formica bar top in front of them.

"That'll be fifteen for the shoes," he said before he took a swig from a bowling-pin-shaped beer bottle.

"Let me get these," Loren offered.

"Are you sure?" Brooke asked.

"I picked up a lot of overtime over the holidays. The money is burning a hole in my pocket."

"We'll get the food then."

"Deal," Loren said. "The nachos are actually pretty good here."

"You've been here before?" Hannah picked up her bowling shoes, only to immediately drop them in horror. "*Eww!* Why are the laces wet?!"

The counter attendant shrugged. "Could be beer, could be other stuff…"

"Can I get a different pair please? And that can of spray?"

"Your wish is my command," the guy mumbled as he swapped out the shoes and set the disinfectant on the counter.

Hannah grabbed the can and sprayed the laces on the replacement shoes. She sprayed the insides. Then she flipped them over and sprayed the heels. She repeated the process, and was about to apply a third coat, when Brooke stepped in, coughing and waving away the haze of disinfectant.

"OK, OK. I'd say you've eradicated any lifeforms that might have taken up residence!"

"You'd like to think as much," Hannah said, "but for all you know, patient zero was just bowling in those things."

Brooke inhaled, then nodded at the other shoes on the counter. "Hit mine again too, will ya?"

Eventually, the attendant reached out and snatched the can away.

"When the heck did you go bowling here?" Brooke asked as they were pulling on their shoes.

"Cole brought me on New Year's Day, they give you a free game on your birthday, so he thought it would be fun."

"Big spender," Hannah noted.

"Let's see how these badboys look," Brooke exclaimed as she got to her feet. "Ugh, that spray is soaking through my socks."

"Mine too!" Loren said. "It burns a little."

"Whatever," Hannah said. "I hope my feet burst into flames. Fire kills disease."

Brooke was still cringing. "I just hope it dissipates soon!"

"Try to take your mind off of it," Loren suggested.

"You said the nachos are good here?" Brooke asked.

"They'll definitely fill you up."

"That doesn't exactly answer the question," Hannah observed. "But let's order a couple platters before the guys get here."

Loren studied the lanes as they headed to *Jeff's*, the bowling alley's in-house diner. The place was filling up with a mix of college kids and people she assumed were regulars. A DJ was setting up audio equipment at the back of the lanes, while a couple of gangly high school kids went around switching on disco balls and unfurling banners that read "Rockin' Bowl."

The girls took a seat in a big corner booth with red vinyl seats. Loren picked up the menu and ran her finger down the list of appetizers as a waitress with a massive red beehive hairdo walked over. She was in her late seventies, and wore glasses that were easily a half inch thick. Her nametag read "Sally."

"Can I get you ladies something?"

"Yes," Loren said. "Can we get a pitcher of Labatts and two orders of #3?"

"Two platters of Gutter Slop," Sally noted as Hannah's head shot up. "How many glasses for the beer?"

"Five," Brooke said. "And could I get a root beer?"

"Sure thing. Five glasses, two slops, one root beer," Sally confirmed, then she headed for the kitchen.

Hannah reached for the menu. "What the heck is Gutter Slop?!"

"That's what they call the nachos." Loren explained.

"Why?!"

"I don't know. To keep things interesting?"

"This town has a real knack for naming their foods," Hannah observed as she slid the laminated menu into its holder behind the mustard and ketchup. "All right, so tell us about this guy you're seeing."

"Cole?" Loren knew it was coming, but she hadn't decided how much to share with them. "I don't know… he's just your typical guy."

"And?" Hannah asked, trying to coax further information out of her. "What's he like? How old is he?"

"He's a bit older than we are. He's from Grimwood. And his parents own the bookstore."

"Sleeping your way up the ladder," Hannah joked. "That's good. Is he coming tonight?"

"Not tonight."

Loren made eye contact with Brooke, who knew a bit more about the situation than she wanted to get into with the group. The truth was, she hadn't invited Cole. She was still making a half-hearted attempt to keep things casual between them. Plus, she wanted to see how hanging out with Braden went – just as friends – before she went and mixed things up further.

Without warning, half the lights in the bowling alley went dark as Dexys Midnight Runners' *"Come On Eileen"* began blasting through the speakers.

"Have you been to a previous Rockin' Bowl?" Brooke shouted over the music.

Loren shook her head. "I have not."

"Whose idea was this outing anyway?" Hannah asked.

Brooke tapped her finger against her temple in pretend contemplation. "Let's see, a slightly square social event, throwback music, and people *bowling*… yeah, that would definitely make this my boyfriend's doing."

"Where is your boyfriend anyway??" Loren asked.

~

"Jesus," Hank said. "These are steep."

After finishing their shift at the radio station, he and Jason had slipped out the back and cut behind the library toward The Avenue. Though hidden from view, the sound of The Falls rumbled in the air as the two of them neared the President's Mansion. Mist billowed around them, swirling and freezing over everything it touched, including the deteriorating concrete staircase that plunged four stories to the street below.

"They're old school," Jason said as he grabbed ahold of the railing and started down the steps. "But they'll save us at least ten minutes."

Hank had serious misgivings. The blowback from the falls had glazed the stairs with a dangerous layer of ice. It was difficult to see what awaited them in the poor light. "You've gone this way before?"

"Tons of times," Jason reassured him. "Usually in warmer weather… but just hold on tight."

They worked their way down the shadowy steps, ice crunching under their feet as they got closer to street level.

"Is Braden coming, tonight?" Jason asked when they reached the shallow landing halfway down.

"He said he'd be there."

"How are things between him and Loren?"

"You mean now that she's seeing that guy from the bookstore? I think he's trying not to dwell on it. Personally, I don't get it. I thought for sure the two of them would end up together."

"Same here," Jason replied.

"Do you know if Loren is bringing what's his name tonight?" Hank asked.

"I have no idea."

"I thought you were the mastermind of this operation," Hank said.

"Me? I'm just trying to get everyone to hang out again. It sucks to have everything screwed up now."

"Yeah. I guess this kind of stuff is bound to happen though."

"I suppose you're right," Jason said as they reached the bottom of the stairs. "I just liked our little group of friends the way it was. I'd hate to see it fall apart if one of us disappeared."

"I'll tell you one thing," Hank mused as he looked up at the staircase from street level. "I'm glad that's over with. Let's *never* go this way again."

They crossed the street and headed north past Brick's and the bookstore. They were passing DiBellas when Braden came hustling out the front door.

"Hey guys, I was just on my way to meet you," Braden exclaimed as he polished off the last bites of his sandwich.

"You know, they do have food there," Jason said.

"Yeah, I know, I'm just a little wary of bowling alley food."

"I've been wary of this whole event from the get go," Hank interjected.

"Are you hating on *Rockin' Bowl?*" Jason asked incredulously.

"Not hating," Braden said. "Just… on guard."

"It's gonna be great, trust me. I've been going to these since I was a kid."

"That's what scares us," Hank teased.

~

Hannah stood at the end of the ball return, drying her hands under the vent by the roundabout. Until then, Braden had never even known what that blast of air was for.

"Nice ball," Hannah called over to him as he selected a glittery, pink bowling ball from the courtesy rack.

"What's wrong with it?" Braden asked defensively.

"Not a thing," she replied as she stepped up to her lane and slipped into game mode.

Braden was beginning to wonder if Hank's girlfriend was some sort of under-the-radar, 10-pin assassin.

Her first throw confirmed his suspicions.

Hannah released her ball with a flourish, watching calmly as it arced across her lane, caught traction less than ten feet from the end, and hooked gracefully towards the center, hitting the pins like a guided missile.

"Strike!" she shouted as she dropped to one knee and kissed her fist.

"At least you're not one to gloat," Braden noted as he stepped forward to take his turn.

His own throw went wrong from the get-go, landing with a *thunk* before it bounced into the gutter and rolled languidly to the end.

"It's pretty the way the glitter catches the light as it rolls down the channel," Hannah said.

"Channel?"

"She's talking about the gutter," Hank replied. "My girlfriend is a bowling hustler."

"Wait, what?" Brooke asked as she stepped up to take her turn.

They were playing boys against girls.

"I may have bowled a little more than I let on," Hannah admitted.

"But what about all that stuff about the shoe spray?"

"Oh, that's *still* disgusting!"

"So, my teammate is a plant!" Brooke exclaimed. "You hear that, Loren?"

"Best news I've heard all week," Loren called from the bench. She looked up at Braden as he stepped down from the deck and walked over to the seats. "Hey stranger."

"How's it going?" Braden replied.

"Not bad. Sorry about your gutter ball," Loren said.

"Thanks. I'll get over it."

"I haven't seen you at the store in a while."

"Yeah, Mary Ellen must be doing something different with the schedule."

The truth was, he'd been requesting hours he knew Loren wouldn't be working.

"How is your quarter going?" she asked.

"Oh, you know, nothing notable, which is probably a good thing." Braden watched Brooke throw a gutter ball that was nearly as sloppy as his own. "It's good to see Brooke is playing on my level at least."

"Good try, babe," Jason said, clapping his hands encouragingly as Brooke walked back and sat down beside him.

"In my defense, there aren't a lot of bowling alleys in the city," she said.

Jason nodded in Braden and Loren's direction. "It looks like they're talking at least," he whispered.

"That's the best we can hope for, right?" Brooke whispered back.

"Well, not the *best*, but it's a start."

"Braden, can we talk?" Loren asked once they'd each had another turn.

"Sure. What about?"

"I… have a feeling you know what's going on with me and-"

"We don't need to talk about that-"

"I can't help but feel I owe you an explanation."

"You really don't," Braden said, perhaps a bit too sharply. "If you're not interested, you're not interested, right?"

Loren looked him in the eyes. "The truth is, I really don't know how to explain things with Cole, except to say he's not the guy you think he is. If you ever got to know him-"

"Why in the world would I *ever* want to do that?" Braden blurted out.

Loren took a deep breath, fighting back a flare of temper. "Fair enough."

A chill blew through the conversation as they sat in silence, watching their teammates play.

The game continued for a while longer, but thanks to Hannah's outsized skill, the girls pulled ahead quickly and easily, ultimately winning by a landslide.

"Anybody want to get a drink?" Hank asked as they were taking off their shoes at the end of the night.

"I just want to get out of here," Loren muttered as she got to her feet and turned to go.

10.

As HE HAD SO many times before, Braden sought refuge in books. When he wasn't working at the store, he haunted the library, tackling his coursework late into the night. Afterwards, he would take out his notebooks and chip away at his new project.

Slipping into a world of his own creation kept him from thinking about Loren, and wondering what she was doing. And who she was doing it with. Tucked away in Ashton Study Hall, in the wood-paneled niche farthest from the windows, Braden lost himself in his writing. Some nights, the words came easy, as if he was copying them down direct from his subconscious. Other times, like tonight, he struggled to maintain his focus as he felt his thoughts beginning to drift.

Braden leaned back in his chair, his fingers laced behind his head as he stared up at the ceiling, rocking the chair forward and back until he nearly lost his balance. In trying to recover, his chair slammed forward, and his outstretched foot struck the wall beneath the desk with a hollow *thunk*.

The odd sound caught Braden's attention.

He slid his chair back and ducked under the desk, crawling forward on his hands and knees to study the intricate paneling that covered the lower wall. His fingers worked their way along the trim, feeling the wooden edges, until he found the detail he was looking for.

***

Loren lay in bed, studying the morning light on the low, angled ceiling in Cole's studio apartment. Steam from his shower was filtering in from the open bathroom door. The apartment was tucked into the attic of an old house on Greenwood, just one block from The Ave. It was small, but cozy. Something about the ceiling and the dormer windows reminded her of the kids' bedroom at the start of *Peter Pan*, which was fitting, as Cole seemed to be eddying somewhere between youth and manhood himself.

Loren climbed out of bed, pulling one of Cole's shirts from the floor and slipping it on as she walked into the kitchen. She poured a cup of coffee and reached into the refrigerator for the milk, noticing – not for the first time – just how packed the shelves and vegetable crisper were with wine and beer pilfered from author events at the store. Loren poured milk into her coffee and flipped through the pile of comic books scattered across the counter.

There was something free spirited about Cole, but ever so slightly… stunted. He *acted* as if he was a graduate student, and he still took the occasional class on campus, but as far as Loren could figure, he'd never actually completed a degree. She wondered if his parents had somehow psyched him out at some point.

But what did that matter either way? The important thing was that she liked him. It felt good to act upon her desires for a change.

***

It was a surprisingly quiet night at the bookstore. Braden sat at the front counter rereading two poems for Sarah Gridley's poetry class. The first made him think of Loren. The second, Elizabeth Bishop's *The Art of Losing*, made him think of Pops and Jeremy. He closed the poetry book and looked up. Heavy flakes were tumbling past the front window. He glanced at the clock. 8:50. He'd be closing up in ten minutes. His stomach was growling. He planned to stop at Brick's for a late dinner after work.

An orchestral version of Gershwin's *He Loves and She Loves* drifted from the speakers overhead. Braden walked over to one of the display tables and started flipping through a book. The front bell jingled, and he looked up to see someone in a large ski cap slip into the alcove by the bestsellers. Braden strolled to the front to check on the new arrival.

"Can I help you with anything?" He asked as he rounded the corner, but stopped short when he recognized the customer. "Oh, hey. How are you?"

"Hi, Braden," Kate Murphy said with a wide smile. "I was wondering if I'd run into you."

Though he'd spotted her on campus a few times this quarter, Braden hadn't seen Kate in the store, or exchanged a word with her since that night in the fall when he was working with Jan.

"Were you looking for something?" he asked.

Kate shook her head. "Just browsing. Are you open until ten?"

Braden shook his head, "Nine, but take as long as you want."

"That's like, five minutes from now though."

"It takes a little while to close up the registers and shut everything down. If you find something you like, I can ring it out a little late."

"Thanks. I'll be quick, I promise."

Kate flashed that smile again and turned back to the books. Braden felt his face flush.

"Take your time," he said as he started back toward the register. "It's been a quiet night. We could use the sales."

"Thanks, Braden."

Kate arrived at the register a few minutes later.

"How are your classes going?" Braden asked as he rang up her books.

"They're OK. I'm missing Price's class though."

"I know what you mean," Braden said as he slipped her purchases into a bag and slid it across the counter. "Thanks for coming in. It was good to see you."

"It was good to see you, too," Kate replied. She held his gaze. "I wish I'd stopped in earlier. I'd love to talk to you more."

"Have you eaten yet?" Braden asked, even before he knew what he was saying. "I'm going up to Brick's after closing if you want to join me."

"You *eat* there?"

Braden laughed. "I do. My friends and I are sort of regulars."

"What's it like?"

"Surprisingly good."

"Do you get that plate thing people are always talking about?"

"The Brick Plate? Not always, but I *was* actually thinking of getting it tonight. You should have one with me. You've gotta try it at least once, right?"

~

"Do you know what you'd like?" Betty asked as she set their drinks on the table.

Kate set down her menu. "As long as I'm here, I suppose I might as well go for the full experience."

Braden held up two fingers. "Two Brick Plates, please."

"What are the bathrooms like here?" Kate asked after Betty left.

Braden smiled. "You wouldn't believe how often girls ask that question when they eat here."

"Oh yeah? You come here with a lot of girls, do you?"

"Not a lot, just three, and they're just friends."

The unspoken suggestion in Kate's joke seemed to be that this was a date. As the night progressed Braden found himself hoping that it was.

Kate was different than Loren. A little louder, clearly more impulsive. She was briefly hesitant when the plates arrived, but she quickly dove in and claimed to enjoy it, even though she left half of the food untouched.

Braden on the other hand cleaned his plate.

"I guess you were hungry," she observed.

"*Starved.* But even if I wasn't, you sort of *have* to eat the whole plate."

"You do?" Kate asked as she glanced over her shoulder.

"Well no, not literally. I just mean if you're going to get into the spirit of the place you might as well give it a go. To be honest, I wouldn't really recommended eating an entire plate if you have any sort of plans for the rest of the night."

"*OK.*" Kate said. "I'm glad we did this, but now I'm a little nervous about the after effects."

When Betty came by with the check, Braden set enough cash on the table to cover both their meals. "Is it OK if I get this?" he asked.

"Sure, but only if you promise we'll do it again."

* * *

Snow was blowing in their faces as they walked past The Little Theater and took a left at 78th. Loren clutched the warm bag from Bomber's Burritos against her chest. She was starved. It had been a long night at the store.

Event nights were always extra work. Setting out the chairs upstairs. Hauling up the books. Extra crowds. Extra everything. It was nice when the author was someone interesting. Then it at least felt like she was learning something. But lately there were a lot of events with the kind of one and done authors that dominated the New York Times bestseller list for a week or two, then passed the baton to the next writer with a trendy premise and an overheated PR machine behind them. Tonight's event was for a book about a widower who begrudgingly takes a trip to Italy, where he finds new love at a cooking class for American seniors. The author had read a long, painfully-detailed passage from a seduction scene involving the crushing of stewed tomatoes in age-spot-riddled, arthritic hands. It was enough to put Loren off pasta sauce.

"What did you think of that book tonight?" she asked Cole.

He grunted. "I never pay attention to the Polaroid transfers."

"The what?"

"You ever take an art class where you take one of those old Polaroids, pull it apart, and press one side down on watercolor paper so it prints like a painting?"

"Yeah, I'd forgotten all about that."

"You notice the cover tonight? Anytime the customers come in murmuring about some 'fabulous,' overhyped book with that kind of cover art, I just ignore it."

"That's a pretty good rule of thumb, actually."

Polaroid transfers. She wished she could tell Braden that one.

They were half frozen by the time they got to his apartment.

"Do you have anything to drink?" Loren asked as she kicked off her shoes and headed for the kitchen.

"Indeed I do." Cole removed two barely touched bottles of red wine from his backpack. "The good thing about Polaroid transfer events? My mother always shells out for good wine."

"I'm surprised there was that much left over."

Cole smiled. "It's the ideal demographic crossover. The old and the trendy like good wine, but they're all on diets, so they barely touch it." He poured them each a glass as Loren plated their food.

She took a sip and nodded. She had misgivings about the amount of alcohol Cole pilfered from the store, but this was delicious.

"Tasty, right?"

Loren took a bite of burrito, her eyes rolling back in her head. "That's good."

"Wanna watch a movie?" Cole asked as he headed for the futon and flipped on the TV.

Loren took another bite of burrito, picked up her wine, and carried their plates across the room. "I don't care what we do, just as long as I never have to stop eating this burrito."

She plunked herself down on the futon and leaned her head against Cole's shoulder as he flipped through the channels. Loren studied him from the corner of her eye.

"What?" he asked when he felt her eyes on him.

"I'm just watching you." She took another sip of wine and sighed. "I feel like I should be reading a book or something."

"*Why?*"

"I don't know, this just seems so... indulgent."

"Indulge!" Cole leaned over and kissed her on the forehead. "You spend half your week reading and writing and going to school. And you spend the other half working at a bookstore. Trust me, despite what my mother would have you believe, vegging out in front of the TV now and then is just as important as reading a book."

"Oh really?"

"Yes. *Really.* I've done the research."

"What kind of research?"

He raised the remote in his hand. "You're looking at it. It's grueling work, but someone has to do it."

Loren laughed inwardly and decided to go with it.

Snow continued to fall outside as the food and wine warmed their stomachs. And for the moment, Loren couldn't think of any place she would rather be.

11.

"What do you *do* there until all hours?" Kate asked.

"At the library?" Braden sighed into the pillow and rolled onto his side. "I work on schoolwork, and if I have time, I work on my own stuff."

"Writing?"

"Yeah."

"What kind of writing?"

"…A novel. Does that sound pretentious?"

"It's not pretentious if you're actually *doing* it." Kate lay on her back, the sheets pulled up to her chin. "So you're pretty serious about the whole writing thing?"

"Yeah. Aren't you?"

"I'm not so sure anymore. I always liked writing stories in high school, but to be honest, now that I'm here, I'm starting to lean toward something more on the publishing side. Maybe marketing."

"Really?" Braden asked. "Does The Writing Center have an emphasis for that?"

"I guess I should find out."

Kate's room was gray with morning light. Braden's eyes wandered, following the outline of his girlfriend's body beneath the sheer fabric sheets.

"It's cold in here," he murmured absentmindedly.

Kate's eyes darted down to her chest, then up to Braden as she hit him on the shoulder. "Yeah, I bet you hate it."

"What?" he said – caught. "I was looking at the goosebumps. On your shoulders."

She slipped out of bed, wrapping the blanket around her body. "If my room is so cold, maybe we should stay at *your* place sometime. I'd like to meet this roommate of yours, and some of the friends you're always talking about."

"Well, the wait is almost over, you'll get your wish tonight."

Kate opened her dresser and began rummaging through her clothes. "I can't wait. This has been a long week."

"It's had some good points though, right?"

"Yes, it has." She leaned down to kiss him, then stood and looked around. "Where's that colossal backpack of yours?"

"Oh, I must have left it at my dorm when I stopped there last night."

"You said you came right here."

"I was just freshening up for you. You don't want to hear about *everything* I do, do you?"

"Probably not," Kate said as she started toward the bathroom. "I'm just going to rinse off. Will you be here when I get out?"

Braden looked at the clock. "I'd probably better get going."

"Then I'll see you tonight."

"I'll pick you up at seven."

~

"Any idea what Jason has planned for us?" Braden asked as he was getting ready to go out.

"How do you know *I'm* not the mastermind behind the evening's events?" Hank asked defensively.

He and Hannah were stretched out on his bed, facing in opposite directions as they worked on their assignments. They'd been spending more time there now that Braden was at Kate's place so often.

Hannah lifted her head at her boyfriend's question. "He knows because you never plan *anything* ahead of time."

Hank gave Braden a look. "She's on me about Valentine's Day. I told her I still have a week to plan something."

"Don't look at *me* man," Braden exclaimed as he pulled on his coat. "I've got my plans made."

Hank scowled.

"Don't give him that look, Hank!" Hannah turned to Braden, "He knows I'm right."

"*Anyway,*" Hank interjected. "Jason didn't say what was happening, but he wants us all at The Shack by 8 o'clock at the latest. Must be a show. Hopefully someone good."

"So, Braden, do we finally get to meet this girl tonight?" Hannah asked.

"That's the plan," Braden said as he headed for the door. "We'll see you guys there in about an hour."

~

The eight ball and the cue ball flew into the corner pocket one after the other in rapid succession. It happened so quickly that it took Hank a moment to realize what he'd done.

Hannah raised her hand. "Can I swap teammates?"

"Shit," Hank sighed as he lowered his stick. "I *knew* that shot felt too easy."

"It's OK, baby," Hannah said. "It's not like I *enjoy* winning or anything."

Brooke leaned against the back wall, nursing a root beer and suppressing a smile. "Hannah, you wanna switch it up, play us against the boys?"

"What if Hank and I just go ahead and sit this one out?" Jason asked.

"Fine, if that's the way you wanna be." Hannah watched the guys take a seat nearby, then she turned to Brooke, arching one eyebrow as she set up the table, "How about you and *I* play a game?"

Brooke rubbed chalk on the tip of her cue. "Mind if I break?"

"Hit me with your best shot," Hannah replied as she slipped the rack under the table.

No sooner did the words escape her lips, then Brooke fired off a shot that sent the balls rocketing around the table, sinking a handful in the process.

"Nice!" Hannah exclaimed.

"Thanks. I dated a guy in high school who thought he was Eddie Felson. He had the whole Paul Newman thing down *cold*, except for the pool game ironically."

Jason looked over. "What does *that* mean?"

Hannah patted him on the shoulder. "You don't want to know."

Brooke gave Jason a reassuring kiss as she rounded the table. "Trust me, you have nothing to worry about. He didn't have a brain in his head."

"Not that that mattered, I'm sure." Hannah noted.

Jason didn't look any more relieved, but redirected his attention to The Shack's main room. The atmosphere was completely different than the last time he and Brooke had been there; the night of the infamous overdose. Rather than thrashing music and an exuberant crowd, tonight the place was mellow, with half the audience members gathered in booths along the edges of the bar, and the other half standing around pool tables, sinking shots and talking quietly, very much in keeping with the vibe coming from the group onstage.

"Are *they* the reason we're here?" Hank asked, nodding toward the band.

"The dude in front is," Jason explained, indicating the lead singer, a tall guy in his 30s with long, curly, blond hair, and a smattering of tattoos up and down his arms. His stage presence was a little stiff, but when he strummed his guitar and opened his mouth to sing, the sounds that came out were jaw-dropping.

"Who is he?"

"His name is Asa Flynn. I saw him performing with a band two years ago called The Dingleberries." Jason raised his hand and pointed his thumb down. "Then he was with a group called The Sugardaddies. There was one other lineup after that. The bands have all been terrible, different styles, different members, all bad, but the one constant has always been him."

"What do you think of the guys he's playing with tonight?"

"The Alley Cats? About what I thought of The Dingleberries…"

The room grew quiet as Asa launched into his next song. His voice was deep and rumbly like a seventies crooner, but his lyrics had a distinct Eddie Vedder quality to them: You couldn't tell what the heck he was saying, but it was impossible to resist that deep, honeyed growl.

"He's like a grunge Neil Diamond, isn't he?" Jason whispered. "I've got this fantasy,"

"About Neil Diamond? I've got that too."

"No, about making a record with this guy."

"Does he ever do stuff on his own?" Hank asked.

"I have no idea. I've always thought he could do an awesome solo album if he found the right session players. But I'm really hoping he'll eventually settle on the right band."

"Do you have any guys in mind?"

"Funny you should ask," Jason replied. "I know this great rockabilly band. If they ever switch up their lead singer, this guy could completely transform their sound. I'll have to take you to their next show…" Jason grew quiet as Asa really started to let it rip. "Can you *imagine* what this guy could do if he relaxed a little and hooked up with the right bunch of musicians?"

"We should put him in our talent rolodex."

"We should also get a rolodex," Jason noted as he looked toward the main entrance and saw Braden and Kate walking in. "Hey, they made it."

Hannah and Brooke looked up as well, watching the newcomers as they crossed the dance floor.

"You must be Kate," Hank said as Braden and his new girlfriend approached the table.

"And you must be… Hank," Kate guessed.

"How do you know that?" Hank asked suspiciously.

"I've heard a lot about you."

"All good I hope."

"All… interesting," Kate said with a teasing smile before Braden introduced her to the rest of the group.

"How long have you guys been here?" Braden asked once all of the introductions had been made.

"Long enough for the game to get ugly," Hank replied.

"He's just sore because I kicked him off my team," Hannah said from the pool table. She lined up her shot and sent another ball zipping into the pocket.

"You're good!" Kate exclaimed.

Hannah pointed at Brooke. "She's even better."

"If you're hustling pool, you apparently want my girlfriend on your team," Jason said.

"Yeah," Braden said. "But if you're working the bowling alley, you want Hannah on your side."

"I don't know if I like the implications of 'working the bowling alley,'" Hannah joked.

"Do you play?" Brooke asked Kate.

"I do, but not as well as you two."

"What do you say we play a little two on two when Loren gets here," Brooke suggested.

"Do you know our friend Loren?" Hannah asked. "She's studying in The Writing Center too."

"Loren?" Kate seemed uncertain. "I'm not sure I do-"

Hank gave Braden a curious look.

"I'm sure you guys have met," Braden mumbled uncomfortably.

"What does she look like?"

"That's her," Hannah said, pointing to Loren, who was headed across the room toward them.

"Oh yeah, I know *her*," Kate said as she turned to Braden. "She was in one of our classes last quarter."

"Sorry I'm late," Loren said as she reached the group.

"No Cole?" Brooke asked.

"Not tonight," Loren said as her eyes darted around the group. "I wasn't sure what our plans were, and he's working an author event 'til closing."

"Maybe next time," Hannah said.

"Yeah… next time." Loren looked uncertainly at Braden and Kate. "Hey Kate – Braden."

"How's it going, Loren?" Braden answered quietly.

"Oh, you know how it is. Just… getting through the week…"

Loren's voice tapered off when she realized Braden wasn't really paying attention. Unsure how to respond, she turned instead to the game at hand.

"What are you playing?"

"Eight ball," Hannah said. "But as we were just discussing, it turns out your roommate is some type of hustler."

"Like you at bowling?" Loren asked.

Hannah just smiled.

"You know, if you want to play teams, I'm not too bad myself," Loren said. "My dad's brewery has a bunch of tables, so I've shot a lot of pool."

Hannah's mood brightened. "You wanna play you and me against Brooke and Kate?"

"Do you want to play?" Loren asked Kate.

"Sure," Kate replied. "But what about the boys?"

"There's another table," Hannah noted. "The boys can play their own game."

~

If Brooke's first break caught Hannah off guard, Loren's opening shot was just as surprising. Only this time, Hannah was pleased to realize the secret weapon was on *her* side.

The balance shifted yet again when Kate stepped up for her turn, powering through a run that quickly cleared half the table. "I used to date a guy who loved *The Color of Money*," she explained.

"Didn't we all," Brooke sighed knowingly.

Braden stood off to the side, observing both tables as he waited to play the winner of Hank and Jason's game. His stomach was in a knot, but so far it seemed everyone was getting along just fine. The only person who *couldn't* seem to relax was him. Though he was trying his best to go with the flow – smiling inwardly as he watched Kate sweep the table – again and again, Braden felt his gaze drifting to Loren. Yet, whenever she turned his way, smiling casually to break the tension, he would quickly look away like some shy high school kid who was afraid to make eye contact with his crush. He was getting frustrated with himself.

~

Eventually, as the music got louder, they gave up their pool tables and found a booth in a far corner, where they could pick over plates of nachos and listen to the band as they talked.

Loren stuck around, but she spent most of the evening either making small talk with Brooke and Hannah or looking down into her glass.

It felt like Braden was making a point of ignoring her.

"So, I'm picking up tickets for the Will Baker Band concert in a couple of weeks," Jason announced. "If anyone is interested in going, just let me know so I get enough tickets."

Hank and Hannah were interested. As were Braden and Kate.

"Can I check with Cole first?" Loren asked as she watched Kate lean her head against Braden's shoulder.

"Absolutely," Jason said. "I just need a total by Tuesday morning."

Loren's eyes narrowed. "I'll get back to you the moment I know what's going on."

***

Lightning pulsed through the churning, black clouds as Loren climbed the steps to Grimwood Library.

The air inside smelled of wood polish and yellowing paper. Students were scattered across the vast expanse of the main floor, turning brittle pages and jotting notes down on fresh paper. Aside from the occasional flash of light through the narrow, leaded windows, the thick stone walls blocked out any signs of the impending storm.

Loren headed for the back stairs, one hand gripping the strap of her leather satchel, inside of which was tucked a bundle of notebooks and papers secured in a drawstring fabric bag: Everything she and Braden had prepared for *Dead Men Don't*.

They hadn't discussed their neglected project since before Christmas, but now that they were both in relationships, Loren was hoping the spark of their creative collaboration might lead them back to their friendship. She missed their conversations – talk of books, and people, and inside jokes – but most importantly, she missed *Braden*. The fallout between them had left her feeling off-balance.

Loren made her way up the winding steps. Now and then, bursts of lightning bloomed in the stairwell, slowly fading into the corners as she made her way to the library's top floor. She stepped into Ashton Study Hall and walked down the creaking wood aisle until she stopped at Braden's workspace.

He looked up from his reading. "Hey."

"Hi, Braden. You're here late."

"I'm *always* here late," he said.

"I thought there was a chance you might be at Kate's."

Braden paused before answering. "I'll probably head over there later. What brings you here?"

Loren took a wary breath.

How to launch into it?

"Braden, can we be friends?"

"How do you mean?"

"You and me, can we be friends again?"

"We are friends."

"Technically, yeah. But not the way we used to be. I think you're mad at me. Or hurt. And I suppose I can understand why. But I'm not happy about it. I know how you feel. Or how you felt-" She stopped and Braden lowered his head. "But look, I'm with Cole now. And you're with Kate. So whatever was or wasn't happening between us, we need to put that aside. We were close, and I miss that. I miss talking and working on our book together. Can we just *forget* about any other feelings we might have had, just sweep them off the table, and focus on what works for us *now*?"

Braden looked up at her again as he braced his palms against the arms of his chair. "Umm… no. I don't think we can."

Loren exhaled. *"Why?"*

"I mean, we can *try*. But I can't say I don't have those feelings for you anymore, because I still do. And sooner or later that's bound to complicate things."

"But you're with Kate now." The words came out like a plea. "Why does anything else matter?"

"Because I wouldn't *be* with Kate if things were different between *us*."

"But, that's not where we are. I'm sorry-"

"I'm sorry too. But I can't just compartmentalize how I feel so I can work on a project with you, and hang out with you when you want company, then have to-"

"Have to what?"

"Have to push my feelings down so *you* can have things both ways. I mean, *why?* Why is it that you'd rather be with some *asshole* like *Cole Phillips?*"

His words hit her like a sucker punch.

"Forget it, Braden." She pulled out the cloth bag with the notebooks, and slung the satchel back over her shoulder. "I know it's not easy for you, but that can't be the reason I don't do something. From now on, if there's a group event that *I* want to go to, I'm bringing Cole. We're together, and we're going to do things *together.* I don't care if you don't talk to me. Or if you give me the cold shoulder like you did last weekend. I don't give a shit anymore. The hell with it." She raised the bundle in her hands. "And the hell with our book too."

"Loren…"

Braden got to his feet, watching her as she turned and marched back the way she'd come. She stopped at the exit, raised her arm, and threw everything they'd prepared for *Dead Men Don't* into a trash bin to the side of the door. Then she stormed off down the corridor.

* * *

"Look, if it works out, I can try to keep your schedules separated, but I'm not making any guarantees."

"Thanks, Mary Ellen," Loren said.

"Whatever is going on with you and Braden, don't bring it into work. If you two can't get along on your own time, that's your business, but don't make it mine. I don't have the patience. If I had to start changing the work calendar every time Cole screwed over one of the girls working here, well… let's just say I'd be even grumpier than I am now."

"Understood," Loren said as she headed out the door.

Jan, who had clearly overheard the entire conversation, gave Loren an understanding smile as she emerged from the back office and hurried downstairs.

Loren was relieved Cole wasn't working at the store tonight either. She needed some time by herself. If luck was on her side, it would be a quiet night.

"Don't hate me," Dan said as he rolled a load of hardbacks out from the receiving room and started transferring them to the shelving cart.

"Don't worry. I like to see what's coming in."

"You and me both, but believe me, when you unpack *every* book that comes into the store, it's hard to keep a handle on your spending. My fiancé is ready to kill me."

"I can see how that could be expensive."

"I'm supposed to be saving for the wedding, but I keep coming home at night with coffee table books stuffed in the back of my sweater. I look suspicious as hell."

Loren laughed. "If that's all she has to worry about, she's lucky."

'That's what I keep saying!" Dan said as he turned to leave. "I've gotta sort some more shipments in the morning, but that's it for now."

Loren scanned the titles on the cart. "This should be more than enough to keep me busy. Have a good night, Dan."

She was still looking through the cart when she heard the front bell jingle, and looked up to see Jason Paper approaching the front counter.

"Jason."

"Hey, Loren," he said. "I'm sorry to bother you here, but Brooke said you were working tonight."

Loren couldn't recall ever having seen him in the store before.

"Is everything ok?" she asked.

"Oh yeah, totally. I'm just getting the Will Baker tickets in the morning, and I wanted to see how many you needed, assuming you're going that is."

That had been a whole issue the night before. Apparently the Will Baker Band was one of the *many* things Cole felt were too mainstream to be appreciated. Loren on the other hand liked their music and wanted to go.

"Oh definitely. I need two."

"For you and Cole?" Jason confirmed.

"Yes. Is Braden…?"

"Bringing Kate?" Jason finished. "Yeah, he is."

"OK."

"Do you still want those tickets?"

"Yeah, or course. Thank you for organizing everything as usual."

"Not a problem," Jason said. "I just like to get everyone together."

"You're like the hub of the group."

"Well, I don't know about that," Jason said as he pulled out a piece of paper and added two slashes to the total. "OK, that's everyone. I'm actually headed back to your place now. Will we see later?"

"Probably not," Loren said. "No need to put the sock on the door."

Jason's face flushed, but he couldn't help smile. "I'll talk to you tomorrow, Loren."

"Have a good night," Loren said as Jason slipped out the front door.

The bell chimed softly in the empty store as Loren walked back to the shelving cart, lost in her thoughts.

Something on the bottom shelf caught her eye. It was a new title. A biography with a familiar profile stretched across its cover. She snatched the title up in her hands: *Alan Grimwood: A Biography*.

* * *

Considering the number of books that arrived each week, the bookstore's receiving room was far too small to maintain any sense of order. Anytime Braden ducked in back, he marveled at Dan's ability to find *anything* in the chaos.

"Dan?" he called over a teetering skyline of stacked paperbacks. "You in here?"

Dan leaned into view. "What do you need?"

"Mary Ellen is wondering if any more Jean-Claude Renoir cookbooks have come."

Dan patted a pile of boxes just behind his chair. "Tell her they're the next thing on my list."

"Will do." Braden started for the door.

"Braden, I have something I think you might be interested in."

"What's that?"

Dan handed him a black, hardbound book. Even before he saw the title, Braden could tell from the design that it was an Alan Grimwood title. He turned it over in his hands. A new special anniversary edition of *Revenant*. An embossed seal on the front promised newly discovered author introductions and a previously unpublished alternate ending.

"Holy shit," Braden exclaimed.

"You like it?"

"Heck yeah. This is as good as sold!" He flipped through the pages and looked up. "Hey, do you happen to have another one of these?"

"I had a hunch you'd ask that." Dan pulled another copy from behind the stacks. "Tell Loren I hope she likes it."

Before they closed the registers that night, Braden asked Virginia to ring him out for the two copies of the Grimwood book.

"Guess you're a fan," Virginia observed as she slid the books back to him.

Braden slipped one of the copies into a paper bag and jotted a note on the outside before he ducked into the break room and slipped it into Loren's staff mailbox.

***

Brooke hung up the phone and brought her hand up to her forehead.

"Long call?" Jason asked, though he already knew the answer.

She'd been on the phone with her mother when he arrived an hour beforehand.

"Long doesn't begin to describe it."

"Don't worry, once they go on vacation again, she'll have other things to keep her busy. Right now you're like her… sudoku."

"Annnd, thank you for *that*." Brooke deadpanned.

"In all fairness, it can't be easy to find the right balance of worry and distance as a parent."

"Probably not," Brooke admitted as she played with a curl of hair behind Jason's ear. "But to be fair, *your* mother worries. My mother judges."

Jason yawned and looked at his watch.

"Oh, excuse me," Brooke said. "Am I keeping you up?"

"Sorry. I was just remembering I need to get those tickets in the morning."

"Who's going?"

"Everyone I think."

"*Everyone* everyone? Loren and Cole *and* Braden and Kate?"

"That's the plan."

"Well *that* should be interesting."

***

"My father keeps alluding to the fact that every time he calls, all I seem to be doing is hanging out with Hank."

"You get that too?" Brooke asked as she and Hannah settled into the gang's usual table at Brownie's. "My mother was just on me about the same thing the other night."

They turned to watch Hank and Jason talking animatedly with someone from their production and engineering class.

"I think I hate my major," Hannah said out of the blue.

"Architecture? Haven't you wanted to do that since you were a kid?"

"Yep. But for some reason I just can't keep my mind on it now. And the funny thing is, I don't even care."

"Maybe you're just caught up in all the first year experiences and figuring out what you really want to do with your life. I doubt you're the first person to get to college and realize it isn't everything you'd imagined."

"How are *you* doing?" Hannah asked.

"Me?"

"What's your major again?"

"Graphic design. And if you want to know the truth, my grades are nothing to write home about either. Only I was never much of a student to begin with."

"So, how did you pick graphic design?"

Brooke pulled a notebook from her backpack and randomly flipped it open to one of the countless pages she'd covered with elaborate drawings.

"I've just always liked art. Even at my most dysfunctional, I was always sketching. I took every class my high school's art department offered. Senior year, when I realized I still needed a couple credits to graduate, one of my teachers spitballed a graphic design class for the balance, and helped me get a portfolio together for college applications."

"So your teacher pointed you to your major?"

"Yeah, but it seemed right to me. I mean, I'm enjoying it. The classes are interesting. I'm still doing art, but my priorities have shifted for the time being."

"Do you have any idea why?"

"I *know* why," Brooke said as her eyes went to Jason across the room. "I'm in love."

"Holy shit…" Hannah murmured. "Do you think that's what's wrong with me?"

Brooke laughed. *"Probably."*

"How did I let this happen?"

"You don't have any control over it." Brooke watched as an athletic looking girl with short brown hair passed their table. Her eyes fell on a small tattoo on the inside of the girl's left wrist. "The right person crosses your path, and you find that missing piece. I would *never* have expected to end up with Jason, but something about him just… clicked with me."

* * *

"Do you hear that?"

"Hear what?" Cole asked, without looking away from his copy of *McSweeney's.*

Loren gazed up at the apartment's low, slanted ceiling as a soft crackling was followed by the sounds of tumbling ice and snow.

"The beams in the roof are creaking from the cold. I love that sound."

"You're not going to love it if the roof caves in." Cole noted.

"Could that *happen?*"

"Probably not, but this building is pretty old."

Loren burrowed under the thick wool blankets on Cole's bed and watched him reading in his old Eames lounger. The chair, like so many of the items in his apartment, was a sign of his parents' background. While she knew Cole's mother was a self-made woman, she didn't know all that much about his father. Judging by Cole's moth-bitten wool blankets and hand-me-down classic furniture, she suspected Mr. Phillips was descended from old money. Half the stuff in Cole's apartment had likely come from his father's New Haven college digs. The furnishings, combined with rigid social standards, and an unspoken sense of financial security betrayed a mindset that can only come with the certainty that an unseen safety net was in place at all times.

Loren returned to her reading, trying to focus on the subject at hand, but her thoughts kept drifting like the snow outside. She had two papers to complete before Monday morning, so *why* had she chosen to spend yet another weekend at her boyfriend's place?

Time passed as she reread the assigned poem, jotting down notes in the margin of her textbook.

"What are you reading?" Cole asked.

Oh, just a poem for Gridley's class."

Cole pivoted in his chair. "What poem?"

"One Art, by Elizabeth Bishop."

"The art of losing isn't hard to master… She won the Pulitzer Prize, didn't she?"

"She did. How did you know that?"

"I'm not an idiot, Loren. I like that poem."

"So do I. She had a difficult life."

"True," Cole said, "But at least she never needed to get a real job."

"That's pretty cynical."

Cole grinned. "You *do* know who you're dating, right?"

"I think you're more of an optimist than you pretend to be. Anyway, I have to write an analysis for Monday, so I really need to buckle down."

"Who is the friend she's speaking to in that poem?" Cole continued. "I know I heard someone give her name once."

"I assumed it was a lover," Loren said.

"Well yeah, friend, lover, that's what I meant." He gave her a funny look. "You might want to read more about Elizabeth Bishop."

"Weren't you an art major?" Loren snapped, suddenly annoyed.

"I dabble," he replied, giving her a bemused look before he returned to his reading.

~

Loren lay awake in bed that night, long after Cole had fallen asleep beside her. The beams were still creaking and popping overhead, even as her legs sweated under the heavy bedcovers.

Finally, unable to quiet her mind, she swung her feet out onto the icy wooden floor, and padded across the studio to the corner where she'd left her book bag. She unzipped the bag's main compartment and withdrew the bundle she'd found in her staff mailbox that morning. The paper bag crinkled as she withdrew the anniversary edition of *Revenant* that Braden had left for her. She studied the new cover in the moonlight, running her fingertips over the embossed surface, then she slipped into the dining nook in the kitchen, flipped on the pendant light above the table, and began reading.

* * *

Jason flipped his laptop open on Hank's desk and powered it up.

"You want one?" Hank asked as he pulled a bottle of Genesee from the fridge.

"Sure, why not?" Jason said. "We're mixing a rock song, we might as well get into the spirit of things."

"I'm sure that's just the type of commitment Professor Demaa is looking for," Hank said, handing Jason his beer and opening another for himself.

Hank stopped midsentence as someone knocked on the door. "Come on in!"

The door opened slowly until Loren peeked her head around the edge. "Hey, guys, I was just wondering if you'd seen Braden tonight."

"Not yet," Hank replied. "But you're welcome to stick around."

"Oh, that's all right. Would you mind if I left something for him?"

"Of course not," Hank replied.

Loren walked over and set a book in the middle of Braden's desk. "Just tell him I found it at the store the other day and thought he would like it."

Hank nodded as Loren started to leave. "Will do."

"Will we see you and Cole tomorrow?" Jason asked.

"We'll be there," Loren said as she stepped out into the hall again. "Have a good night, guys."

"You too, Loren."

Hank shut the door quietly after she left.

"Are she and Braden talking again?" Jason asked.

"Not that I know of, but maybe the ice is cracking."

Jason leaned over to look at the cover of the Grimwood biography Loren had left on Braden's desk.

***

Kate awoke with a start, a little voice whispering in the back of her head as she left Braden sleeping under the blankets and slipped into the bathroom.

She turned on the shower and stepped under the spray of hot water. They were meeting up with Braden's friends after breakfast to head to the Will Baker concert. Hank and Jason would be driving. Although they'd gone on a few fun outings with the group, Kate still wasn't at ease around his circle of friends. She wanted them to like her, but the truth was, she couldn't help but notice a degree of tension, particularly whenever Loren was around.

The steam pulled away suddenly as the bathroom door opened. A moment later, Braden stepped into the shower behind her.

"Why didn't you wake me up?" he asked sleepily.

"Because you looked so cute lying there with your mouth hanging open." She turned to face him as he wrapped his arms around her.

"Are you excited for our little getaway?"

"Yeah," she replied. "It should be fun…"

Braden looked her in the eyes. "But something's on your mind-"

"It's nothing."

"Don't you want to go?"

"I do… it's just-"

"Just what?"

"I don't think your friend Loren likes me."

His arms loosened.

"Sure she does."

"No, Braden. She doesn't. Girls know these things. I just don't know why."

"Kate, you don't need to worry about Loren."

"Why not?"

"Listen to you," he laughed. "Are you dating *me* or are you dating Loren?"

Kate forced a smile.

"You," she replied.

But she was really wondering if she should be asking Braden the same question.

~

"Have you ever been to Rochester?" Loren asked Cole as the car merged onto The Thruway on the way out of Grimwood.

"Once or twice when my folks had business there."

They were riding in the backseat of Cathie Pepper's car, which Jason had borrowed for the weekend. Brooke was in the passenger seat while Jason was seated at the wheel.

"What's it like?" Brooke asked.

"Let me put it this way," Cole said. "If Grimwood is *Die Hard,* then Rochester is *Die Hard 2.*"

Jason rolled his eyes, but kept his focus on the road.

"What does that even mean?" Loren asked before Brooke could do the same.

"Let's just say Rochester is like Grimwood's unbathed, blue collar cousin."

"I know I'm from Manhattan…" Brooke said as she glanced over the seat, "but *snobby* much?"

"*What?* I'm not saying it doesn't have its charms," Cole said, easing back on the disdain, "But it's certainly not some world class city." He turned to Loren, but she seemed to be avoiding his eyes.

"Jason, what's the plan once we get there?" Loren asked in an attempt to change the topic.

"Well, the concert isn't until tomorrow, so tonight is wide open," Jason said. "Dinosaur Bar-B-Que has a sister restaurant down the street from the hotel. I was thinking it might be fun to meet up there after everyone was settled and see if they have a band playing."

Cole turned toward Loren again – clearly less than intrigued by the idea – but she was looking out the window.

"That sounds fun," Loren said as she watched the scenery drift by.

~

"Whose idea was it to go to an out of town concert on a Sunday night?" Hannah asked.

"I'm pretty sure it was *all* of ours," Hank said.

Hannah was seated in the passenger seat of Hank's car, with Braden and Kate squeezed together in the back.

"It's just stressing me out to miss a full day of classes this early in the quarter," Hannah said as she flipped down her sun visor, checking her makeup in the mirror.

"Babe, this is college," Hank reassured her. "You can't be the class valedictorian your *entire* life. There are better ways to pass the time."

"That's good to hear, because at the rate I'm going, I'll be lucky to get a certificate of attendance."

"Actually, I'm pretty certain you won't get that either," Braden chimed in.

"Why is *that?*" Hannah asked.

"You just said it yourself, you're missing a day of classes. That will torpedo your attendance record."

Hannah's glowered at him in the mirror. "Thank you so much for pointing that out to me, Braden."

"It'll be worth it," Hank reassured her as he stepped on the gas. "You just have to *try* to enjoy yourself."

~

They reached the hotel in the late afternoon. Fans in town for the first night of the band's two-night stint were already packing the streets around the river and gathering outside the Blue Cross Arena as Hank followed Jason's car over the bridge and into the parking lot of the riverside Hyatt.

Brooke walked over to Hannah as they filed into the lobby with their luggage. Cole and Loren had walked inside ahead of them, and Loren was now standing at the reception desk, handing the manager her credit card as she and Cole checked in. Hank and Jason, and Loren and Kate were lined up a short ways behind them.

"How was your ride?" Hannah asked.

Brooke shrugged. "It was all right. Cole is a piece of work."

"How so?"

"He's so condescending and dismissive of everything."

"Wow, and *you're* from New York…"

"That's what I said!" Brooke exclaimed.

"I thought his folks were loaded." Hannah said as she watched Loren take her card back and pick up their key. "Is Loren paying for their room?"

"Probably."

"Can she afford it?"

"I have no idea," Brooke whispered. "Just remember, we're here for *her*, so we have to try to be nice to him. I know it's tough, believe me."

"Hey guys," Loren said as she walked over. "We're gonna head upstairs for a bit."

"Will we see you at dinner?" Brooke asked.

"I'm not sure-" Cole began…

…as Loren simultaneously answered, "I'd like to."

"What room are you in?" Hannah asked.

"1116," Loren replied. "What time are you all heading over for dinner?"

Brooke looked at her watch. "Like… seven?"

Hannah touched Loren's arm. "We'll stop by your room before we go."

~

"What do you think of Cole?" Hannah asked Hank from the shower.

He was standing at the bathroom counter, drinking a beer and brushing his hair in the fogging mirror. "He's a putz."

"I know that's the official Braden-support response, but what do you think personally?"

"Personally? I haven't really spent any time around the guy."

The shower stopped, and Hannah pushed the curtain open.

"Neither have I," she said as she wrapped herself in a towel. "Brooke thinks he's obnoxious. I kind of get the same impression, but I think we should talk to him more tonight before we make up our minds."

"Sounds like a plan," Hank said as he stretched out on the bed and turned on the TV.

~

Braden stood at the floor to ceiling window, looking out over the Genesee River. Snowflakes were swirling in the arena lights across the way as concertgoers lined up outside the building to get in. With any luck, the crowd at the restaurant would die down by the time they headed over.

Kate was getting ready in the bathroom. Now and then he would see her reflection in the glass as she stepped out to grab something from her bag.

He couldn't have *hoped* to meet a better girl. And they were having a good time together. But occasionally, Braden could feel something in the back of his mind disengaging. He wasn't sure what it meant. He didn't like it. But he wasn't sure how to stop it either.

~

Braden studied the pin-up art covering the walls of the Rochester branch of Dinosaur Bar-B-Que as Kate spoke with the hostess at the reception stand.

Braden felt a tap on his shoulder and turned around to see Loren standing beside him.

"Hi, Braden."

"Hey," He replied, a little too exuberantly.

"How was the drive up?"

"It was good. Hank played plenty of…interesting music for us." Loren chuckled.

"Where is Cole?"

"He's out front with Hank and Hannah, talking to some guy about his motorcycle."

Braden's eyes narrowed. "I'm… not sure I can picture that exactly."

"I'm not sure I can either," Loren said as she tried to imagine Cole discussing Harleys with the leather-clad bikers in the front lot. "Listen, I wanted to thank you for the book you left for me the other night."

"I wanted to thank you too. I brought the Grimwood biography with me actually. I'm about halfway through. It's good."

He looked over Loren's shoulder as Kate turned and began walking back to where they were standing. "Anything interesting in the new edition?"

"Yeah actually, maybe we can talk about it later. Hey, Kate."

"Loren-" Kate said, sounding unusually muted. "I've got us all down for a table, but it might be a while."

"Maybe we can find a pool table around here," Loren mused with a half-smile.

"Maybe we can skip that this time," Hannah chimed in as she walked in with the rest of the crew close on her heels.

~

"Yeah, he's an asshole." Hannah whispered to Hank.

"I'm inclined to agree," Hank confirmed as he looked to the end of the table, where Cole had been holding court on the inadequacies of the Will Baker Band. "Of course, Braden is giving him a run for his money tonight."

"Yep. And it's not going unnoticed." Hannah nodded toward Loren, who was glaring across the table at Braden.

Kate meanwhile was seated to Braden's right, studying Loren from the corner of her eye as the conversation grew increasingly tense.

"So, what I'm getting is that you look at the band *and* their fans as being totally without merit," Braden challenged.

"Maybe it just comes down to perspective," Cole replied. "I see the majority of their fanbase as meathead frat types, and the guys in the band aren't exactly the greatest minds of our time, either."

"We're still talking about *music* here, right?" Brooke chimed in. "Because 'great minds' suggests this is some sort of life and death issue, like eradicating Polio."

Cole leaned back in his chair. "But *shouldn't* music aim to be on that same level?"

"*As curing Polio?!*" Hannah interjected.

"I mean striving to be *art*, not just background noise for getting laid on a Saturday night."

"Hey, booty music is a valuable commodity!" Hank joked.

"And I happen to *like* their music," Hannah added.

Cole looked from Hank to Hannah with a smirk. "I'm *sure* you do."

Loren brushed her hair behind one ear and cautiously entered the debate. "I just think it's nice to have something you can put on to take your mind off things. When I think of the band, *that's* what I think of, playing their albums while I worked on my homework after a shitty day in high school."

"Maybe it's just comes down to who was popular when you were a kid," Cole said. "For me, I'd much rather rock out to The Cure when I want to change my mood."

"But that's not exactly your generation," Jason observed.

"What do you mean?" Cole asked defensively.

"They must be at least ten years before your time," Jason said. "More even."

"I'm not interested in safe choices, like only listening to the most popular music of '*my generation*,' I'm talking about the quality of the work. You should engage with things that *challenge* you, not just what everyone your age is into."

"It's often harder to *like* something than it is to judge it from afar," Jason observed. "I think it's important to at least be in touch with the culture of your time."

"Negative reactions are a reflection of a lazy mind." Braden added.

"Really?!" Loren said. "Come on, now you guys are being stupid."

"Lazy mind?" Cole asked, a split-second slower on the uptake.

"I think everyone is getting a tad hyperbolic," Loren noted.

"Maybe we should change the subject," Hank said.

"*That* sounds like an excellent idea," Loren agreed.

"What about 'favorite Will Baker song?'" Hank asked with a mischievous grin.

Loren gave him a look.

Cole went silent.

Loren turned to Braden, but it seemed he was avoiding her eyes, which was probably just as well. She was peeved with him at the moment as well.

"Anyone interested in dessert?" Kate asked.

"Absolutely!" Jason he flagged the waitress down for menus. "*Anything* to get off this topic!"

The group grew quiet as they looked over the dessert options.

"I'm having trouble deciding," Braden announced. "Does anyone happen to know which of these desserts is the most popular choice for the members of my generation?"

Kate elbowed him in the side.

"I think I'm done," Loren said as she set her menu down and took out her wallet.

~

Loren and Cole started for the hotel early, leaving the rest of the group behind. Deep bass rumbled across the river from the arena as they walked along the sidewalk toward the Hyatt.

"Sorry if I was pissing you off," Cole said.

"That's OK. Fortunately for you, Braden was being the bigger dick."

"Yeah, why does he seem to have it out for me anyway?"

Loren didn't answer.

They strolled silently for a ways, their breath fogging in the winter air.

Loren stopped and looked at Cole intently. "They're all really good people." Her eyes glistened as she spoke. "I hope you know that about them."

Cole nodded.

"They *are* though. You just need to ease up a little and not be so judgmental about everything."

"I know," Cole replied softly.

Loren stepped forward and gave him a gentle kiss.

"I don't know about you, but I'm ready to get the hell out of this cold."

~

Jason and Brooke met up with Hank and Hannah for breakfast the following morning. The two couples spent the majority of the day exploring the city together. Braden and Kate passed the day by themselves, as did Loren and Cole, not crossing paths with the others until early in the evening when everyone met up in the lobby to head to the arena for the show.

Loren's talk, along with the time they'd spent alone during the day, had improved Cole's mood considerably. By the time they took their seats after the opening act, Cole almost seemed *excited* for Will Baker and his cohorts to take the stage.

Braden on the other hand seemed increasingly ill at ease when he saw how well Loren and Cole were getting along, which was curious, since Kate was holding his arm so affectionately, and seemed to be legitimately hitting it off with the rest of the group. She'd even exchanged a few one-liners with Loren throughout the evening. But no matter what happened, Braden remained visibly on edge.

"You OK?" Kate asked Braden when the band was between songs.

"Yeah, I'm fine."

Kate wasn't so sure.

The night stretched on, and after two encores, the concert eventually came to a close. As the gang made their way back to the hotel, Kate split off from Braden a bit, walking with Jason and Brooke as the other couples walked slightly up ahead of them. Braden dwindled in the back by himself.

"How is he doing?" Brooke asked Kate as she gestured back toward Braden.

"I have no idea," Kate said. " I thought we were having a good time."

~

The somber mood had yet to lift when they were checking out of the hotel the next morning.

"We'll wait to make sure everyone is ready before we get going," Jason said as he and Brooke were heading to the garage with their bags.

"Sounds good," Hank replied.

Loren and Cole started for the garage as well.

While most of the group acknowledged Loren's exit, Braden simply stared down at his feet.

For the umpteenth time that weekend, Kate took note.

The drive back to Grimwood was tense. Hank and Hannah tried to make conversation, and Kate repeatedly attempted to draw Braden out of his funk, but nothing much came of their efforts. Kate sat in the back seat and studied Braden's face from the corner of her eye. At one point she reached out and gently squeezed his hand. He squeezed back, lightly, but never looked her way.

~

"Can I ask you something, Braden?"

Kate took Braden's hands after Hank and Hannah had dropped them off in the circle behind Lavery Hall.

"Of course."

"Did something ever happen between you and Loren?"

Braden was quiet. "Why do you ask that?"

"I don't know, you just seemed to get… down the more time we all spent together this weekend. And it seemed like you were sort of out to get Cole with a few of your comments."

"Nothing ever happened with us," Braden replied, but there was no force behind it.

Kate studied his face. "Do you have feelings for her?"

"Does that matter?"

"I'd like to know where I stand. So yeah, of course that matters."

His eyes met hers, then he looked away, pressing his lips together tightly.

They stood there, silently, the temperature dropping as the sunlight began to fade.

Finally, Braden raised his hands at his side. "I don't know what to say."

"Neither do I," Kate replied.

Braden turned and walked away, heading around the corner toward the quad.

Kate stood and watched him go. "Is that it?" she called after him, unsure if she was talking to Braden or just to herself.

~

After a week had passed with no word, Kate went looking for Braden one evening after work. She didn't have any classes with him that quarter, and she'd never succeeded in finding his secluded workspace in the library, so she went to the *one* place she knew she could find him, R.K. Phillips on a Tuesday night.

The Ave was mostly empty as she made her way up the street, mentally reviewing the things she wanted to ask him. But the moment she stepped inside the bookstore, all of her carefully formed questions slipped away.

Braden was chatting with the store's shipping guy. The two of them were laughing about something together, but the smile on Braden's face froze when he looked over and saw her approaching. After an uncomfortable silence, his co-worker excused himself and slipped into the back.

"Hey, Braden."

"Kate."

"So… what's the deal?"

"The deal?"

"Am I ever going to hear from you again? I thought things were going pretty well with us before we all went away."

"They were," he replied.

"So then what happened?"

A pained expression passed across his face. "You asked me about Loren…"

"And that's why you haven't-" She stopped short. "What about Loren?"

"I *do* have feelings for her."

"OK." She looked down at a stack of books on one of the front tables, silently straightening the top copy as she gathered her thoughts. "So, *did* something ever happen between the two of you?"

Braden shook his head.

"Then, who cares? That doesn't mean we can't make things work." She forced a smile. "I mean, I have feelings for John Cusack, but that hasn't-"

"I don't think it would be fair to you."

"Since when are relationships fair?"

"The thing is… I *want* to be with Loren."

Kate sighed. "Even if she's with someone else?"

Braden nodded slowly.

"So that's it?" she asked.

"I guess so."

Kate stared at him, hoping for more, but an invisible wall had gone up.

"Good luck with that, Braden," Kate said finally as she turned and walked out of his life.

* * *

After he coolly ended things with Kate, Braden spent the majority of his time alone, much of it in the upper reaches of Grimwood Library, safely hidden away as he worked on his novel between class assignments. As Winter stretched into the deep gray of March, Braden purchased a laptop computer and began assembling the rough draft of his book. His fingers tapped the keys relentlessly. If he paused too long between passages, his thoughts would drift to feelings he had no wish of entertaining, so he continued to write.

Meanwhile, his friends were drawing even closer together.

Jason and Hank continued their collaboration in and out of the classroom. Their friendship growing tighter by the day. When they weren't hanging out as a foursome with Brooke and Hannah, they were prowling music venues, checking out bands, and brainstorming their professional dreams for the future.

To some degree, even Loren was finding herself drawn deeper into the tightly knit group. She still detected a wave of apprehension whenever she brought Cole along on their outings, attributing it partly to his differences with the other guys, but mostly to their loyalty to Braden. But whether they took to her boyfriend or not, it had no bearing on her. The truth was, however much she cared for Cole, she'd come to realize that *his* natural inclination was to retreat into relationships. It was a tendency she found isolating. Perhaps too late in life, she was realizing she needed close female friends, and Hannah and Brooke were becoming just that.

Jason remained the hub of the group. He organized the outings and checked in on everyone individually from time to time. Along with his sunny disposition, he had an optimistic quality that Loren and the rest of them found endearing.

One night at The Shack, after perhaps one beer too many, Jason looked around the group somberly and asked, "Why in the hell isn't Braden out with all of us tonight?"

Brooke put her arm around him and gave him a little kiss on the cheek. The moment left Loren feeling a little wistful herself. The truth was, she missed Braden too.

* * *

There was a palpable sense of loneliness in Ashton Study Hall. Braden wondered how much of that he brought with him, and how much of it was inherent to the space's dark history. Though he felt largely at home in his workspace of choice, there were times, like tonight, when that feeling of isolation seemed more intense than usual.

Weeks had passed since he'd last spent any notable amount of time with his friends. Kate was slipping from his mind, already a strangely distant memory.

He stared at the slowly blinking cursor on his screen, then shut down his whirring laptop. The sound of the fan disappeared in a vacuum, but the dimly lit room hummed with silence.

Braden pulled the Alan Grimwood biography from his backpack and set it on the desk, thinking of Loren as he stared at the cover.

Sooner or later, he would need to summon the courage to fix that friendship.

~

Braden left the study hall shortly before midnight, carrying the Grimwood biography in one hand and his winter coat in the other. The library was silent as he stepped into the dark corridor and started for the stairs. Long pools of blue light stretched beneath the windows along the wall to his right. He was halfway to the stairs when he sensed the air shifting, as if a vacuum was drawing the oxygen from the far end of the corridor toward him, and pulling the shadows along with it. Braden stared straight ahead, his eyes quivering in their sockets as his mind struggled to discern what was happening.

A muted highlight off to the right caught Braden's attention. He watched from the corner of his eye as a silhouette emerged from the shadows.

"Deborah-" a voice whispered.

Braden turned to the sound, squinting in the dim light as he tried to make out the face beneath a backlit aura of long hair. His mouth had gone dry.

"I'm looking for Deborah," the figure said again.

This time, Braden could tell the person speaking was male. Judging by his build and the sound of his voice, the two of them were around the same age. Braden watched as the figure looked down at his hands, slowly opening and closing his loosely clasped fists.

Something about him seemed vaguely familiar.

"I'm afraid I don't know anyone named Deborah." Braden said as he studied his counterpart's shadowy features. "Actually, I thought I was the only person up here-"

The figure looked up sharply and shouted, "Nobody asked you a *goddamn thing!*"

Braden stepped back in surprise, the book falling from his hands. He silently studied the figure standing before him. He was wearing a plaid shirt and faded jeans, flared at the bottom. The edges of the clothing were unusually frayed, almost threadbare. The longer Braden studied him, the more the guy himself seemed worn as well, almost translucent. Then it hit him-

He was a flare.

Seeing Braden's evident shock, the figure stepped forward, "I'm sorry, I don't know what's happening with me. I don't feel like myself lately."

Still Braden didn't speak.

"I have these… blackouts." He wiped at his eyes. "I think I might have done something."

Braden suddenly knew why he recognized him.

The incident in the library.

This was the shooter.

"Have I done something?" the figure asked.

Braden nodded. "What's your name?"

"Bryan."

"Bryan…" Braden swallowed slowly, trying to speak clearly. "What do you remember?"

Bryan took a step backward, toward the window. "What did I do?"

"I think you know."

"Did I hurt anyone?"

Braden hesitated before he answered. "You did."

Bryan stepped closer to the window. "And Deborah?"

Braden was silent.

"No," Bryan whispered. "No." He was rushing backward now, repeating the word over and over under his breath.

Then, like a wink, Bryan's expression changed from tortured, to enraged, and in the same flash, he was gone, leaving Braden standing alone in the middle of the empty corridor.

* * *

Jason and Hank were in Hank and Braden's dorm room, listening to tracks they'd mixed in the audio lab that morning. Jason hit pause, and the two of them turned to Braden for his reaction, but he was lost in his thoughts.

"Yo! " Hank snapped his fingers. "Earth to Brady."

Braden blinked and looked at Jason. "Your uncle, the one who worked in the library, what was the term he used for the unusual stuff that happened over there?"

"The midnight visitors," Jason replied. "He had a bunch of stories about that part of campus."

"Stuff that happened to *him?*"

"That's what he claimed."

"Did he ever… *talk* to anyone?"

"About what he saw? Sure."

Braden's eyes darted to Hank, then back to Jason "No, I mean did he ever talk to any of the… visitors?"

"You mean *flares,* don't you?" Hank asked skeptically.

"He said he heard voices sometimes," Jason said.

"Did he ever mention a name?" Braden hesitated. "Bryan, or Deborah maybe?"

"I don't think he ever said anything like that, but… Deborah. That does ring a bell for some reason."

~

"Deborah Payne was the girl he was obsessed with," Loren said as she spread out a pile of reprinted newspaper articles. "She was the first person Bryan Miller killed when he stormed the library."

"That's who I saw then. Bryan."

They were seated in a booth at Brownie's. Braden had been nervous to contact her, but he was pleasantly surprised when Loren answered the phone and didn't hang up as he explained his reason for calling. It was almost as though they'd both been waiting for a safe topic to help break the ice between them.

"Let me look into it," Loren said once he'd brought her up to speed.

An hour later, they were seated at Brownie's, coffee mugs and printouts spread out on the table between them. Braden studied the gentle creases under Loren's eyes as he reached for his coffee.

"So, here's the big find," Loren said as she rummaged through her bag. She withdrew a hardbound yearbook and set it down in front of Braden. "Look at the dedication."

The cover read: *Grimwood – Class of '73.*

The incident at the library had occurred one week before Thanksgiving in 1972.

Braden flipped the book open to the front page. The caption at the top read: *In Memoriam.* A dozen color photos – one for each of the victims – were spread across the page.

The first picture was of a radiantly happy girl in an emerald green dress. Her arm was around a young man with a moustache and slicked-back hair.

Loren pointed to the young man's smiling face. "Recognize him?"

Braden leaned in closer. The eyes seemed familiar, but he couldn't quite place the face. Finally, he looked down at the caption. It read: "Deborah Payne with fiancé Mark Price.

Braden's head shot up. "Is that Professor Price?"

"I think so," she replied somberly. "Class of '73. That would be about the right year."

"That's terrible. I can't believe he wants to be anywhere near this campus after that."

"Maybe he feels close to her here." Loren pulled the yearbook back and studied the picture again. "You notice the green dress?"

"The same shade Price is always wearing."

"I think it must be his silent tribute to her. She's wearing the same color in all of the class photos."

"Can you imagine losing someone like that?"

"I don't even want to go there," Loren mused.

"If that were me, I'd want to get as far away from this place as possible."

"Maybe you wouldn't though."

"Why do you say that?"

"Well, you stayed at your grandfather's house after he passed away, right?"

"That was a little different," Braden said. "But I see your point. I guess it's just the violent nature of it that I can't imagine…"

"Did I tell you I saw Alan Grimwood again?" Loren asked.

"When was this?"

"Our first week back from break. I was walking back alone, when suddenly I could just *sense* him standing there, even before I turned."

"It's like a mood, right?"

"Exactly," Loren agreed.

Until then, they'd maintained an unspoken agreement not to discuss anything beyond the incident, but the tension between them seemed to have faded, and before she realized it, Loren was asking Braden something she knew she probably shouldn't.

"Are you still seeing Kate?"

"Not anymore," Braden replied as he gathered the papers together and placed them on top of the yearbook.

"She seems like a nice girl."

"She's just about perfect," Braden said as their eyes met. "But she's not the right one."

He slid the stack of materials back to Loren, who said nothing, and felt no need to.

An unacknowledged truce had been forged between them.

Loren knew what he meant, so their conversation pivoted to other topics. A weight had been lifted from both of their minds. Whether or not they were together, at least they were speaking again.

"I keep thinking about the flare I saw at the library," Braden said at the end of the night as they were preparing to go their separate ways. "Do you think we could ever talk to Price about the incident?"

"I was wondering the same thing," Loren said. "I really don't know."

12.

THEY KNEW APPROACHING PROFESSOR Price with questions about that long ago tragedy crossed a line of acceptability, but eventually, Braden and Loren decided it was a risk they were willing to take.

Mark Price's dimly-lit office was tucked into the southeast corner of The Writing Center's top floor. The rain-speckled windows provided a view of The Lookout, The Falls, and most-strikingly, the Library's infamous tower. He was dressed in a dapper grey suit, with his shirt collar unbuttoned. Today's touch of emerald green came from a neatly folded pocket square in his breast pocket.

Price turned slowly in his chair, his shoulders drawing up as their inquiring words sank in. He opened his mouth, pausing to compose himself before he spoke. "First, I have to hand it to you, if anyone has ever before made the same connection between me and *that*," he nodded to the tower, "None of them had the nerve to mention it to me." He was clearly pushing through a web of complex emotions as he struggled with what to say next. "Second, what exactly are you two looking to get out of this?"

Braden and Loren were still standing in the doorway. Braden's eyes darted around the room uncomfortably, settling briefly on a teacup on the Professor's desk. He watched wisps of steam swirl in the air above the rim.

Loren was the first to step forward.

"Candidly, sir, we don't really know. Braden and I are just trying to understand some… things that we've encountered in our time at Grimwood."

Price studied their faces, his shoulders relaxing slightly, his expression softening, as he read between the lines and decided their motivations were sincere.

"So, you've seen them too…" He motioned for them to sit. "Not everyone does."

Braden and Loren took a seat, feeling their way around the topic. This was the first time either of them had discussed *any* of this with a third party, let alone someone who *believed* what they were saying. They began to fill Mark Price in on the flares they'd encountered in their time on campus. Braden discussed the victims of the incident that he had seen that first day at The Lookout. Loren detailed both of her encounters with Alan Grimwood. And finally, Braden walked him through his unnerving run-in with the flare of the shooter himself.

Price leaned back in his chair, heavily. "Alan Grimwood. That's a new one," he said with a cryptic smile. "He haunted the campus when he was alive, so it shouldn't surprise me that he's still here." He met Braden's gaze. "The ones I've seen have almost all been *here*, on the academic side, mostly down around The Lookout, same as you. Once or twice I've caught a fleeting glimpse in the library-"

"Have you ever encountered Bryan Miller?" Loren asked.

"No." Price's expression went flat. "Not in this life anyway. Thank God for that."

The phrasing caught Loren's attention. "Did you know him at some point?"

"I knew *of* him. I wouldn't say any of us really *knew* him as it turned out. He was in a class with Deborah our sophomore year. That's where it all started, his unsettling obsession."

"What did Deborah think of him?" Loren asked

"She just figured he was harmless. Everyone did. Lots of guys had crushes on her. He just seemed to be especially… persistent." Price looked at Loren, his expression remorseful. "I'm not proud of this, but there was a group of us who used to joke about his annual Valentine's gifts. They were always over-the-top and creepy, but our friends would kid me that I'd better step it up, or Deborah might eventually leave me for Bryan. We should have known better. He was clearly unstable. Unfortunately, it turned out he was much more troubled than any of us ever realized."

"You couldn't have known that though," Loren said, trying to reassure him. "Did he know you two were engaged?"

"Yeah. I've often wondered if the ring was what set him off. I gave that to her a week before it happened."

Price grew quiet.

"What about Deborah?" Loren asked eventually.

"What about her?"

"Have you ever seen her flare over all these years?"

"Never."

Price brought one hand to his chin as he again leaned back in his creaking desk chair.

Braden shifted in his seat uncomfortably.

"I have a theory about the ones we see," Price began. "It's nothing unique. I've heard countless variations of it over the years, but I believe the individuals we encounter after their deaths are here because they were pulled away with something in their lives left unresolved. Messages undelivered. I've spent a lifetime on this campus, teaching and writing, but I could have done those things at any university. I suppose deep down I've stayed here for a reason, but there are times I can't help but wonder if I've wasted a lot of years waiting for something that just isn't going to happen."

Price grew quiet as a bemused look flashed across his face. He turned to Braden.

"I like that term your grandfather used. It's so much more vital than the old standbys. Instead of living lives full of dreams and passion, only to blink out without a trace, it's reassuring to think they can flare back from time to time, if only to scare the shit out of us."

* * *

Hank slipped a shot of Howard's Kahlua into his mug of microwaved coffee as he looked out the window. Snow that was blowing in sideways in the driving wind. "You want some in yours?" he asked Jason, raising the bottle of booze as he handed him a second steaming cup.

"No thanks. I'm supposed to pick up dinner at Red Tomato and meet up with Brooke after my shift. I feel funny if I get there with booze on my breath."

"I'm not sure Kahlua really counts as booze, but that's cool. She still doing OK?"

"She's great." Jason said with a smile. "Honestly, she doesn't even care if I have anything to drink, I'm just trying to make things a little easier for her in the long run. How are you and Hannah?"

They walked out of the kitchen, heading down the quiet corridor to the broadcast booth where Jason would be manning the next shift.

"I think everything is good," Hank said. "I mean, she's wound as tight as a guitar string, but so far I haven't done anything to make her snap. I'm heading over to her place after this."

They stopped and sat in the lounge area outside the studio. Hank reached for a copy of *The Reporter*, Grimwood's free weekly paper, and flipped to the music listings in the back. "We should check out some more bands soon."

"I'm game," Jason said. "There's no time like the present, right?"

"No there isn't." Hank slugged back his coffee as the muffled sounds of the broadcast indicated the current DJ was signing off. "And at the present, I'm heading over to my girlfriend's place, hopefully to get laid." He tossed *The Reporter* down on the table, where Jason picked it up, slipping it under his arm as he got to his feet.

"I wish you luck," Jason said. "Tell her I said hello."

Hank gave him a funny look.

"I mean, at a time when it won't seem strange."

The studio door opened, and the previous host, an upper-classman in an oversized parka, gave Jason the thumbs up as he turned to go. "It's all you."

"Stay warm out there, " Jason replied. He looked at Hank as he stepped into the studio and started to close the door. "I'll see you around, man."

~

None of WGRM's shifts could be called particularly taxing, but Jason was especially fond of the weeknight blocks between 9 p.m. and 10:30, when the unstated rule was that hosts could play whatever they wanted – within the realm of common decency – before switching the feed over to a loop of Howard Lester's greatest hits to close out of the broadcast day. Jason had worked out a fairly eclectic playlist for the next few hours, and was largely there to make small talk during the transitions. The rest of the time he was free to do as he pleased.

Just before the end of his shift, Jason flipped to the weekly music section in the back of *The Reporter*, where he caught sight of a listing that made his pulse quicken. He reached for a red pen and quickly circled a show announcement, then he folded the paper open to that page, and tucked it into his backpack so he'd remember to show it to Hank first thing the next morning.

A light blinked on the console, letting him know it was time to end the live feed for the day. He reached for the microphone and watched the needle as it bounced and quivered in time with his voice.

"That will just about do it for tonight. Before I leave you to the soothing sounds of Uncle Howie, I want to wish you all the most pleasant of evenings. Wherever you are, and whatever you're doing, I hope you have something or *someone* to keep you warm. I'll catch you on the flipside. This is Jason Pepper, signing off."

~

Jason stepped outside and locked the station door. The bolt slipped into place with an audible ping. He tucked the keys back in his pocket and pulled on his gloves as his fingers grew stiff in the cold. After hours of radio station din, the nighttime world of Grimwood campus was especially peaceful. The snow was still falling – but slower now – the flakes drifting over to the icy crust that encased the ground.

Red Tomato was at the far end of The Ave. He briefly considered cutting across the snowy field that stretched from the front of the Student Union to Eldredge Drive, and making his way down the hill, but the nighttime snowfall inspired him to take the closer route, where he could savor the quiet.

The ever-present sound of The Falls rumbled in the distance behind the Library as Jason trudged around the back of the Student Union toward the glowing lights of the President's Mansion. The freezing mist from the unseen falls created a ribbon of whirling flakes, which swept westward, filling the trees overhead with thick, drifting limbfuls of snow. Jason gazed upward, marveling at the beauty of the scene as he made his way around the farthest corner of the mansion.

It wasn't until he reached the staircase that Jason remembered *why* he so seldom took this route. The white of the snow amplified the light, making the steep old steps appear less foreboding than they might have on any other night. Still, when he saw the glistening shell of ice on the surface of the snow-covered concrete stairs he nearly turned back.

His mouth tightened as he weighed his options.

Brooke would be hungry. And he was anxious to see her.

If he held the handrail and made his way slowly, one step at a time, what was the worst that could happen?

He took hold of the thick metal rail, gripping it tightly in his left hand as he took his first step. His foot broke through the icy crust, punching down to the underlying snow, and slipping ever so slightly on a layer of ice that had formed directly over the concrete treads below. That undermost layer was the one to watch out for, but he could handle it.

He took another step. And another. Each time, gently pressing his foot down through the frozen layers, until he found a rhythm he felt comfortable with. At this rate, he'd be at the bottom, trudging up The Ave towards pizza and Brooke in no time.

But as tight ropewalkers say… You might *think* you're as good as there, but it's the steps you have left that kill you.

Jason's foot slipped out from under him on the next step. He twisted to the left, grabbing for the rail with his right hand, but his other foot got away from him as well.

The last thing Jason Pepper saw was the handrail rising up to meet him as he fell. His temple smashed into the thick metal bar – his arms and legs shooting out to the sides, as if from an electric shock – then he tumbled to the bottom of the concrete stairs, where he lay motionless under the silently falling snow.

* * *

Brooke woke with a jolt.

The light was dim, but it was unmistakably morning.

She sat up in her bed, looking around the empty dorm room.

Loren's coat was draped over the back of her desk chair, but she wasn't there.

Brooke looked to the side of the door, where Jason always threw his jacket and shoes on the nights he stayed over. The floor was bare.

He'd never arrived.

Maybe something had come up at the last minute. But things didn't feel right. When the phone rang a split second later, her first instinct was to cry out.

~

Loren came back from the bathroom, dressed for the day, her shower caddy in one hand. If Brooke was awake, maybe the two of them could head over to Brownie's for breakfast. She opened the door cautiously, afraid to wake her if she was still asleep, but when she stepped inside, she found Brooke slumped on the floor between their beds, the phone in her hands, and tears streaming down her face.

~

"What happened?" Braden asked Hank as his roommate greeted him at the elevator and led him down the hospital corridor.

"Some kind of freak accident." Hank's eyes were red and swollen. "He fell and hit his head."

"How long before someone found him?"

"A while. He was in a coma when they brought him in."

In a strange case of life coming full circle, Hannah and Loren were seated in the same waiting area where they'd all gathered the night Jason had found Brooke passed out in the club bathroom.

Hannah squeezed Hank's hand as he sat down beside her.

Braden hesitated at the edge of the room, his mind suddenly awash with memories of a similar scene the previous year. The day he'd arrived at the hospital in Huntington, and met up with Jeremy's family. They were all in a similar state, paralyzed by grief and sadness. In his naiveté, Braden had initially mistaken the atmosphere in the room as shock, the family gathering together, summoning the strength to push through to their loved one's recovery. Then Jeremy's uncle had walked over and broken the news.

Braden inhaled deeply, raising his emotional defenses as best he could.

Loren walked over and gave him a hug as he quietly cleared his throat.

"Where's Brooke?" Braden asked.

Loren nodded toward a partly open door, where a light board and clouded X-ray were briefly visible before the door closed. "Cathie brought her in to hear the latest. Based on the bruise on his head, and his condition when he was brought in, they think it's an epidural hemorrhage."

"What would that mean?"

"Depending on the amount of bleeding, and the time he was out there… it's not good." Her voice quivered as she took Braden's hand. "They have him hooked up to a machine in there now."

Braden looked over at Hank, who was holding his head in his hands.

The door opened with a creak, followed by a murmur of voices. Then a doctor stepped out into the hall, voicing his regrets before he disappeared down the corridor.

Cathie Pepper stood in the background, looking to an unseen bed in the darkened room. Brooke stepped out into the hall, anguished tears glistening on her face.

"Take care of your roommate," Braden whispered in Loren's ear.

She nodded toward Hank. "You take care of yours, too."

~

Even as the doctors were working to stabilize him that morning, Jason's body was shutting down. Eventually, as the afternoon light began to fade, Cathie told them she had decided to donate Jason's organs. A short time later, they were allowed to step into the room to say goodbye to their friend. Then Cathie and Brooke stayed behind.

The doctors removed the ventilator, disconnected the machines, and left the three of them alone.

His body relaxed.

His breathing gradually slowed to a stop.

His heart grew silent.

And Jason Pepper died.

13.

ONLY THE DEAD KNOW what happens when they slip through the looking glass. On this side of existence, the process – no matter the culture – is fundamentally and reassuringly the same.

The news goes out.

Arrangements are made.

The loved one's remains are taken away and prepared for burial.

Those who remain talk. They attend to the business at hand. They search for the memories, and if they're lucky, they recall the laughs.

Food is shared.

Life goes on even as it ends.

Braden went with Hank to buy a black suit; Olga had shipped his up earlier in the week.

"I always thought I would be older when I bought a suit for my friend's funeral," Hank said as he swiped his credit card at the register.

The wake took place on a Friday. They were all there. Even Cole. Brooke was quiet, quiet in a way that made everyone a little nervous. Except for Loren, who stood by her through it all, squeezing Brooke's hand, doing whatever she could to be there for her, as Brooke was there for Cathie.

At the end of the night, just as visiting hours were drawing to a close, a mousey girl in a grey dress arrived to pay her respects. She shook Brooke's hand, and hugged Cathie Pepper.

"Susie," Cathie said. "Thank you for coming." Then she led the girl to the casket.

"Who is that?" Loren asked Brooke.

"Jason's ex-girlfriend," Brooke whispered as she sized up her predecessor. "Her shins are longer than her thighs. It's freaky."

Loren laughed.

~

The next day, Jason Pepper's friends and family followed his body to Grimwood Cemetery, and said their final goodbyes.

* * *

Weeks later, Brooke jolted awake in the middle of the night, sitting bolt upright as she gasped for air, like a swimmer breaking free of the waves, starved for oxygen. Then she slumped over the edge of the bed, her body racked with silent sobs.

Somehow, she had continued on. Numb. Going to classes, passing the days and weeks in a daze.

She hadn't seen Jason's mother since the funeral, when they'd held each other tight. Brooke could still feel Cathie Pepper's hand on the back of her head, her fingers tangled in her hair.

"I'll be in touch," Cathie said.

Brooke hadn't heard from her in the time since, but she couldn't blame her. If *she* was sleepwalking through the fog of heartache, Jason's mother was facing down eighteen years of memories, the loss of her only child.

In the first days, it had seemed to Brooke like a bad dream. As if someone had made a mistake, signals had been crossed.

Jason was simply traveling, but he would return at any moment, and when he did, the bewildered look on his face would make up for the needless anguish his loved ones had been feeling. Yet over time, the realization slowly sank in that this was how things would be from now on. He would never be back. He would never again peek around the edge of her door. Flash her that smile. Or look up at her from beneath the covers of her bed.

Jason Pepper was dead.

Brooke saw the words in her mind, as clear as if they were printed on a page. She felt the ache in her chest, as she once more tried to accept what had happened, and what she had lost.

14.

When you live upstate, there comes a time at the tail end of winter, when it feels as though the ground will never thaw. The sky will never clear. And the pursuits of the warmer months will remain only memories. But inevitably, the frost melts away, and the roots and seeds hibernating beneath the surface awaken and wriggle through the layers of earth into the filtered light of spring. Around the same time, people begin to emerge from the worlds and routines that have sustained them through the frigid months.

Life went on. But if Jason was the sun that held his friends in orbit, when his light went out, the shock of his loss blew them apart, sending them spinning off on their own paths. Hank and Hannah were in their bubble. Loren was with Cole. And Braden and Brooke drifted away in the outer reaches, each following their own isolated and uncertain trajectories…

Braden stepped out of The Writing Center into the blinding sunlight on The Lookout. He dropped his head, shielding his eyes from the glare as he waited for his pupils to adjust. When he looked up, a silhouette was moving toward him from the library.

"Hi, Braden," a girl's voice said.

He squinted toward her, the light pulling in around the edges of her body as his vision returned.

"Brooke… " he replied. "I don't know if I've ever seen you on this side of campus before."

"Yeah, I usually stick to the art and design end of campus, but I had to do some research for a report."

"How are you doing?" Braden asked.

"I'm OK… I miss him."

"I do, too."

Brooke touched a knuckle to the corner of her eye. "It seems like everyone has been busy."

"I suppose we have," Braden said. "Have you seen much of Loren?"

"She's around now and then, but she's mostly staying at Cole's place."

"That's what I figured."

"You guys still aren't in touch, huh?"

Braden shook his head. "We aren't avoiding each other – I should give her a call."

"I'm sure she'd like that."

Brooke grew quiet, and Braden tried to think back to just what he had been *doing* for the last few months. Just his same old solitary routines, nothing unusual. There was no good reason *not* to have seen Brooke or any of his friends. But then again, he hadn't heard from them either.

"You know, Jason really kept us all together," Braden observed

Brooke looked up, shielding her eyes from the sun. "He did, didn't he?"

***

The good thing about Cole's apartment being so close to the Dinosaur was that takeout was just a short walk away. That was both a blessing and a curse. Beef brisket and dirty rice and beans were great comfort food in the winter months, but they'd definitely stuck to Loren's ribs more than she would have liked. When she dug her clothes out for the warmer weather, her jeans were uncomfortably snug at the hips.

"I like it," Cole told her when she complained about the extra weight.

But she didn't.

She wasn't comfortable with a lot of things lately. And it wasn't just the fit of her clothes. More and more it seemed she wasn't doing the things she felt mattered. It was an all too familiar feeling.

Music was drifting in through the kitchen window as Loren filled her mug with boiling water. That was one of the other problems with living so close to the Dinosaur, whenever the bands played on a Friday night, she wanted to head over and see what all the excitement was about. Unfortunately, Cole liked to stay in, partially because he didn't have the money, but largely because that was just his way. She dropped a teabag into the water and swayed her hips as she watched Cole listening to music in his chair. His headphones made her think of Jason.

Cole glanced up, lifting one of the earpieces. "Did you say something?"

"No, I was just watching you," Loren said. "I… think I should be checking on Brooke more."

"Why is that? Did she say something?"

"No, it just seems like I should make sure she's doing OK."

"How did she seem the last time you saw her?"

"Surprisingly good, considering."

"She probably wants her space."

Loren wasn't so sure.

"Girls are different, Cole. We don't always say what we want, but we *need* to talk about things. I think I should be doing more."

"Suit yourself, but if it were me, I'd spend less time thinking about what I *should* be doing, and more time thinking about what I *want* to be doing."

He dropped his headphones back into place.

Loren watched him again.

She didn't care what he thought. She missed her friends. And if she felt the distance, she could only imagine how Brooke was feeling.

~

"What drink is that?" Hannah asked over the sound of the music.

Hank's head lolled her way, a befuddled expression crossing his face. "It's a *beer*," he answered in a tone that asked '*what-else-would-it-be?*'

"I mean what *number* is it."

He leaned back, hitting his head on the back of their booth as he tallied his drinks on a mental chalkboard.

They were seated in the back of the Pig 'n Whistle. The crowd around them was made up largely of fraternity guys, who were, amazingly, even more drunk than Hank. And that was saying something.

Hank raised his glass, splashing beer across the table. "This is number… seven," he mumbled. "Why?"

"Do you think it might be time to call it a night?"

"*Why?*" He asked again, speaking at an almost comically shrill volume.

"No reason," Hannah said as she wiped up the beer with a handful of napkins. "I just thought you might want to cut your losses. Half your booze is ending up on the furniture anyway."

"Ah," Hank grunted, as if that put a cap on the topic.

"I ran into Brooke today," Hannah said.

Hank peered down at the top of his drink, watching the bubbles rising from the bottom of the glass.

Hannah watched him from the corner of her eye.

"Did you… hear me-?" she asked finally.

"How's she doing?"

"She misses everyone. She asked about you."

"Me?" He wiped his mouth. "Why's she wondering about me?"

"She's worried about you."

"Jason was *her* boyfriend," Hank replied, his expression slackening. "She shouldn't be worrying about *me.*"

"He was *your* best friend, Hank," Hannah said. "It's OK to admit that you're hurting. I know you are. You wouldn't be staring into your eighth pint of beer if you weren't upset."

"It's my seventh…" he started.

"It's your eighth. I was just seeing if you had lost count."

Hank looked up from their table, turning his head to watch the partying crowd drift past his bleary gaze. *"Come On Eileen"* was playing, and for the first time in memory, the song didn't make him want to get up and dance. It made him feel terribly sad. Hank leaned over, resting his head on his girlfriend's shoulder.

"I think we need to get the band back together," Hannah said as she ran her fingers through his hair. "I'll take care of it."

* * *

Dinosaur Bar-B-Que seemed like a natural choice, but as Hannah was making the plans, she suddenly realized that *all* of their previous BBQ excursions had been masterminded by Jason. His absence would be felt, but then again, that was kind of the point, wasn't it? If their circle of friends had any hope of pulling together to heal, they would need to acknowledge their loss. Wherever they went in Grimwood from here on out, Jason Pepper would be the missing piece.

When the night came, Loren even convinced Cole to join them.

Brooke arrived to find the five of them gathered in a booth, sipping their drinks and catching up. Braden was the first to see her approaching their table. He stood up and gave her a hug, then he moved to the side to let Loren and Hannah do the same.

Tears pooled in Brooke's eyes, but it wasn't until Hank stood and met her gaze that she blinked, and her emotions spilled over.

"Hank," she said as she wrapped her arms around him.

They held each other tightly for a long time.

Then the music picked up, and the night began.

15.

THE SCHOOL YEAR DREW to a close. Dorm rooms were packed. Final papers were typed up and handed in. At some point, between the close of final exams and the first day of summer break, Brooke managed to arrange one final group dinner at Brick's.

The summer weather and the passing of time had healed their wounds just enough that they could begin to smile again whenever something reminded them of their departed friend. And even when they weren't invoking his name, Jason was always there, between the lines of every conversation and quiet moment.

They took their spots in the usual booth and put in an order for a round of Brick Plates.

"You guys are mean," Hannah grumbled, still uncertain about her peer-pressured order.

"Something to remember us by," Braden said.

"I'll be cursing you all for this in an hour," Hannah noted.

"I doubt it will be that long," Hank joked.

They discussed their summer plans as they ate their meals. For the most part, everyone was spending the break at home. Hank would be working his old job in Albany. Hannah was planning on helping her father with his business. Even Brooke was heading back home to the city, though she was clearly wary of dealing with her parents again.

"What about you, Braden?" Loren asked.

Braden looked up. "I'm going home. I'm not entirely sure what I'll do there, maybe see if The Book Revue will have me for a few months." He shrugged. "Other than that? Who knows."

"I'm sure you'll be writing," Loren said.

"Hopefully."

"What about you?" Brooke asked Loren.

"Oh, my plans are always sort of up in the air."

"Are you going back to Wyoming to chase Buffalo?" Brooke teased.

"You… know that's not where I'm from, right?" Loren replied.

"I know. I know. You're from Colorado," Brooke admitted. "I just can't remember the name of the town."

"Durango," Braden interjected.

Loren met his gaze.

"What's summer *like* in Durango?" he asked her.

"It's beautiful," she said.

"I've gotta admit, I'm a little jealous."

Loren looked him in the eyes a moment longer before she changed gears. "So, how is everyone getting home?" she asked.

"I'm driving back just as soon as I take Hannah to the airport," Hank said.

"My parents will be here tomorrow afternoon," Brooke said.

What about you?" Loren asked Braden.

"I'm taking the train back in the morning," he said.

"Want some company at the station?" she asked.

"Absolutely."

Later, after they'd paid the bill, the group made their way outside, where they exchanged hugs on the sidewalk.

"There's no need to get maudlin folks," Hank said. "We'll all be back here in a few months."

"Ignore him," Hannah said as she hugged Loren and Brooke, and took Hank's hand to leave. "My boyfriend is afraid to feel human emotions. But I'm working on him."

"We know he's a softie at heart," Braden said as he started back toward campus with Hank and Hannah. "I'll see you in the morning, Loren."

"See you then," she replied.

Then it was just Loren and Brooke standing together on the quiet sidewalk.

Brooke watched Braden and the others as they crossed the street. Then she turned and gave Loren a funny look.

"Have a good summer, roomie," Loren said as she leaned in for one last hug. "I'm expecting to see you back here in the fall. Do *not* leave me with some stranger next year."

"Don't worry," Brooke said. "I'll be back. I promise."

~

Braden and Loren drank their morning coffees and watched through the bus windows as The Avenue and Grimwood slipped out of view.

When they arrived at the train station, Loren took a seat on one of the long benches, watching their bags as Braden went to the ticket window.

"Are you all set?" she asked when he returned.

He held up his ticket. "How about you?"

"I'm good. It looks like your train will be here soon."

"Yep." Braden sighed as he sat down beside her.

Loren could feel him looking at her from the corner of his eye.

She heard him take a deep breath.

"You know… I meant everything I said this year, Loren."

"I know you did."

He inhaled again, but Loren spoke before he could get the words out.

"Let's not say anything now, Braden. Things are good. We should leave on a high note."

The air shifted around them as the train drew closer.

"We did have some good times this year."

"Yeah, we did," Loren said.

The train rumbled into station.

Braden and Loren got to their feet, gathering their bags as the waiting area filled with the commotion of disembarking passengers. An announcement came over the speaker system.

"The eleven o'clock to Grand Central is boarding now. All passengers, please board at track fifteen."

"Are you leaving soon, too?" Braden asked.

Loren nodded.

"I guess this is it then."

They hesitated, then hugged each other tightly.

"Take care of yourself, Braden."

"You too. I'll see you in the fall."

Braden picked up his bag and joined the other passengers as they headed for the door.

"Have a safe trip home!" Braden said as the crowd swept him out to the platform.

Loren stood in the middle of the station and watched him go.

The train doors closed, and the final boarding announcement went out.

Then the sound of the departing train shook the old station, the deep rumble picking up strength as the train chugged down the tracks.

Loren stood alone, thinking about everything that had happened that year. The friends she'd made. The unusual things she had seen.

Then she thought about Braden. The night they'd gone to see Dan Buckley. The times they'd spent working on their book together; the way Braden had looked at her as they brainstormed ideas. The way he *always* looked at her.

It's funny the way the heart works.

Love isn't fair.

The train engine whistled in the distance and Loren's attention snapped back to the present. She looked at the station clock overhead, picked up her bags, and headed for the exit to the street.

The sun broke through the clouds, bringing the early Summer heat out in force as Loren emerged on the sidewalk in front of the station. Heatwaves rippled over the asphalt as Cole's weathered Saab pulled up to the curb. The passenger side window was rolled down as Cole leaned over from the driver's seat.

"Get ready for the Summer of your life," he said with a wide grin.

Loren's mind was suddenly clear.

"Is that a promise?" she asked.

"It's a guarantee."

Loren tossed her bag in the back, climbed into the passenger seat, and they drove away.

About the Author

Mike Attebery is the author of ten novels, including *The Grimwood Trilogy*, *Chokecherry Canyon*, *Firepower*, *Seattle On Ice*, *Bloody Pulp*, and *Rosé in Saint Tropez*. He lives with his family on an island off the coast of Washington State.

You can find Mike online at:
www.facebook.com/AtteberyBooks/

on Instagram at
https://www.instagram.com/mikeatteberyauthor/

and on his website http://www.mikeattebery.com